THE

FANATICS

MAKE UP YOUR MIND

Simon Tomlin

Published by

Hakon Books

Text Copyright © Simon Tomlin, 2010

The Fanatics Second Edition

ISBN 978-1-4457-5442-0

To Susan Breach, best wishes for the future,

Simon

TABLE OF CONTENTS

PROLOGUE

One man's sacrifice is another man's freedom, in theory at least. But nothing is gained in this world from sitting on the sidelines of life complaining about the things we dislike. Ultimately, we have to take action and hopefully lead by positive example. The example I am trying to set here is to detail the truth about a group of people who believe they are destined for power. They believe that the cyclical force of history is on their side and that nothing can stop them. This is the story of my battle to uncover the reality of life inside the far Right as it gathers momentum and socio-political power across the Western World in the wake of 9/11 and the 'war on terror'.

In 1989, I began to flirt with neo-Nationalism in its Derbyshire birthplace in the heart of rural England. A storm was gathering a steady pace but most people were unaware or thought the phenomenon might just be a storm in a teacup – they were wrong. A band of young fanatics who called themselves *Blood & Honour* were beginning to make a noise through the far Right music scene. As a patriotic but naïve young man I saw something 'strangely appealing' in their controversial world and decided to investigate it. It was not long before I was seduced and sucked into a whirlwind of human conflict.

Back then, I was young and learning about life and in the ensuing years I was to learn more than most that violence as a means to attain political goals can be avoided. Violence begets violence and revenge. Eventually this leads to a tit-for-tat spree of carnage which leaves whole families destroyed. Who can forget Northern Ireland or the internecine Israeli/Palestinian conflict and the awful abuses of humanity?

I was subjected to political violence and extremism of the worst kind during five years (1990-1995) inside the British National Party. These were formative years and they left me saddened that I had lost my youth in a vortex of human conflict. I rose from the starting point of campaigning activist to become a senior elections officer organising the BNP across the country and liaising with similar groups abroad.

But in 1995, I left the BNP and began a new life free of political constraints and free of looking over my shoulder for our pursuing enemies. My new life was quite difficult at first - I missed the excitement and buzz of being in a crowd of people dedicated to 'winning at any cost'. The camaraderie was gone and all that was left was a set of memories that sometimes I wanted t forget. But I was winning a new life and with deep commitment I succeeded. I trained as a journalist and secured an honours diploma with distinction from the *London School of Journalism*. I rebuilt my life and the far Right was a distant memory for me or so I thought but events were to take a fateful and decisive turn that left me with little choice other than to rejoin the 'New BNP' led by a Cambridge graduate.

In early 2000, I was invited to a BNP meeting in the East Midlands by a former colleague and friend. The new BNP leader Nick Griffin was the main speaker at the event. Griffin had taken over the BNP operation just a few months before following a bitter power struggle with John Tyndall - the diehard who led the British far Right for nearly 40 years. I'd heard a lot about the 'new BNP' in the media and was not convinced by it. Had Griffin really removed the extreme skinhead element? Had Griffin truly transformed the BNP's hardcore neo-Nazi image and severed links with its militant creation Combat 18?

I had no real idea but Griffin's 'New BNP' intrigued me nonetheless and I decided to investigate this apparent damascene conversion to ascertain the truth of it. I accepted the offer and turned up as planned, meeting with the quixotic Griffin after his impressive speech. He took me by surprise from the outset, offering me a leading position as a press officer in the BNP's Media Monitoring Unit. Realising time was of the essence and seeing my opportunity to get close to the leadership and advance through the party ranks, I accepted the offer and this book was born.

By sharing my story with you I hope to educate you of the deepening dichotomy between the declining Political Establishment and the changing political attitudes of the general public. This is an entirely human story about human-beings and the lives they lead. It's not just my story but a story which should provoke a wider debate in all sections of society. The issue is by far bigger than me, it is an epic that documents the seemingly unstoppable rise of the far Right across the world.

This book documents a socio-political struggle and the main players behind it but in no way at all do I seek to glamorise violence. Nor do I level the blame entirely at the door of the far Right because their enemies are just as violent, if not more so. My intention is to encourage debate and help people to better understand why some people resort to politically motivated struggle after realising there is no voice for them in society.

Ultimately the British National Party and all far Right political organisations have come into existence as a result of the rush to Globalisation without first seeking the permission of electors. Every nation in the Western World has witnessed this type of betrayal and now the backlash is gathering pace. Throw in the admixture of Islamic extremism brought to international attention in appalling detail on 9/11 and the scene is set for a clash of civilisations.

Before you undertake this voyage into this mysterious and for the most part completely intriguing world, I urge you to be open-minded and cast aside all preconceptions of what you think this book is about. Perhaps the book cover has helped you to believe it is all about neo-Nationalists trying to take over the world?   No, the purpose of this book is to ask you to consider who are the real extremists and what causes so-called extremism? Be assured, as you reach the final pages, your attitude will change from excitement to shock and terror, and then wonderment, confusion and reasonable doubt. You are the juror who stands in judgment not only on this book but rather on those who stand out so prominently in it.

If anyone is in the wrong, by the last chapter you will be unsure who to blame. The reason for this is quite simple to explain: There is good and bad in all human-beings, right and wrong in very argument, entrenched dogma in every political movement on earth. Opinion, by definition is subjective not objective. Judge me according to my merits and faults of which I have many in equal abundance. I am after all not perfect but simply *human, all too human* and I make no bones about it for the sake of the truth.

At the dawn of a new century and one that offered the promise of peace and economic prosperity, a thunder bolt stuck from the clear blue skies on the morning of 9 September 2001 and with the ensuing catastrophe all hope of peace was lost. Thousands of souls cried out in pain as the terrorists struck but to some it was a 'Godsend' and the tide of history had turned. Militant Islam immediately gained a vehicle for worldwide publicity as the American war machine sprung to life to exact deadly revenge.

Across Britain and Europe neo-Nationalist groups said they had been proved right and that mass immigration had to be confronted as the far greater threat to Western civilization. In Britain under Tony Blair's premiership an immediate crack down came not in the form of attacking radical Islam but rather a vicious assault on civil liberty, apparently for our own protection. Millions of people across the political spectrum rejected the 'protection' racket offered by the New Labour regime and began to fight back against the Orwellian assault on the right to privacy.

It was the moment so many factions had been waiting for across four decades; a perfect socio-political storm through which to chart the path to salvation depending on which side you took in the clash of civilizations. 9/11 did not create socio-political and religious extremism, it simply fanned its flames that had been simmering for many years since the end of the Second World War and the creation of the state of Israel.

Both America and Britain had stood by and adopted a nonsensical policy of appeasement of the foreign militants invading their countries, apparently for asylum, in the form of mass immigration. In a blinding stroke 9/11 exploded support for the anti-immigration far Right and soon clashes were spreading out on to the streets as neo-Nationalism mobilised. The tide of history had turned away from peace as Afghanistan and then Iraq were invaded by American and British armed forces. The scene was set for fundamental socio-political unrest across the West.

In the yawning gap, neo-Nationalist organisations rose to prominence and continue to rise as Europe and America are threatened by militant Islamists and mass immigration. What now for the future of the West as the far Right march forward to win political power at the ballot box? Is the clash of civilizations inevitable? Can the far Right really win power at the ballot box? You will find many of the disturbing answers here but what you do with the knowledge is your business.   This is not a hatchet job of the type so beloved of Establishment journalists for political reasons dictated by editorial 'demands'. This is the truth and you would do well to take note. After all, you were warned and this warning from history will soon become perfectly clear.

CHAPTER 1

JUST A REBEL SONG

"And it is not enough to have memories." - Rilke

With an arrogant swagger I'm turning the corner onto Nottingham Road, the main road running straight through the heart of my hometown Eastwood. It's a small and greyish sort of town set in the heart of the British Midlands with a population of eighteen thousand inhabitants. There are only two black families in the entire town and two newsagents are owned by Asian families. It's pretty much white and proud of it. I live on the Nottinghamshire border with Derbyshire, surrounded by wonderful leafy green countryside which seems to me like an Elvin playground.

Eastwood has been put on the world map by the controversial novelist D H Lawrence whose saucy novels caused so much controversy back in the swinging sixties. I'm twenty-one years old and full of life and energy. Like all young people I want some excitement in my life. I've done all the usual stuff of going to nightclubs and bars, chatting up girls and getting drunk. I've been courting a great girl for the last two years and we're pretty happy but I'm missing something - there' seems to be a void in my life? Life should be great really. I've got a good job in the construction industry with a good income and a lovely girl who adores me. What more can I ask for?

There's something missing though. I can't put my finger on it to be sure but inside I know that something is missing. Maybe I'm just bored with 'normality' and the small town world I've grown up in. I've always been hyperactive and need lots of things going on at once to keep me interested in life. I've always been a rebel, you see, and tonight I'm going to a skinhead 'concert' in the nearby town of Ilkeston across the border in Derbyshire.

It's only three miles away but it may as well be another planet for young Eastwood lads like me. You know, we really don't like each other. Eastwood and Ilkeston lads have been fighting each other for decades and that's just the way it is. Sad really when I think about it but I try not to. We're going to the Mundy Arms pub at the bottom end of Ilkeston town. I'm nervous, not just because I'm going to Ilkeston but because I've not been to a skinhead 'concert' before.

I have no idea what to expect but I'm sure I'll soon learn. I've heard all the rumours about fighting and getting plastered but they're just unsubstantiated rumours to me. Seeing is believing as far as I'm concerned and I'll just have to wait and see what happens. Won't be too long now before I'm there.

I've covered the last two hundred yards from the war memorial to the Lord Nelson pub in a flash. My mind has been elsewhere though. My girlfriend Catherine does not know I'm going to this concert tonight but every man should have his secrets, shouldn't he? But in a small town like Eastwood, secrets don't last too long. I've always hated the nosey attitude that small town people have. It's my business what I do with my life right!

"A pint of lager please Alan." I sip at the creamy froth and take my place with the lads by the open coal fire. Sounds quite cosy doesn't it but the Lord Nelson is quite a grimy pub really with carpets you could resurface a road with. We're always joking about Alan's tarmac carpets but he's only interested in taking our money and good luck to him. He's not a bad landlord really and he puts up with a lot from us. But he's no soft touch either and soon lets you know when you're out of line with his pointed finger and strong stare. I like him a lot.

The Jones brothers, Richard and Steve, are sat with about ten other guys I don't know too well but I remember their faces from my school years not so long ago. We chat for a few minutes nothing important just small talk. Steve tells me not to worry about going to the concert - he's been to several and he says the skinheads are a decent sort - our sort. Our sort is the type of person interested in Nazism, Adolf Hitler and the Third Reich. I've always been fascinated by the swastika since I was about twelve-years-old.

The swastika is just fascinating to me and I've always been intrigued by the dark side of life but never really experienced evil - at least, I don't think I have. I mean, my Dad was really harsh on me when I was growing up but he was that way with my brothers and sisters too. I have two sisters and two brothers, all older than me. As the youngest child it's hard to get noticed at times so I fig-ure I've got to do radical things with my life to make an impression on my parents and my siblings. That's where all this rebellion comes from, I suppose.

Mum and Dad divorced when I was seven and my family has never been the close loving type. I've not had any real love and affection from my family for more years than I can remember. But Catherine, my lovely little redhead whom I have adored for years is my salvation. I think she's the mother I've never really had even though I'm three years older than her. Mum left when I was six-years-old. She suffered from my Dad's violent temper and aggression for the best part of twenty years.

After two nervous breakdowns caused by Dad's violence and selfishness, Mum left for her own good. I was devastated at the time but that's years ago and I have a life to lead now. Life is for the living after all. Even so, I do not have any respect for my Dad. I think he's cold, cruel and violent when he can't force me to do what he wants. He's tried to raise me to become a radical socialist like him but internationalism does not interest me and I'm tired of his unrealistic left-wing lectures. I just want to free myself of his overbearing presence in my life.

His views have got him no further in life than 30 years in a filthy coal mine breathing in deadly dust and fighting to organise one strike after the other. Each time the miners' objective is to bring down a government, as far as I can see. The National Union of Mineworkers (NUM) dresses up its reasons for striking in the language of demanding better pay for miners and working conditions. But, like many people, I feel the miners, most of them good, hard-working men, deserve better pay but are being led astray by neo-Marxist radicals in the NUM.

On the other hand, my Dad can't be badly paid because he's spent most of his wages on alcohol and gambling for years now. I have grown to dislike my Dad; a feeling that borders on total contempt for him because he's been violent to all of us, especially Mum. I am not interested in his radical socialism and already I hate his turgid leftie friends in the Labour Party. I think they have no grasp of realpolitiks at all in economic terms. But then, I'm young and arrogant like my Dad before me and I probably think I know it all too.

We finish the small talk and my mind drifts back to the present. Steve Jones stands up and announces, 'the taxi's here lads'. I finish my beer quickly and it mixes with the nervous adrenaline flowing in my stomach. I'm feeling quite queasy now. We get into the taxi and make off straight through the town centre - the road I have just walked down. It's a warm and sticky summer night and we're all thirsty for some more beer and excitement.

Our red taxi winds and winds through country roads so idyllic and beautiful they remind me of Constable's Haywain. Swallows rise and sweep over the bursting yellow corn fields, zooming in on their insect targets like Spitfires attacking a Luftwaffe bomber squadron. I amuse myself with these thoughts for a few minutes. Every time I think of my Dad I get angry with him for what he's done to his family. In a sense I am here because of him and I am being driven by his actions. With a jolt our taxi draws up outside the venue and hard reality kicks in.

My close friend Karl Burns has decided to come with us to the Mundy Arms pub in Ilkeston. The lead band tonight is a skinhead group called Skrewdriver about which I know nothing other than it's members think they are neo-Nazis, part of the Blood & Honour music scene, I believe. I don't know too much about Blood & Honour either but I'm sure I will soon learn. Secretly, I think the whole scene is just for a bunch of big kids who can't stop playing with toy soldiers in their minds.

We walk straight into the Mundy Arms, a typical old English style pub with oak beams hanging clumsily from the ceiling, smothered with grey cobwebs and dust, that's been gathering for decades. It's writhing with skinheads, all of them plastered in Waffen SS badges and swastikas are everywhere. There seems to be two swastikas for every man and I'm bedazzled by them, they're like bright stars in a dark night sky. Richard Jones or 'Bones' as we call him buys a round of drinks, whisky chasers and lager. I walk over to the pool table with Karl and put down some money to get the next game - winner stays on.

I'm not very good at pool but it seems a good way to break the ice with the experienced skinheads. They eye us up with suspicious and malicious eyes at first, wondering if we're 'legitimate volunteers' or just trendy boys looking for something weird to play with. I love fashion labels and spend most of my wages on smart expensive clothes. Sure enough I'm knocked off after five minutes and Karl takes the table. He's a good player, so he'll be on for a while. I start talking to a young skinhead about the same age as me.

He tells me that he's called 'Benny' and I'm not sure if this is his real name but what the hell - at least I've made contact. We chat about National Socialism and he seems to be impressed that I have read William Shirer's *Rise and Fall of the Third Reich*, his *magnum opus* on the Nazi regime. The book is over a thousand pages long and printed in dense typescript. I read it when I was fifteen-years-old, during a two week suspension from school for outright disobedience. I hate being told what to do and take orders from no one, as a free spirit my life is my own.

The school eventually expelled me a year later for refusing to take orders from Marxists masquerading as schoolteachers but I got a job a week after that so I wasn't too bothered. Benny tells me that he's been raising money from supporters to finance the skinhead bands. He's been in the game for five years since he was sixteen. I get the feeling that Benny doesn't like me. Maybe it's because I'm a newcomer and he's suspicious or maybe he just doesn't like me as a person full stop. As he turns to leave he tells me that I should read Hitler's Mein Kamp if I want to become a "real Nazi". I tell him that I will - become a real Nazi, that is.

We've been in the pub for about an hour now and the skinheads seem to be taking us for real. I'm pleased about this because I've been wondering whether to leave because of the constant cold stares. There must be close to three-hundred skinheads in this pub. We've taken over the ground floor, the meeting room upstairs and the cobblestone courtyard. It's quite a sight as I look around me but this is no ordinary music concert - this much I can tell.

There's a latent air of aggression swimming over our heads and already I feel that I am being sucked under the waves into it and the air is bristling with electricity. I can feel myself getting colder and harder emotionally because this is a hard town that I'm in and these are hard looking men that I'm drinking with. If I show any sign of weakness I think they'll use it against me. I'm no softy anyway. I'm not a hard man but I have built up a reputation of being able to look after myself from my school days and these 'rumours' stick with you, like it or not and I don't like it.

I can hear some sort of weird sounding punk music blasting out upstairs but I can't make out a single word of it. It's my turn to buy the drinks, whisky chasers and lagers all round. Well, for three of us anyway. I love whisky; especially the quality brands and I sip at the amber fluid, savouring every drop of this lovely hot moisture. Benny comes racing down the stairs about ten feet away. *"Quick lads. Skrewdriver's about to start. Come on - get upstairs now."* There's a rush for the stairs and play fights break out among the skinheads. It's frenetic and my pulse races.

They're shoving each other around like cattle in an overcrowded slaughterhouse. I think back to the times I spent during my childhood watching the pigs and cows being slaughtered at an abattoir close to my family home in Eastwood. The men there didn't mind grimly fascinated kids watching them work providing we didn't get in their way. Little did I realise that I too would work at the same abattoir when I left school but only for a few weeks thankfully - my older brother was my supervisor and I hated him with a passion.

After ten minutes the snake of skinheads is tailing off and now it's time for me take my first tentative move upstairs. I'm still a little apprehensive but the adrenaline and whisky is spurring me on. I'm behind about ten skinheads now, a few feet from the door when the music erupts with a deafening explosion. I still can't make out the words clearly but it sounds like some Dixie rebel song from America's Deep South. The track ends and I'm still not in the room yet. Someone shouts out from the stage for everyone to move forward to let the stragglers in. So now I'm a straggler - great start.

But with a sudden surge forward, I'm in the hall. I suppose it's a bit like a man losing his virginity really, hesitancy than ecstasy. The skinhead 'musicians' are strumming at their guitars and the drummer is beating away furiously. It looks like a scene from a Nuremberg rally in macrocosm. The stage is bedecked with Nazi flags, black Swastikas stare out menacingly at us and of course our Union flag, the good old Union Jack. Over on my right by the tall windows there's a Confederate flag and beneath it there's a handwritten message in large black letters which reads: **THE SOUTH WILL RISE AGAIN**. This is strange but I like strange and detest co-called normality. It must be some sort of Ku Klux Klan thing, I reason but who knows?

A stocky and cocky skinhead walks to the edge of the centre of the stage, his animus so impressive. He's tattooed down both arms but I can't make out the designs. He's wearing a black T-shirt with a red and black motif in the centre but again I can't make out the design clearly. I'm right at the back getting very frustrated so I decide to push forward to get closer to the stage. I manage about ten yards and that's enough. The lead singer is Ian Stuart Donaldson or just Ian Stuart as he's known to the skinheads. He's the boss and the men adore him.

He's got a really menacing face, a bit like a bitten bulldog's. He starts blurting out some speech about how we are the new elite of the white race, reborn warriors of the *Waffen SS*. He says we are the vanguard of white nationalist resistance against ZOG (Zionist Occupation Government) - it's a term I don't understand yet but men know what it means and they hate ZOG.

Stuart promises that one day we will triumph and cleanse Britain and the Western World of "coloured scum". I have never heard anyone speak so openly about their hatred of immigrants. Eastwood people are passively racist for the most part and don't speak like this in public. But this wasn't Eastwood or indeed Ilkeston talking, it's the far Right's 'skinhead messiah' and his presence is mesmeric, his message bewildering. Stuart's stamping on the stage now, his right arm flailing about like a hedge cutter throwing Nazi salutes and cutting down imaginary Communists. *"Sieg Heil!" Sieg Heil!"* he bellows and a barrage of stiff right arm salutes that festoon like a hedge of glistening spears are raised to meet his salutation.

Ian Stuart shortly before his violent death in 1993

"Rock against Communism, the evils of the world have gotta be rid yeah! Rock against Capitalism the evils of the world they gotta be rid yeah! Long live the Nationalists. Take me apart from my nationalist stance; take a knife to my heart without givin' me a chance yeah. Shut down my papers, don't tell the truth and send us off to prison with no real proof yeah! Rock against Communism, the evils of the world they gotta be rid yeah! Rock against Capitalism, the evils of the world they gotta be rid yeah! Long live the nationalists!"

The mood of the crowd is electric. I know this guy is no great singer or lyricist but he's enchanting and has a huge stage presence. The skinheads love him - they adore him and I'm beginning to like him as well but then again, maybe I just want to have his power to whip up a crowd, it's fascinating. Ian Stuart is a magnetic man for sure. We're jumping up and down on the floor so hard I wonder why we've not fallen into the bar downstairs.

Some of the skinheads are having mock fights which I'm told are the norm at these events so I don't get too worried when a skinhead pushes me a couple of feet back spilling my beer. I just turn round and push him back but not too hard though. We jump up and down together and sing along with Ian Stuart: *"I'll never forget you didn't believe, you'll beg for mercy, get down on your knees - I got the power, I got the power. With these hands I'm gonna save this land, I got the power"!*

I'm impressed with his song, it sounds good to me and I like the strong lyrics. I'm starting to realise that I like power and I like it a lot. The void I've carried with me from my childhood, when Mum left, is gone and I feel empowered. I seem to have real camaraderie with people who share my interest in neo-Nationalism and I don't feel the need to hide my interest any longer. I feel like I have been liberated from the brain drain that has duped so many people into believing the Establishment's propaganda. But I still don't believe these skinheads are real 'Nazis', they are obviously just playing at it or are they?

"Hail, the New Dawn! Hail, the New Dawn! Hail!" Stuart rocks from the stage, Skrewdriver Security (a skinhead stewarding group) flanks him on both sides and we rock with him. The aggressive 1989 drumbeat is thumping in my head and it's shaping the sound and focus of my political future. I know I have entered a world completely different than the one my peers live in but then I hated their artificial world and I also know now that there is no turning back! I'm gripped by it all. I feel happy that after years of looking for a just cause, this rebel has finally arrived – a rebel with a cause and the path of violent rebellion against the State is wide open before me.

CHAPTER 2

THE COMMANDER

It's Friday night again and time to go to the pub with my new 'Nazi' mates. I've been shovelling concrete all day and I'm pretty exhausted but not too tired for a few drinks. Tonight, I'm meeting up with the British Movement boys at the Red Lion pub in Heanor; another gritty Derbyshire town with strong support for the far Right. Heanor is not a tough town in the genre of Ilkeston but there's strong rivalry between all the local towns on the Nottinghamshire and Derbyshire border.

That's the way it's always been as far I'm concerned - it's all I know but then I'm only twenty-one. One thing I've noticed at the skinhead meetings I've been to, is that the inter-town rivalry is non-existent in the far Right. The whole organisation seems to unite everyone behind a common ideology: Britain for the British.

I like being able to drink with my new mates in local towns which previously would have been off bounds to an Eastwood lad out on his own, unless he had a death wish. I just don't get any hassle from local youths anymore and I guess they sense that we're part of something bigger than them. Essentially, we're in a bigger but politically motivated gang and that's the way it is.

Tonight, the Mr Big is coming over from Hucknall, another Nottinghamshire town just two miles from Eastwood. I've heard this man has a fearsome reputation for gang beatings and punishing the enemies of National Socialism. His name is Gordon Jackson, he's in his late thirties, built like a bull dog and everyone is clear about who's in charge when he's around, so I'm told. But I've never been impressed with rumours and reputations. Seeing is believing as far as I'm concerned - it's the only proof!

There's about thirty of us tonight but the Jones brothers aren't here. Steve Jones does not like Jackson because Mr Big has been trying to muscle in on the Blood & Honour music scene. But I want to meet this Mr Big and learn something if I can. It's cold and wet outside now that summer is quickly turning to autumn. In a couple of weeks I'll be twenty-two and winter will be here again. I was born on a dark November night in 1968 and I constantly joke that 'I was born in darkness and have lived in it ever since'.

It's good to get out of boring Eastwood at weekends even if the place I'm going to is only a few miles away. I like experimenting with different things and the far Right is about as different as you can get. Some of my school mates are starting to use drugs for recreational purposes but I need something a bit more real than tripping off to 'paradise' at weekends and that's why I'm in the far Right and proud of it.

We're swilling down the lager beers and having a right old laugh, when in walks a huge man wearing a black bomber jacket, green combat trousers and Doc Marten boots. This must be Mr Big from the way some of the lads are rushing over to him fawning like all creeps do everywhere. I'm not into adulation or self-infatuation - I just want to be sincere about who I am and not make a big thing of it.

Jackson heads straight over to me and sits down beside me at the small round table. Benny has asked him to speak to me - an introduction of sorts, I guess. Jackson is plastered in the usual neo-Nazi paraphernalia: SS and Swastika badges. On his right hand there sits a menacing silver deaths head ring - the skull and crossbones glimmer at me sending a shiver down my spine and they seem to promise a cruel fate.

Jackson likes to play the silent type in an attempt to unnerve a person. He's been sat here for nearly ten minutes without saying a word. His eyes scan the bar looking for threats, real and imagined, with the precision of a hunting hawk. He's getting on my nerves. Just when I'm about to get up and walk over to the bar he speaks: "Heard you're looking for some action, Simon?" I pause wondering what to say. I don't want to sound like an amateur even though that's what I am.

"I might be if there's a good cause to fight for Gordon." He spits back, "You can call me 'Gordy' - everyone else does and there's a good cause for all of us to fight for - racial nationalism." I pause for thought and say, "tell me some more Gordy." He spits back again, "Go and get a couple of pints young man and we'll talk some more." But now he's commanding me or so he thinks.

I buy the drinks and walk back over to our little round table. I try not to stare at Gordy but he's fascinating me in a menacing sort of way. The other skinheads are staring at us whispering among themselves as I sit down. Gordy stares straight at me; his eyes are as cold as steel and the smirk that develops at the corner of his mouth is entirely sinister. He strikes me as being a man of the world but I must not let him overawe me, if I'm going to make the right impression. I want to be seen as an equal and not just another subordinate in his little gang which seems to number no more than forty men at any one time. Maybe he has reserves up his sleeve like a card shark but I don't think so; I think he's bluffing when he talks of big numbers - he's got no ace, he's really full of shit.

Jackson's face is a block of fierce determination and his eyes filter out icy steel from beneath his sharp mousey brown crew cut. Each hair looks like a poisoned talon to me. He looks every inch a hitman, even though I've never met one but I imagine they look like him. He has risen to the position of Midlands commander of the British Movement through a combination of bullying and brutality against his rivals. He sits at the table swilling his beer down his fat throat like a great ogre, ranting about the evils of democracy and Zionism. Without warning he slams his glass down hard on the table. "So, how many men can you contribute to the revolutionary army, Simon?" He demands.

Me: "I've got several mates interested in paramilitary action if you can get the weapons, Gordy." He seems happy.
Jackson: "Not many ugh! I can get over three-hundred involved if we can get the weapons." He's bragging again.
Me: "Well, I'm pretty new to this Gordy and you'll have to give me some time to raise more men." I was bluffing, will he call it?
Jackson: "I'll give you until December [1989] to get thirty men together for action, or you'll get nowhere in the BM, my lad!" As well as being a bully, he gets a kick out of patronising me.
Me: "I'll do my best Gordy - that's all I can say."
Jackson: "You'd better, young man. I don't tolerate people letting me down. No fucking idiots around me understand!" He bellows, drawing chuckles from his sycophantic henchmen.
Me: "Yeah, of course, Gordy. I understand what you're saying." I'm shaking inside but trying hard to disguise my fear because I know he'll feed off my unease.

Gordy lifts his pint and swills another frothing lager down his throat - the waste spills down his bulbous purple lips. He's not a handsome sight but at the same time he's not to be trifled with either. But I'm determined not to be taken over by this bully; I've never lost a battle in my life and I'm not going to lose this one either. Gordy's an arrogant bastard but then my Dad's always been pretty much the same, so I'm used to this behaviour, although my Dad was vastly more intelligent than this evil brute and already I despise the man.

Gordy sits joking with his mates and the air is thick with plumes of nicotine smoke billowing from the tables around us like small chimneys and I wonder if these are the dark satanic mills of William Blake's imagination. Unlike Blake's visions, there are no angels of deliverance seated here tonight just race hating thugs who probably don't know what they are hating and why. I've had enough for one night and I'm thinking that these British Movement boys are not for me, far too extreme. I walk out of the Red Lion pub with Karl Burns in tow and he's clearly agitated about something.

Me: "Come on then Karl, what's up mate?" I ask him. .
Karl: "Simon, you've got to stay away from Gordy, he's bad news. Some of the lads reckon he's killed people before now who've opposed him. Stay away from him - he's a sadistic bastard. He's got it in for you because you're a threat to him." He finishes his speech nervously.
Me: "Well, he ain't gonna kill me. That much I can tell ya Karl. Gordy's no one without his mates. He's just a fat arrogant dictator." I shoot back, acting the tough guy but inside something about Gordy is worrying me. I know this is going to end badly.

I know that Karl has my best interests at heart but I'm not going to give in to Gordy. I'm not a weak man like the rest of his victims but I guess I've just sat and supped with the very Devil himself or at least another incarnation of his earthly malice.

It's late December 1989, the Yuletide festivities are over and I'm recovering from a series of hangovers. I'm looking forward to the New Year and getting involved deeper with Blood & Honour. I've become quite friendly with Ian Stuart and some of his Skrewdriver Security boys. One in particular, Cat Mee, has been a real help in getting me closer to Ian. I feel more in touch with his personality than Gordy's. Ian has got quite a reputation for fighting with the far Left and Nigerian immigrants but he's not aggressive with me and very different than evil Gordy.

Whereas Gordy's a big thug who likes to dominate everyone with the threat of violence, Ian leads by inspiring his followers, not intimidating them. Yeah, of course, Ian can be violent when he wants to be but at least he does not patronise me the whole time like Gordy and his BM boys. I've already made a decision not to get involved with Gordy and the British Movement; they are too violent and extreme for me.

I don't mind mixing it if I have to but I don't want the whole of my life to revolve around street violence because it's not the way forward for the far Right. I'm pretty sure of this and I've not seen any of the legendary street battles yet that so many of my peers brag about. I want to get deeper into the ideological side of neo-Nationalism. I want to read Hitler's Mein Kamp and Alfred Rosenberg's Myth of the 20th Century, so I can speak confidently of my new ideology; I still don't know what the ideology is yet or that it actually exists.

I want to satisfy myself that this is not just a violent pastime for skinheads who think they're Nazis. And I am not going to become a skinhead either; I like my hair too much to have it shaved off. And anyway, the skinhead image of boots, bomber jackets, SS badges, scarred faces and shaved heads is a real turn off to the majority of the British electorate and this battle has to be won at the ballot box. We British have fought in a world war to defeat the Third Reich and open shows of Nazism will not work favourably on British voters. After just a few months, I'm beginning to understand that we need to clean up our act and wear suits and ties which is my favourite garb.

I'm going to be starting my own construction business in early 1990 and I hope to use some of the profits from this venture to fund my political activities but I'm not wasting any money on the skinhead scene. I've been working as a construction worker for two years now and I feel confident enough to branch out on my own as a sub-contractor. One of Maggie Thatcher's babes and capitalism must be made to work for us.

But there's serious courting work to do yet before I secure a contract from a major house builder. I'm sure I'll get there eventually and I never give in when I want something deeply. I have a fanatical willpower to succeed at everything I want to do but if I don't want to do it, then I'm not interested full stop. I'm going to use my thirst for success to propel me through the ranks of the far Right as well - nothing will stop me and the extra money from my business venture will be the icing on the cake.

New Year's Eve is out of the way and I've had another chance meeting with Jackson. He shook my hand in the Lord Nelson pub and wished me a 'happy' new year. I returned the compliment out of a sense to placate him really; there was nothing genuine in my heart when I wished him a happy new year as well. I'm certain it was the same for him.

Anyway, I've read half of Mein Kamp and I can see parallels with my own hard upbringing and that of Hitler's. He suggests that such experiences make a man stronger but I'd rather have had a happy childhood if I'm honest with you. But still, I cannot change my childhood now and must deal with what I have.

I'm going to another Skrewdriver concert on the 20th January 1990 and am looking forward to meeting Ian again. They regard Ian as the Great Father of the far Right in skinhead circles and already his influence is spreading across Western Europe and the United States. Blood & Honour and the skinhead bands led by Skrewdriver are fast becoming a force to be reckoned with on the streets of Western cities but I still feel that I need to join a real political party to further my ambitions.

I think the only way we're going to win power is through the ballot box but the skinheads believe in armed revolution which I feel is surrealistic rather than unrealistic. But I'm going to persevere with Blood & Honour until the right political party comes along. I like Ian Stuart and I think he can teach me a lot I need to know about far Right rivalries and factions. It's minefield and a false step could prove deadly and Ian knows the circuit better than anyone.

It's a Monday morning and I'm up to my arms in mud and concrete, building an extension to a petrol station on the outskirts of Nottingham. It's bloody freezing and my tender parts are as cold as a brass monkey's. Snow is beginning to drift across the landscape and from my trench the whole scene looks like something from *All Quiet on the Western Front*. I imagine what life in the wars must have been like for my ancestors, secretly hoping that one day I will have the opportunity to fight for my country. My great-grandfather Private William Meller was killed in action in Belgium in 1917 and my Mother always talks about him with great pride and love.

I don't mind dying for a good cause because we've all got to die one day anyway. General George Patton once said *"better to fight and die for something than live for nothing."* I'm inspired by the Viking belief in a glorious young death for a warrior as a means to gain entry into an eternal paradise: Valhöl, the spiritual home of the Germanic warrior fallen in battle. My ambitious train of thought comes to an abrupt end when my supervisor Glynn shouts at me to 'get back to work Simon.' Well, it won't be long before Saturday night at the Mundy Arms in Ilkeston.

I slam my shovel into the concrete and start shovelling - back to the grind but destiny will catch up with me for sure. It's Saturday afternoon on the 20th January 1990, the sky is grey and it's freezing cold outside. I lift myself from my bed and walk over to the window to look out into my Dad's well tended garden. I think he cares more for his precious plants than his children but to hell with him. I turn and look at my beautiful Red lying in bed asleep, her vibrant red locks flowing onto the cream embroidered pillow.

William, Harriet, Mary & Jennie Meller in 1915 pictured in Nottingham before embarkation for France. On 4 October 1917 at Ypres in Belgium, William was killed in action in a British infantry charge on German trenches. His body was never recovered and he laid down is life for his country on this thirtieth birthday.

I feel deep love for Catherine and she's the only girl I've ever loved. I've been unfaithful to her many times and I'm sure she knows but does not make an issue of it. Maybe she does not know and is oblivious to the truth. I've made a pact with myself never to betray her again for another woman. We were both virgins when we met two years ago and after a nervous start our lovemaking soon became very passionate and fulfilling. But I've suffered from a wandering eye and girls find me attractive too. I guess I was too young for a serious relationship but we can't choose who we fall in love with can we?

Red is my fond term for Catherine. She hates being called Cath' and will not allow anyone to refer to her as Cath'. "It's Catherine or nothing!" She tells anyone who slips up on this point. We're both stubborn to a fault and sometimes clash over religion. I'm interested in astrology and soon learn that Leos and Scorpios have passionate and fiery relationships but then I've always had a sting in my tail. Red comes from a staunch Roman Catholic family of Irish origin and her family home is just two-hundred yards away from mine. Red's mother is a devout Catholic and she does not like the fact that I've got involved with the far Right.

Carmel is from Dublin in the Republic of Ireland and she thinks that I hate all Irish people which is not true; I only hate the IRA because they murdered two of my former army colleagues at Balleygawley in August 1988. I joined the British Army in August 1987 as a young craphat at Winchester Barracks; the home of the Royal Green Jackets Regiment. After just six weeks I was medically discharged after injuring my knee during an exercise on the assault course.

The army left it open for me to return to training with the Royal Green Jackets once my knee injury was healed but I met Red and the army just didn't matter anymore. I hated being ordered around anyway and did not want to become an automaton. I am not cut out to take orders from anyone. I have lusted after Red since she was fourteen. She used to walk by my living room window and those intense red curls just inflamed my imagination. I've always preferred redheads and I guess it's because they appeal to my passionate nature. There seems to be something very sensual about redheads that I cannot resist and they make the best lovers also, in my experience.

She's waking now and those lovely blue eyes in unison with her infectious smile melt my heart again and again. She rises gently from the duvet taking care not to expose her breasts - she's a respectful lady my little Red - and she winks at me. I wink back at her and see that she's troubled. You get to know your partner's moods after two years together. Suddenly, she blurts out: *"Simon, I don't want you to go to the skinhead meeting tonight. I've got a feeling that something bad is going to happen to you."*

We've always had a strong psychic connection, so I take everything she says like this seriously. *"I've got the same feeling babe, but I have to go. If I cancel now, I'll lose face with Ian and the rest of the lads. Please don't pressure me."* I finish in a reassuring tone. "*Then please be careful and don't take any risks, OK!*" She orders me. I love it when she gets bossy in an affectionate way - it really turns me on. *"I'll take good care babe - I promise you!"* Again I reassure her.

CHAPTER 3

FOREVER YOUNG

The Mundy Arms is packed with skinheads again and Gordy's here with his nasty BM boys and there is real friction, no one seems to like them. Apparently, he's been trying to muscle in on the control of the skinhead bands' finances. He's got a mole inside Blood & Honour too, I've heard from Tommy Swift but then Tommy has always been a loose cannon with his mouth in the few months I've known him. I wonder how Tommy can know such information when he's just another foot-soldier but maybe he's better connected than I know.

(Alistair Bulman – centre – fronts neo-Nazi rock band Whitelaw)

It seems that Alistair 'Benny' Bulman has been 'persuaded' by Jackson to do his bidding, or else, I presume. Poor Benny has been dealing with Blood & Honour's finances for some months now - he's in for hell if he does not comply with Gordy's diktats. Maybe these allegations are just rumours but from the tense atmosphere here tonight I can tell clearly that something is brewing up.

Ian comes walking over to me with a broad smile on his face and shakes my hand vigorously. *"Good to see you again, Simon."* He says with sincerity and I return his warm greeting with heartfelt sincerity. I like Ian a lot despite his fearsome reputation and the fact that he's loathed by the far Left which makes him even more popular in the far Right. He's a guiding force in my life and I trust his judgement. Now, Jackson… well enough said about that evil brute.

I buy the beers and sit with Ian and Cat Mee at a large oblong table in the smoke room. There are old men sat around the tables trying to look disinterested but despite their cloth caps they are incongruous because they're not wearing any Nazi regalia. I guess most of these men have fought in WWII against the Third Reich. Still, we don't bother them and they aren't interested in us and many seem sympathetic to the mantra of rave and nation which was they fought for in WWII. There must be about two-hundred skinheads here tonight not as much as the summer concerts but then winter sorts the men from the boys.

I'm talking to Ian about my belief that we should form a proper political party and wear suits and ties to make our ideology seem innocuous. 'Never judge a book by its cover' - but people do all the time, don't they? First impressions count for a lot in my book and many people share this view. Ian tells me that he's been trying to knock his skinhead followers into shape for years but they will not accept a change in their scene - it's become a club for them and they're happy with their image. I tell Ian that I don't agree and that I need to be part of a political party. *"Well, you can be Simon, if you want to. Just go upstairs and join the BNP. They're into the suited-n-booted image you're looking for mate."* He tells me in his legendary firm but polite manner. *"What's the BNP then Ian?"* I ask him in a serious but puzzled way. *"I've never heard of the BNP."*

"BNP stands for the British National Party and some of their activists are upstairs tonight recruiting. Go up and see them." He instructs me. *"So who do I speak to up there Ian?"* I want to be sure of this. *"A bloke called Karl Brown, he's a well dressed skinhead and he's got another bloke with him who wears his hair long like yours, you little poofter."* We all laugh together and I'm not offended by the 'poofter' comments because I know Ian's just joking. *"Should I go up now Ian?"*

I ask again quite nervously - somehow I know this is going to be a life changing decision. *"Put your nerves aside and get on with it Simon. It's what you want ain't it!"* He's telling me not asking me. I nod back without speaking. *"Then get on with it and tell Karl I sent you up, right!"* I nod again and walk through the smoke room into the adjoining pool room to speak with Richard Jones about the BNP thing. He tells me to turn around and look on the table near to the bar. There's a pile of leaflets on the table printed red and blue on a white background. I walk over and pick one up. The picture depicts a typical scene of debris and burned out cars on some British sink estate. Beneath the picture the BNP lists some of its main policies:

1) An end to non-white immigration and a start to repatriation with generous grants paid to immigrants returning to their homelands.

2) Restoration of the death penalty, particularly for child murderers and a return to life-means-life imprisonment for other serious crimes.

3) British withdrawal from the European Economic Community.

4) Withdrawal of British armed forces from NATO. British armed forces will then protect British interests from a position of armed neutrality and a return to national conscription.

This is for me certainly. I want to find out more about this party and probably join it. There's a post office box address in Kent near London. Not too far away I suppose. My mind is made up and I head off for the stairs to make my way into the music hall. I look around for a couple of minutes then spot a skinhead wearing a smart cream shirt. This must be Karl Brown, so I head off in his direction a mighty ten yards away. I get to his table and see an assortment of BNP leaflets laid out neatly in four separate piles, well presented and disciplined, the very antithesis of the skinhead mob.

Me: "Are you Karl Brown, mate?" I ask him in a firm but polite tone.
Karl: "Yeah that's me mate, who are you." He's quite well spoken like me.
Me: "Ian Stuart sent me up to see you. He tells me you're a BNP activist recruiting for the party tonight. I'm interested in joining."
Karl: "What's your name?" I tell him and he asks me to sit down.
Me: "I'm looking for a political party that has a smart image but believes in racial nationalism to rebuild Britain and save our folk."
Karl: "Well, you've found it in the British National Party, young Simon." I just hate that patronising tone and tell him so. He looks a bit peeved but I think he respects me for being frank with him. Or maybe he's just desperate for recruits.
Karl: "Point taken Simon. Let me introduce you to my colleague Dean."

I shake hands with the long-haired Dean who's also nicknamed 'Lentil' on account of his hippie hairstyle. At first I'm not impressed with the scruffy Dean but he certainly knows his ultra-nationalist position. So I ease off with my impetuous judgements. We sit and talk together for about twenty minutes going over my concerns about presentation, presentation, presentation. I think they get the point and Karl explains that the BNP's leader John Tyndall, does not allow any Nazi badges to be worn on BNP activities and no references to the British people being Nordic or Aryan, just British people.

I get his point and understand him perfectly when he tells me that the media use such references against us by using the 'BNP Nazis' smear. Nothing untruthful here and this BNP lot understand the meaning of realpolitiks. I have had enough of the uncouth skinhead scene and after tonight I'm going to get into the BNP instead but I'll still keep in touch with Ian Stuart.

I promise Karl and David that I'll send off for an information pack and hope to become a member. They give me a BNP newspaper to read, The British Nationalist, and I'm happy-as-Larry. I make off for the bar downstairs. I'm already drunk but a couple more won't do me any harm. Oh God, Gordy's at the bar and I just know he'll starting harassing me to join the British Movement again.

"How ya' doing Gordy?" I ask him with complete disinterest. "I'll be better when new boys like you honour their promises to me." He looks completely pissed off with me. "What promises have I made to you then Gordy?" I tell him with a mean look on my face. I really do not like this man but then he doesn't like himself either, so I'm not alone. In fact, I detest him, he is a just a violent gangster out to make money and he needs to be stopped.

Jackson: "You said you were gonna join the BM."
Me: "I never said any such thing Gordy. I was interested for a while but now I've joined the BNP."
Jackson: "Yeah, they're a bunch a soft wankers. You'll get on fine there." He laughs.
Me: "What'd ya fucking say, ya fat wanker." The beer's talking now but it's time to get things sorted out at last. He turns and looks at me as if he wants to tear me apart but I'm standing my ground. I'll have him if he starts because I'm younger and faster than him.
Jackson: "Look! You give me respect and I'll respect you. Simple enough innit."
Me: "You got that right Gordy. So let's start again shall we... I never told you that I was going to join the BM and you fucking well

know it. So don't start coming the heavy hand with me. I always honour my promises, unlike you." Oh dear, he now looks ready to explode.

Jackson: "I wouldn't fucking have ya now anyway. You're all mouth you young lads. I wouldn't take eight quid off you if you offered it me." (£8 was the subscription for BM membership in 1990.)

Me: "Well now, that is a surprise Gordy. Cos' I've heard you've been taking liberties with membership fees for some time now. It's common knowledge mate! Yet, you're the only one who doesn't seem to know what's going on behind yer back." I chuckle at him. I really hate this vile thug stood before me and I want him to try it on.

Jackson: "Who the fucking hell's been telling ya shit like that. C'mon, I wanna fuckin' know, now ya' little twat."

Me: "You wanna have a go then Gordy." I square up to him, looking him directly in his eyes, they're cold and lifeless like a shark's but he hasn't got the nerve without his gang.

Jackson: "I just wanna know who's been spreadin' these slanders about me."

Me: "Apparently, this person who told me says you've been spending membership fees on leather furniture for your home and new computers as well. Any truth in it?" I'm quite cocky now that I've got him on the defensive.

Jackson: "It's bullshit Simon. I never stole a fellow believer's money in my life. So who's told ya this crap then? I'm gonna sort him out big time." He's like a raging bull.

Me: "That's for me to know and you to find out Gordy. I don't betray my mates, got it!"

Jackson: "I'll find out eventually, you can be sure of that!"

Me: "Not from me you won't!" I tell him. If I tell him, Tommy Swift's a dead man.

Jackson: "Look Simon. We believe in the same thing but have different ways of doing things yeah. Let's agree to disagree. Let me buy you a drink, you've proved yourself." So, he's been testing me all along and boy do I know it.

Me: "Yeah, sure thing Gordy. I'll have a pint of lager please." I never forget my manners, you know.

He orders pints of lager for both of us. We stand and drink our beers for a couple of minutes - then he asks me to watch his pint while he goes to the toilet. And that's when the alarm bells should start ringing but I'm over-confident and drunk. I stand at the bar feeling happy with myself for standing up to the big brute when Richard Jones tells me that Skrewdriver's act is about to start upstairs. *"I'll be up in a minute Bones. Just waiting for Gordy to come back from the toilet."* He nods and disappears.

Seconds later Gordy returns from the 'toilet' with six other skinheads - strange that. They swarm all over me at the bar like wasps waiting to sting me. OH SHIT! What have I got myself into this time, I wonder. My mother should have called me Frank Spencer because like him I'm a prat-n-a-half. This is not going to end well at all. I've made a big mistake coming here tonight.

"I see you've called for the cavalry then Gordy." He tells me to *"shut it"* but I just laugh. Another skinhead postures up to me. *"He said fucking shut it, right!"* This little 'hard man' means 'business'. He's about five foot nothing with a scar from his left ear to the corner of his mouth where it forks off at his lips. He's Scottish as well and guess what: he's called 'Jock'.

Well, fuck me, what a surprise that is. But he's got his mates with him and that's a powerful currency in any man's world. Gordy's gang close in on me and there's nothing cool about them. They're hot and bothered and, like bitches on heat, I know they mean to chop my balls off. But first they've got to get to my zip and I'm staying stumb. I'm just gonna play this one out see how it goes.

But I've got a really sick feeling in my stomach as I think back to the weird vision in the dark alley-way just a few hours before. A sense of fatalism washes over me, enveloping me in its cold and unforgiving grasp. I sense that Gordy and I represent one another's nemesis. His pack of skinhead dogs are snarling for my blood and Jock seems particularly intent on scarring me for life. Violence begets violence, oh yes!

Gordy's closing in on me now, his chest bursting with an hitherto unseen hugeness. It was a different story a few minutes earlier when I faced him down. But he was just fomenting this episode in his twisted and evil mind. There's no escaping this reality, whether I like it or not. Gordy moves in for the kill asking me who's told me that he's on the take. He doesn't seem to be denying it now. Obviously he's buoyed up by the presence of his skinhead cavalry, remiss of yellow scarves but they've got yellow hearts. Only weaklings hunt in packs because a real man can stand alone against the tide of time if necessary, and I hope I'm such a man. Inside I'm shaking with fear.

Jackson demands to know who's told me that he's on the take. Again I tell him that I'm not going to betray my mates even though they have deserted me. They're so close to me now that I can smell the sickening stench of sweat and beer on them. What's going to happen next I wonder. Gordy's trying to get the 'truth' out of me but I'm not playing truth or dare tonight. Suddenly the great oaf walks off to speak with a man wearing a long black crombie coat, in his late forties. I bet he's the boss man - I'll never forget him, the grey haired old bastard.

Gordy's pleading with him and certainly not for my life either; I know he wants to kill me. They're having a heated discussion and the old guy seems quite reluctant to give in to Gordy's demands but eventually I hear Gordy shout: *"So what else should I do with him then, hey - you tell me?"* The old guy looks at Gordy with a sense of reluctance and says: *"Just take him out and do him, right Gordon!"* Gordy nods at him and makes straight for me.

My heart does not just sink, it bloody capsizes. *"Boy are we going to have some fun with you Simon. We've been known to hang people from meat hooks before now, haven't we lads?"* They nod in agreement, each one smirking at me, their eyes fuming with latent hatred. Well, I guess this is it then, I'm done for. I could have made a run for it earlier but I've waited too long, gambling that they were just bluffing. And my mates are upstairs listening to Skrewdriver...oh God, 'no man is an island entire of itself...'

Gordy grabs me by my shoulder length hair and tells the others to grab my arms. In front of everyone, even the old guys wearing flat caps, they frog march me out of the bar through a small passageway that leads outside into the courtyard, execution style. My willpower takes over from the fear as I know I'm going to need it. Gordy is dragging me by my hair across the dimly lit courtyard. He pauses next to a brick wall and slams my head against the sharp engineering bricks. Bloody hell!

I see stars and bluebirds and feel blood dripping down my forehead and Gordy shouts: ***"Fucking kill him!"*** The skinheads lunge at me and shove me over. I land against the brick wall and in a flash draw my hands up to protect my face. I can feel the winter frost biting through my jeans into my warm flesh. BANG, BANG, BANG - the kicks rain down on my head. I can hear the pack snarling and groping with one another to get the best kick at my head. They're kicking the hell out of my head but I'm not damaged, my hands and arms are taking the brunt of their vicious and brutal assault.

I'm finding it hard to breathe now after a couple of minutes of pounding from their heavy Doc Marten boots. My nose is bleeding profusely and I can smell scorched rubber and skin. I'm starting to feel extremely sick but fight it back. The kicks are getting harder and harder but I tell myself that I can take it - that I can take anything. My Dad has beaten me black and blue in the past, so I guess this is nothing knew but even his brutality never descended into this bloody awful savagery.

My eyes are stinging and my hands are in agony as they soak up one hammer-like kick after the other. Oh God above, how much longer can I take this? But Gordy stops the pack and again demands to know who's told me he's on the take. I tell him again that I'm not telling him who told me about his pilfering. I've taken some harsh punishment these last few minutes and I'm hurt but I'm not out for the count yet. So, he orders them to start again. This is a living nightmare.

Whack, whack, whack, the boots rain in. Each kick sounds like an arrow storm whistling into me, ripping pieces of flesh from my head and face. The blood is pouring out of me now and running down my chest. I'm starting to depersonalise this episode as a means to survive but a kick hits me on the forehead jarring me back to reality - **BANG** - my eardrums explode with the shock and my knees go weak and urinate myself. I feel like a drowning man suffocating on his own blood and I can taste the crimson fluid as it flows down my throat.

My teeth are loose and the pain is searing like a hot poker jabbing at my gums. They won't stop until they've killed me and I'm resigned now to a young death, forever young. But still I fight on and the pain in my head from their kicks is so appalling that I depersonalise again and imagine this is happening to someone else. I feel desperately sick and want to vomit but how can I when my hands are covering my face. If I let them down they'll have a turkey shoot on my exposed face. It's agony and the pain is getting worse by the second.

I'm fighting back the taste of nausea and blood like a brave little soldier but a kick comes in at an angle and my right hand is blasted away from my face. Simultaneously another kick thuds straight into my right eye socket and my head just erupts into a world of pain. My head lolls back and I groan, blood and mucus pouring out of my poor broken body.

Whoosh, everything is silent and yellow light surrounds me. I'm in shock. Red lights dance around in the yellow gloom like small but friendly lighthouses warning me to awake, awake. I'm soaring back down the tunnel of reality where in an instant I'm again confronted with horror and torment - no respite this is hell on earth and easy is the road. Only seconds have passed, probably only one or two but I don't know for certain. I'm not certain about any-thing now, I'm just so confused, smashed and crushed like an egg against a brick wall.

My head feels like it's been kicked through two brick walls. My face is ripped and torn apart. I lift my right arm to my face and I can feel my exposed cheekbone and a deep gash pouring out blood. My whole head feels like a crushed pumpkin, oozing blood everywhere. My nose is bleeding so quickly that it feels like a torrential downpour. Oh God, Oh God above, I'm dying, I'm dying - what will my mother think when she knows I'm dead? Catherine, Catherine, I can hear myself calling out into infinity but there's no reply only a deathly quiet and the heavy night frost cuts into my skin with a vengeance, no mercy.

I vomit and the slipstream ruptures through my teeth and pours down my broken body, mingling with my spent blood and urine. I feel desperately humiliated by all of this abuse. I'm finding it hard to stay conscious. Gordy orders his boys back inside the pub telling them that *"the police will be here soon."* They scarper and in a flash they're gone. I feel a bit more relaxed now that they've gone. I don't feel angry like some people might think - I just feel pathetic like a filthy used rag.

Gordy's standing above me and I think he's going to finish me off. What can I do to resist him, I think. Not an awful lot is the answer - in fact, nothing. He bends down and I can feel his breath on my face but there's no odour. It's freezing cold and I'm thinking that I'm lucky this happened in winter because the cold numbs the pain. In fact, I feel numb all over my body now. He demands to know who my informant was and I tell him because it's time for the heroics to come to an end. Many men act tough about surviving interrogation until they really experience it and this is veritable hell on earth where I am.

In a flash he thrusts a knife at my throat which I can't understand because I've told him what he wants to know. But this is not about information, it's about his demented 'pleasure' and he's loving it. He couldn't break me man-to-man but after his mob has crushed me, he laps up the 'glory' of his hollow 'victory' like a typical tyrant. *"I want you to apologise to me for the trouble you've caused me Simon, right!"* He speaks, almost a snake-like hiss, very slowly. I'm disgusted by the thought of apologising to him but I want to see Catherine again, so I bury my remaining pride before he buries me and I do what he demands.

"I'm sssorry Gordon." I blubber back through bubbles of blood but he's not satisfied. *"Say it louder."* He bellows his cold steel cutting into my throat. *"I'm sorry Gordon."* I tell him again. He stands up and laughs, walks a couple feet, stands still, then urinates behind my back. I feel his urine running down by my right leg, my stomach turns again and then he's gone leaving me to fight

for my life. Karl Burns was right about Gordy - he's a complete and utter sadist who revels in his evil work. Still, I'm alive, just about, and I've got a fighting chance yet.

CHAPTER 4

A CHANCE YET

I'm in a serious condition but at least he's gone now and I can now make my fight for survival unhindered by his vicious mob. I paw at my face and the blood seeps through my fingers. My right eye is completely closed and the whole right side of my face feels massively swollen and in parts, crushed and ripped. I panic as I realise what a mess they've made of me. They used to call me 'pretty boy' in Eastwood but after this I'll be disfigured for life - scarface, they'll call me now. I'm sobbing and must just allow myself a few moments of self-pity merely for pity's sake.

The warm trickle of blood flows down my chest and my white shirt must be a 'pretty' sight and I think it's best that I can't see it. I claw the mess out of my left eye and hold my head to the right to allow the blood to flow free. At last, I can see again out of my left eye. It's absolutely freezing out here but at least it numbs the pain. I'm breathing deeply, in short shallow breaths and the moisture from my slipstream makes a dense fog around my broken head. It must be ten below zero or more out here tonight. I look up and see the dark star-studded winter night sky and I know that I must get moving or stay here permanently, forever young, frozen.

So where am I going to go? Can't go back into the pub, it's full of Gordy's boot boys. I think as quickly as I can which is not too fast because I still feel very dizzy. I know! At the bottom of Bath Street, a couple of hundred yards away there's a public telephone box where I can phone for an ambulance. I try to stand but my legs are like jelly so I slump against the wall for a few seconds summoning up every inch of my willpower for this escape to freedom. The blood squirts from my head and face like water pouring from a tap. Just minutes ago I was young and strong but now in a whirlwind of violence I am destroyed.

I force myself to stand erect by leaning against the wall for support. I feel happy to be on my feet again. The blood is squirting out of my face and head but I try to ignore it - I have to concentrate on moving now or else I am dead, last chance. I stumble forward a couple of steps and collide with a large steel dustbin. Shit! I move around it with the agility of a slug but at least I'm moving again. I can see the gates leading out of the courtyard and sense freedom.

I allow myself a painful smile but the blood drips through my open mouth. I'm through the gates and can see Bath Street lit up over to my right. There's two grit car parks between me and salvation - the main road. It's very quiet and no one seems to be around.

Am I imagining this? Am I really dead after all? Everything is surreal and time has slowed down. The searing pain in my eye socket brings me back sharply to reality. I'm alive. The pain has started to kick in again like being hit by a train. It's only about five minutes since Gordy went back into the pub, so I think but I don't know the time and it's too dark to see my watch. I walk on with great difficulty as I wobble and falter every other painful step. This bloody grit car park is a nuisance from hell - just my luck.

There's a slim road between the car parks and I'm half way across it when I trip over and graze my badly bruised hands. How much worse can this get? I try to stand again but my legs are cold like death and numb. Strangely, I still have plenty of strength in my arms. I can see the main road fifty yards ahead but there's no one around to call out to. I'll have to crawl, so I do and it's hell.

This is bloody painful hard work. The blood is pumping out of me again and I feel like giving up but I know that rest at this stage will be final. I scrape on and on and on. My hands are cold and torn from the grit but it's so cold out here that the frost acts like a mild but welcome anaesthetic. But I wish I was at home in bed right now. I'm thinking of Catherine's warm embrace and her gorgeous red locks but I don't know if I'll ever see her again in this lifetime. I want to cry at this thought but I can't - everything is cold and blunt and I must be in shock.

Snap! They'll get a bloody shock when I get my hands on them I think. Good, the anger arrives in time to save me and I'm going to use it to fuel my last few yards to escape. The thought of revenge spurs me on. I'll get those pigs! I'll get those cowardly thugs. I've never fought anyone in a gang in my life, always one on one, the honourable way. I am deeply angry now and feel that I have the strength of thousands with me.

I stand up and stagger forward onto Bath Street. Great, there's a young man walking towards me about twenty yards away but he looks horrified. *"Help me please. Help me please."* I beg him but he screams and runs off. Well, that's it then. I lie down on the tarmac pavement before I fall down. I'm freezing cold and I can see blue and yellow lights exploding in my closed right eye. The pain is unbearable now and I feel sick, very sick. My head is erupting into a raging torrent of pain and unbearable agony. I'm gasping for breath but I must breath slowly lest I start to palpitate but I'm past it now, it's all over; the Goddess of death is coming and I feel little fear.

My head feels like it's stuck to the tarmac. If only this was Alan's tarmac carpets at the Lord Nelson pub...there'd be plentiful help there. But a warm pool of blood is forming around my right ear and spreading out slowly like treacle pouring into a mould of no real shape or consistency. I can see the star-studded night sky very clearly with my left eye. My mind spins and spins and spins but one star seems brighter than the rest - I hope it's my lucky star. I'm getting weaker and weaker now and half of my head feels like it's been chopped off and it's so cold, like a blanket of ice forming over me, and a permafrost beneath me.

I'm deathly cold and the pain is no more, only a numbness envelops me slowly in its deceptive grip. I smile awkwardly and think of my mother and Catherine; the two most important ladies in my life. My breath is slow and laboured. My mind is flickering in and out of consciousness, like a light bulb going on and off, on and off. I must be close to death now and I feel so relaxed - a warm light burns within me. I feel that I'll see everyone I love again on the other side. I begin to wonder how the newspapers will report my death. What will my family think? How will Catherine take it? Oh God above, I'm too young to die....

Clank, clank, clank - the noise is getting closer now and I can hear two voices behind me. This must be the one about the Englishman, Irishman and Scotsman who die and go to heaven, some gallows humour. No. It's a young woman in her late twenties with blonde hair. Well, I've not seen too many angels recently wearing black high-heel boots and stockings so I must be alive.

Then again, maybe I've gone to hell? *"I'm a nurse!"* She tells me. *"Can you hear me?"* I nod to show her I understand. She smiles and tells me that her husband has telephoned for an ambulance. I guess angels must wear high-heel boots and stockings after all. God knows what the husband looks like. She lifts my head and puts something soft and warm under it and I rest back again. I'm going to be alright now.

The nurse is talking to her husband and I don't understand what they're saying but then maybe I don't want to if it's bad. A couple of minutes pass in a timeless age and the screech of a siren fills the night air like the moan of a wailing banshee and blue lights flash on the shop windows like reflections of hope. I'm happy now that the ambulance has arrived. A vehicle draws up behind me. I can hear footsteps and men talking coming closer by the second.

But what's this then? A police sergeant is stood over me like a hovering hawk. *"Come on lad. Let's get you up."* He says in a firm manner. *"I can't move."* I tell him pathetically. *"Look son. You let us move you or you'll be staying on that pavement permanently and in an hour SOCO [Scene of Crime Officers] will be photographing your dead body. So what's it gonna be!"* Charm is not his strong point but his honest and blunt manner is the shock back to reality that I need. *"Where's the ambulance."* I ask him. *"We can get you to hospital quicker, OK!"*

Two police officers lift me under my arms and draw me up slowly. My legs feel like useless vines wilting after the grapes have been plucked. They lift me over to their white riot van where two other officers take me by the arms and lift me slowly into the back. They lay me down across two seats with my legs upright like an old cloth doll. I can't work out why they've put me like this; must be some medical technique. One officer puts a blanket under my head and I feel comfy again. The other officers climb into the van and we're off. Banshee sirens wailing and blue lights clearing the path ahead.

Two young officers about my age (22) sit in front of me, both of them wearing grimaces as they stare at me. I start to panic at this because the police see some very bad sights in their work and they're grimacing at me. Oh shit! I must be in a real bad way. My head feels like its crushed and ripped apart as I finger it nervously. One of the officers senses my anxiety and puts his hand on my left arm. *"Come on mate. Stay calm we're almost there."* I start to cry like a baby and look away. I can feel the van turn the corner and we're here.

Ilkeston Community Hospital is brightly lit and holds the key to my salvation. The side door slides open with a slam. Like helper ants the police remove me gently from the van seats and I feel the crisp cold air on my nostrils again. I still can't move my legs but two officers hold me tightly under each arm and drag me forward. The automatic doors fly open and people look at us bemused. One old man wearing slippers and a nightgown looks like he's seen a bloody ghost, a phantom from hell on a dark and freezing cold night.

A matron stands over by the reception desk near to an open door. They're ready for me then. I force a look up and see the clock striking eleven-fifteen. Gods knows how long this has been going on, I am bewildered. The officers drag me forward and my chin flops onto my chest like a wet kipper with a bloody slap. The blood is pouring out of my head: pitter patter, pitter patter, the noise is soft but all consuming. I can see my feet dragging through the blood on the ceramic tiles; it's a dark red slipstream of human misery. So this then, is the real face of the far Right and I'm learning fast.

The matron wears a mask of distaste and pity on her hard middle-aged face. The officers drag me through the open door and place me on a trolley laden with soft white blankets and lovely soft pillows. I relax and in an instant the matron and a male nurse start fixing white lint dressings on my head and face. Quickly they wrap a bandage around my head and I feel much safer now. They still wear expressions of concern and distaste, clearly at the mess I'm in. (The awful things that human-beings do to one another!) I can hear them talking about calling for the emergency doctor. I panic again. The matron can see my fear and assures me that I'm going to be alright.

I ask why they aren't stitching my wounds to stop the bleeding. *"I'm sorry love but you need x-rays and we can't stitch your wounds until we're sure you haven't got any broken bones."* She's quite apologetic really. *"When are you going to x-ray me then."* I ask her impatiently. *"Well... we've got to transfer you to the QMC in Nottingham because we don't have the specialist equipment here."* It hits me like a bombshell and my heart sinks.

I thought I was safe but this is not over yet by a long shot. *"So what are you waiting for then?"* I demand. *"Listen love, we've got to wait for an ambulance to come from the Derby Royal Infirmary to take you to the QMC. And..."* She pauses, *"...there's an ambulance strike on tonight and services are limited so it might be quite a wait."* What! I can't believe this. *"Look. I'm not gonna last that long. I'm pouring with blood."* I lambaste her, as if she doesn't know. *"You are going to be fine here with us until the ambulance comes, I promise you OK!"*

She's very gentle about it and I calm down again. An eternity seems to pass before the doctor comes to see me. He inspects my face and head and puts new dressings over the open wounds. He tells me that I will be fine but I feel very weak. He turns to the matron and tells her that I must not be given any medication before I'm transferred to the QMC. It's standard procedure with head injury patients I'm told. But it's no real comfort, none at all.

I'm starting to feel desperately weak again and the blood is pumping out of me. The sergeant has been with me all this time. He can see that I'm getting weak again and asks the matron if he can take me to the QMC in the police van. *"Absolutely not! If he dies en route to the Queens then both our jobs are on the line. I understand your concern but the answer is NO!"*

She's in charge here. *"He'll be dead before the ambulance arrives."* He retorts. Have these people forgotten that I'm still here and still alive, I wonder. It's so encouraging to hear them speaking about me in this way. But I'm too weak to speak. I think of Catherine again and my resolve stiffens. I tell myself that I'm going to live and it becomes my mantra - my will to live, not to die young and have a life. Time passes by in a kaleidoscope of emotions. The door opens behind me. At last, the paramedics have arrived. They slide me off the hospital trolley onto their own smaller trolley and whisk me away. The police sergeant follows us and wishes me good luck. It just so happens that he's saved my life and I'm too weak to thank him. Thank you, thank you, I say in my mind.

The ambulance pulls away and we're off on the six mile drive to the Queens Medical Centre on the outskirts of the city of Nottingham. A paramedic hooks me up to a heart rate monitor and holds my hand. I ask him the time and he tells me it's nearly one o'clock. I've been at Ilkeston Community Hospital for just under two hours waiting for this ambulance. I don't feel bitter though - just grateful to be alive. I can see out of the smoked glass rear window and we're passing through Wollaton, close to the beautiful Wollaton Hall and country park. The ambulance turns the corner onto Derby Road and makes the slight ascent up the main road with ease.

A pins-and-needles feeling erupts in my toes and in a flash it sweeps over my entire body. My heart beats rapidly like thunder and then stops, I gasp for breath like a deep rattle in my lungs. Everything goes blank but strangely I'm still aware of everything. and I'm thinking, is this death? I'm hurtling through the dark night sky towards a bright star that seems brighter than the rest. I'm getting closer and closer to this huge crystalline like orb glowing out a radiance of white and silver warmth. Everything is quiet and peaceful and I feel completely loved like at no time in my young life before. But I'm aware of the paramedic ripping at my shirt in the ambulance. I'm thinking the whole time that this is death and somehow it's wonderful and not horrific like I imagined it would be.

I'm about three feet away from the orb when I jerk up with a violent jolt. I'm back in the ambulance, what's happening, and the paramedic is putting down a huge needle. My shirt is wide open and I feel very warm and very much alive. He turns and smiles at me: *"Good to see you back, Simon."* So that was death after all, I think stunned. I can hear the ambulance driver speaking into his radio instructing the hospital: *"ETA two minutes. I repeat. ETA two minutes."* And the ambulance pulls off with great speed.

The doctor is asking me what I experienced when I lost consciousness in the ambulance. I tell him that I don't understand what he's saying. So he puts it bluntly: *"Did you experience anything when you fell asleep in the ambulance?"* His Italian accent is very clear now. *"Yes. Yes I did."* So I tell him what I saw and after a couple of minutes he strokes me gently on the head and tells me: *"We get this all the time in here, don't worry, you're going to make it."* The nurses are laughing and joking with me as we ride the lift to the x-ray suite some floors above the accident and emergency unit. I'm slid in and out of one room after the other and snapped for posterity. After thirty minutes or so the nurses are now taking me to theatre for surgery.

The surgeon stands above me, smiling generously and I feel safe. She explains that my right cheekbone has been fractured in the attack but that she can now stitch my wounds. But because my wounds are mainly facial, it's going to be a long process as the wounds are very messy and uneven. She's going to use a scalpel to straighten up the wounds so they heal neatly. She injects me with several local anaesthetics around my head and face and begins the gruesome task of rebuilding my face.

"Don't worry Simon. We'll soon have you looking beautiful again." But I don't believe her. I believe that I'm going to be scarred for the rest of my life and that no woman will ever want me again because I'm ugly now. I've not even begun to think of the possibility of any lasting psychological damage. I've been handed a lifeline and I think, maybe God wants me to survive for a greater purpose that I don't yet know of....

The surgeon tells me that I've lost close to two pints of blood and I will be kept under observation on one of the wards for a few days. I'm in no mood to argue with her. I fall asleep after a few minutes of her cutting and slicing at my face. I'm so numb I can't feel a thing anymore. Hours later I'm wheeled off to a ward packed with old men coughing and choking - just what I need. I fall asleep in no time, safe in the knowledge that this phoenix will rise again stronger than ever before.

CHAPTER 5

BRANCHING OUT

It's late Sunday afternoon, less than twenty-four hours since I was nearly killed by Gordy's mob. I feel very much changed and I don't mean physically either. I've looked at the damage in a mirror a surgeon brought with him to explain the finer points of a cheekbone fracture. He told me that I may need an operation in six months time if the fracture hasn't healed properly. I feel very tired but very bitter too.

I've got over forty stitches in my face. My sinuses have collapsed and I have a haemorrhage in my right eye. My right eardrum is badly damaged and my front teeth are shattered in several places. My arms are black and blue from the beating and the palms of my hands are raw from crawling over the grit car parks. I've every reason to feel bloody angry with what's happened to me. My face looks like a huge red and blue mess - I now resemble John Merrick, the elephant man. But I have no time for crying, I just want to get out of this hospital quickly. Being on a ward with a lot of old men who are clearly dying is doing nothing for my confidence.

I'm going to phone Dad and ask him to collect me from the hospital around six but first I have to sign myself out and that will be a problem. I call for the nurse and she arrives about ten minutes later. I explain that I will feel better at home. She does not agree and calls for the doctor. Here we go again, yet another clash with 'authority' - it's the story of my life.

"I really do advise you against going home at this time. We expect patients with head injuries like yours to spend at least five days under observation." He explains. *"I understand what you're saying doctor but I'm going home. My girlfriend will look after me. Please just bring me the papers to sign."* I think he's got the point. *"I really do advise against this Mr Smith."* I put my hand up and now he's got the point. He walks off with a sorry look on his face but nowhere near as sorry as mine. The nurse returns with the papers and I sign them immediately. Now I've got to phone Dad and ask him to collect me and I just know that he's going to be a real pain.

"Simon, you should follow the doctor's advice and stay in

hospital for a while." He tells me but I've never been too good at doing what he tells me. *"Look, it's too late for that now Dad - I've signed the discharge papers. Collect me or I'll phone a taxi."* He's persuaded and agrees to collect me. Now it's time to phone Catherine and ask her to come down to my house. She has a go at me too but agrees to come and see me at seven o'clock. I feel awful but I know I will feel more secure at home - familiar surroundings you know. I sit back and decide to get some much-needed sleep.

The nurse wakes me at five-thirty and helps me to get dressed. Dad has brought me some fresh clothes. As I put them on I bemoan the fact that last night's beating has cost me about five-hundred pounds in damaged clothes, all of them the latest fashion labels. PHEW! *"Well, you will get yourself into these scrapes Simon, won't you."* Dad is so patronising, even when he's well meaning. *"Yeah, whatever Dad."* I grumble back.

He's bought my new Hugo Boss blazer for me to wear and it's damned painful getting it on. We sit down and wait for the doctor to bring me a prescription for pain killers and some medical notes for my GP, when Dean Hopewell and his friend from the BNP walk in. *"Sorry to hear about what happened to you Simon."* The tall one says and introduces himself as the Nottingham BNP organiser Calvin Richards. He's got a crew cut with a quiff at the front which makes him look like Tin Tin but with dark hair. *"Yeah thanks for that Calvin. I'll feel a damn sight better when the police catch up with Jackson though."*

He promises to give me any help I want. If I get any problems from the BM that the police can't deal with, then Calvin's BNP boys will be my cavalry - hope they arrive in time. I like Calvin on first impression, even though he thinks he's a bit of a wide boy, but I can see that he's obviously not like the BM scum who did this to me. *"I'll phone you in a couple of days Simon, when you're feeling better, if that's OK with you."* He's polite as well. *"Yeah, that's OK Calvin, look forward to it mate."* He shakes my hand, David does the same and off they go.

Dad looks at me furiously. *"Haven't you learned anything from last night Simon."* Here we go again. *"They could be useful to me Dad. There's no harm in being friendly you know."* God I wish he would listen to me for once. *"Simon, don't be so bloody ridiculous. They might wear decent clothes but their politics are rotten."* He's patronising me again. At times I think that's all parents are good at. *"Dad, you're a staunch Communist by self-confession, so don't lecture me about political extremism, OK!"* The doctor arrives with the goods and prevents a protracted argument between us.

I'm lying in bed when Catherine opens my bedroom door and rushes over to me. *"I bet you thought you'd never see me like this babe. Do I look bad?"* I'm fishing for some TLC. *"Simon, your face will heal in time. I will always love you, you know. You know that don't you."* I tell her I do and I do believe her because she's the golden light in my life. She climbs into bed and caresses me very gently. I can see tears welling up in her eyes and I start to cry as well.

"Please promise me that you will never go to anymore of those horrible meetings Simon." She's serious and so am I when I tell her that the skinhead scene is behind me for good now. I'm not telling her about the BNP though because I'm not serious about it anymore - I don't know what I want. We talk for a few minutes and drift off to sleep. When I wake next morning Catherine's gone off to work and Dad's standing over me asking if I want a cup of tea - yeah that will make it better, won't it.

Dad tells me that an Inspector from Ilkeston Police is coming over to interview me at eleven this morning. Well, I'd better get ready then. I get some clothes on and try to make myself look presentable - ever the narcissus. I'm sitting in the living room next to the open coal fire when the Inspector walks in with a constable. Dad offers them some tea, they accept and he brings it in like a good old trooper. He has his moments, don't we all.

The Inspector starts by saying he's sorry for what's happened to me and I tell him that he's got nothing to be sorry for, he's done nothing wrong to me. Maybe I should just shut up. *"The man who led this gang attack on you is called Gordon Jackson and where does he live Simon?"* I tell him that Jackson lives on a council estate in Hucknall near to the Mason Arms pub, which is his local. The Inspector assures me that the police will arrest him very soon. He finishes by asking me if I will attend Ilkeston Police Station in a couple of days to look at some mug shots to help identify Jackson's accomplices. *"Yes, that will be no problem Inspector."* I tell him and he shakes my hand very lightly. I'm going back to bed to get some well earned sleep.

Dad is shaking me softly. It's already the next morning but he's woken me several times to make sure I'm OK, just like the hospital advised him to. *"Simon, the police are on the phone. They've got some news for you."* He looks happy. *"What's the news then Dad?"* I ask him in a sleepy tone. *"They've got Jackson in custody at Ilkeston Police Station."*

Boy, am I happy now. Jackson the maggot farmer is not quite

the fox he thinks he is - no surprises there, I always knew he was a violent halfwit. I get some clothes on and hobble down the stairs. It's Detective Constable Jim Skinner on the line. *"Morning Simon. DC Skinner speaking. We've got Jackson in custody. We arrested him at six o'clock this morning. Can you come over to the station to identify him for us?"*

"Yes, of course I will Jim but I'll be safe won't I?" My heart is beating like crazy. *"You'll be perfectly safe here with us Simon. You have my word on it."* I've not met Jim but I like the tone of his voice. I've told Dad about the call and he's getting ready to drive me over to Ilkeston. Jim meets us in the car park at the back of Ilkeston Police Station around one in the afternoon. He walks us into the station through the back door. Uniformed police officers are everywhere in the custody suite as I look around which makes me nervous.

Jim tells me that I will have to identify Jackson face to face in a cell with his solicitor, direct confrontation. I'm not scared about this but Jackson is playing the system and wants to unnerve me. He has the right to request this form of identification. He has refused an identity parade and I realise he is desperate, this is his last card and it's no ace either.

Jim walks me to the steel cell door and opens it with a creak. Jackson is sat there with a smirk on his fat ugly face and I feel like killing him on the spot. *"Yes, that's definitely Gordon Jackson. The man who assaulted me on the 20th January at the Mundy Arms."* I speak very clearly. Jackson lowers his head, smirk gone and he looks resigned to his fate. Jim closes the cell door with a bang and I feel very satisfied now that Jackson's caged like the wild animal he is.

Jim takes me to an interview room upstairs to show me some mug shots in the hope of identifying Jackson's accomplices. I spend the best part of an hour looking at some of the ugliest mugs around but without success. I'm disappointed but Jim points out the fact that we've got Jackson. *"We'll get the rest of them in time."* He's confident but I'm not. Something tells me that Jackson will not squeal on his boot boys. The far Right is all about punishment beatings, just like in Northern Ireland, and people who squeal can end up dead.

Jim asks me if I will speak to some senior intelligence officers interested in the far Right's covert activities. No use asking me. I've been to seven skinhead concerts and nearly got killed at the last one. I know the skinheads can be extremely violent but I've not seen any guns or explosives flying around. But then Jim tells me that they found several firearms at Jackson's home in Hucknall this morning. What have I got myself into. When will I ever learn. I guess it's all part of growing up, wish I was somewhere else though.

(Ilkeston Police Station, Derbyshire, England)

Jim explains that two of the seized weapons are high powered air rifles. Another two are deactivated pistols and two more are 22 calibre pistols capable of killing at close range. Unfortunately, the police have not recovered any ammunition so Jackson can't be charged, which I don't understand. Jim says the weapons are going to be destroyed by the police. So, this seems to be the big league then; hence the Special Branch officers who've come to see me.

Jim walks out of the room promising me that I will be escorted home by CID officers when the Special Branch boys have finished with me. Dad is told to go home and leaves immediately. Two men in their forties enter the room and introduce themselves as Frank Bailey and Alan. Frank is over six feet tall and his cocksure swagger shows he loves himself. Alan is my height, five-ten and somewhat more laid back. So, this is the good cop, bad cop routine then. I smile to myself even though it's not really amusing.

Frank looks like a gangster with a gravel face, he sits down and speaks in dulcet tones: *"You know Simon, we see a lot of young kids like you caught up in terrorism and political violence and we do our best to save them from broken lives but most of them never learn. A good few of them even end up dead, like you nearly did. We just want to help you get your life back on track, young man."* Frank's just another patronising prat for sure and he does not seem interested in my welfare at all.

Alan: "You can't be happy about what has happened to you Simon, surely not hey?" I sit silently without replying and my face wears no expression. This is the hard sell.

Frank: "We've been after Jackson for a long time now. He's a real nasty piece of work as you know. We've got good intelligence that he's killed several people in the past but we've not been able to prove anything. He's quite the slippery bastard really. Or, should I say that no one has ever had the courage to come forward before you." Oh dear, he's playing to my ego now but he's got no chance.

Frank: "We need someone on the inside to help us catch up with the likes of Jackson and Ian Stuart. You know Ian Stuart don't you Simon?" I nod without speaking. I feel that these bastards are secretly taping all of this.

Frank: "What do you know about Ian Stuart then, Simon?"

Me: "Only that he is the lead singer of Skrewdriver."

Alan: "Do you know him well enough to have long chats with? Only we've been told that you two have been talking quite a bit recently at his concerts." They have agents already at work undercover in the far Right – he's showed his hand, not every clever at all.

Me: "The concerts are not his. They are for all nationalists who want to make a difference to an unjust system." I really do not like these two SB boys - they're hard as nails and they probably have to be but they strike me as criminals in suits.

Alan: "OK, point accepted but he is the main man, isn't he Simon?"

Me: "As far as I know he's a singer songwriter. I think someone in Blood & Honour runs the shows but I don't know who."

Frank: "Well, we believe that Stuart and Jackson have long been good buddies, if you take my meaning. Splitting the proceeds between them and lying to the members about where the money is going and treating people like you with contempt." I'm boiling inside but that's what he wants - my anger to feed off, pure manipulation.

Me: "There's no way Ian Stuart would ever steal supporters' money. He's too honourable for that. He believes completely in the nationalist cause. Now Jackson would rob his own mother to get ahead in life."

Frank: "Not what we've heard about Stuart anyway, he takes drugs you know, amphetamine addict apparently."

Me: "I don't give a fuck what you've heard. You're just another lying copper trying to destroy the revolution but you won't succeed. We'll triumph in the end." Good God, just listen me.

Alan: "Please calm down Simon, we just wanted to know who was on the take and who not. We've got a better idea about things now. Just stay calm, you're the victim here, we understand that, you know." Alan's a real slimy bastard and there's no sincerity in his voice and I hate these two cold-hearted fuckers.

I start to calm down and I know I've been too hasty with my replies but I could not listen to those slanders against Ian without retort. Ian's been like a father to me these last few months and I know him to be a loyal and honest man. These SB boys are really pissing me off but I must keep my cool - no more mistakes. Alan stands up and suggests a break. Great stuff, get fucked, I think.

The good cop, bad cop team walk out of the room and leave me alone with my thoughts - yet more mind games. I refuse to play their game and just sit and think about Catherine's voluptuous body instead. We're all hot and bothered under the covers when Frank and Alan come back into the room. I switch off immediately - I don't want them poisoning my sexual fantasies.

Alan offers me a cigarette and I refuse it. I don't want anything from these people. Alan draws the look of a studious professor and speaks: *"Well, I bet you're going to be out of work for sometime Simon, what with your injuries."* Here we go… *"It's going to take you quite a while to get back to work, don't you think."* I do not reply to his transparent financial manipulation and find his approach sordid and contemptible.

Frank: "We're willing to pay you very well for any information you can give us about the far Right - especially the activities of Blood & Honour and Ian Stuart." Well, the cat's out now then.

Me: "Let's get something straight shall we Frank. I am a committed nationalist and I will not betray the Cause to you people. If you want to withdraw your support in the Jackson case then just get on with it. Jackson's finished in the far Right now anyway - he's got too many enemies, he's a dead man walking."

Frank: "Yes, we know all about what's going to happen to Jackson once his trial is over. He'll be ready to do anything to survive by then and I do mean anything."

Me: "I don't give a shit what happens to Jackson now. The queer boys can take him in prison for all I care." I laugh in a sick manner, thinking of Jackson's potential horror and my revenge.

Frank: "We'll talk again in several weeks' time Simon, when you've had a real taste of the far Right's power struggles. That's if you're alive in several weeks' time." His voice is cold, his face emotionless. Is this the 'clinical detachment' police officers are taught in training or maybe he's just a cold bastard full stop - I think the latter and detest this bastard, he's just another Jackson with but with a [political] police warrant card.

Me: "Heard something on the grapevine then Frank?" I've bitten and I'm shaking inside.

Frank: "No, just going on our knowledge of the way these things work out usually." He laughs, sick bastard.

He's loving this, I know he is. He's a power freak, just like Jackson. I turn my head away in disgust and look out of the window. Rain is falling lightly on the dirty glass panels, the sky is dark and bleak and the whole scene seems to reflect the dreadful feeling in my heart. I turn and look at Frank and Alan and feel nothing but hatred for these manipulative old bastards. These Special Branch officers don't seem to give a damn about my safety; they're just looking to manipulate my weaknesses for intelligence purposes.

I feel angry again and harbour feelings of hate for the State and its agents. I make up my mind to accept Calvin's offer of BNP protection from Jackson's mob. I'm going to join this racial nationalist party and wage war on its enemies - that's how I feel now. These SB boys have now pushed me over the edge and I feel that there'll be no turning back. One thing is certain: I won't be 'branching out' for them, forgive the pun.

Several weeks later Frank telephones me at home and I'm still 'alive', and getting stronger by the day, to take his call. He wants me to meet him at a pub in Hucknall and I cannot believe the man's sheer audacity. By some strange 'coincidence', Hucknall is Gordon Jackson's hometown and Frank's proposed rendezvous is less than a mile from Jackson's family home. Now why would Frank want me to meet him there? *"I just want to speak to you again. To see if you've changed you're mind about working for us."* Is he for real? *"Frank, get this: I will never work for you in this lifetime or the next!"*

I replace the receiver and feel sick and disgusted. Why is Frank Bailey trying so hard to get me to become an informer, I wonder? And why ask me to meet him in Hucknall? I decide that he's trying to set me up for a hit by Jackson's mob but then he's a [political] police officer and why would he want me out of the way. I guess I'm worth more to him alive than dead - for the moment anyway. But I won't play ball with the not so Special Branch, so that might be the answer. I guess I'll never know the truth of what's happening behind the scenes but I know that I will never trust the cops again, no matter what their rank. I have witnessed at first hand that the police do not give a shit about people – we're all just pawns in their nasty little power games. The only notable exception is Detective Constable Frank Skinner.

This appalling and sinister experience with the dirty Special Branch has taught me that they play a very dangerous 'game' with human life and seem to care little about who get hurts as long as they are safe and well. I know they've got to get intelligence on what the State classifies as 'subversive elements' but they're not getting it from me. I'm not putting my life on the line for them. I'm in enough trouble for now and I've started getting death threats from Jackson's British Movement mob as well, so I'm keeping my head down before it gets blown off – not that Special Branch would care in the slightest.

I've not been out for a drink for weeks but at least I'm going back to work next week. And things are looking good on the business front too - it seems a contract is looming with a major building contractor Sol Construction based in Lincolnshire. A new Chrysalis TV studio is being built in Langley Mill just a mile from my home and Ricky and I are in the running for the job. I used to work for Ricky near Gatwick Airport and he's got a huge amount of experience in the building trade, so we've formed a paper company *Smith & Brooks Groundworks Contractors.*

I've also been invited to a BNP meeting in Nottingham in a few days time and I'm deciding whether to go or not. Life is on the up again and my shattered self-confidence is growing. But nothing will ever erase the terrifying memory of Jackson's brutal punishment beating and at night I feel unable to sleep, not through fear of him returning to kill me, simply the hot sweats and fearful dreams and tremors are haunting me.

How on earth did Frank Bailey and his goons thought I could work for them after all I have suffered and what they have also subjected me to. My hate, such as it is, is directed mainly at Special Branch and I judge them no differently than Jackson's mob. Threatening to kill me if I dared to betray my proposed handler. Now I know what I am fighting against and what I am fighting for and more importantly, why I am doing it. If anyone is going to sell out to the State it will be Jackson not me and that is precisely what Jackson did to save his own skin.

CHAPTER 6

WANTED DEAD OR ALIVE

Catherine and I have been going through a bad patch for months now since I was attacked and I guess our relationship will soon be over. She's not happy that I've got involved in the BNP, despite promising her that I wouldn't. Well, I said that I wasn't going to go to anymore skinhead concerts and I've honoured that part of the bargain but she can't understand that I need the BNP and it needs me. Especially now I've been to my first meeting at The Yorker pub in Nottingham.

John Tyndall spoke at the meeting and I can see why he's our party leader. His speech was packed with patriotic fervour and inspiring talk of building a second British Empire when the BNP takes power. There's also the fact that the BNP boys are protecting me from Jackson's mob. The far Right should be united in a common cause but instead it is beset with internecine warfare and bitter power struggles and I believe the State is behind most of the 'disruptive action'. Tyndall has an Iron Will and he says we must become as steel if we are going to survive and win this war against the "corrupt Establishment".

I've become harder and harsher since I was beaten up. The bruises have nearly gone now but I am very angry inside. I'm still suffering from bad headaches and keep on popping the painkillers. I've not had any more nightmares about the attack though. When I think of it or try to think of it, everything goes blank. I've got plenty of anger though and have started shouting at Catherine a lot, which I don't like because it scares her.

She's been very good to me but I don't know how to control my anger anymore. It just flares up every day without warning and I feel that I want to bash someone or something. I've started punching my bedroom door a lot and I feel better for a while after which is very sad. Being back at work has helped me to exhaust myself physically most of the time but on a mental level I cannot switch off. I've started reading more than at any time in my life. I've ordered a stack of books from the BNP book service and I'm reading John Tyndall's, The Eleventh Hour, his political autobiography in which he promulgates his view of a reborn Britain under his leadership and we are his vanguard.

(Former BNP leader John Tyndall delivers another fiery speech)

Tyndall proposes banning the unions, which are left-leaning; subjugating the power of the City Stock Market to the needs of British industry and making money our servant not our master; all coloured immigrants will be repatriated (although I don't think this can happen without massive bloodshed) and no coloured immigrants will be allowed to enter the country ever again.

This is strong stuff and I'm sold on everything except compulsory repatriation. Surely, voluntary repatriation would work better with electors whether we honour our election pledges or not. If people can see that we (BNP) do not intend to force anyone to leave against their will, then our policy will gain more support. Compulsory repatriation is seen as cruel and extreme and I'm forced to agree with the people who've told me so. The main objective is to win power through force of reasonable argument; armed struggle is not a viable option in Britain and I will not support it - we are not a Banana Republic, yet.

I still believe that I can help to shape the BNP into a 'respectable' political force in mainstream British politics but it's going to take years to materialise this dream. There were a few skinheads at the Nottingham meeting but at least they weren't the British Movement type: all swastika badges and Nazi salutes. So I think there's hope for me in the BNP. Catherine hates the effect the far Right is having on me but I've told her not to make me choose between her and the BNP because she will come second place.

I think it's true to say that the BNP is starting to take over my life but in truth, I don't care. I want to do something memorable with my life and the mainstream political parties do not interest me in the slightest. I voted for Labour at the 1987 General Election but that was more to please my Dad than anything else. *"My family has always voted Labour"* is not a viable argument I'm prepared to tolerate anymore. I've heard this hereditary nonsense so many times that it makes me sick to the core. Anyway, I like the fact that the BNP is different and controversial. I've always wanted to be different than my peers and now I've got what I want - it's just another form of rebellion but now my rebellious nature has purpose and focus.

The new business venture has been going well for the last few weeks and I'm earning more money now than I can spend - so it seems anyway. Sadly, Catherine and I have split up. I have become too aggressive for her and she's had enough of my violent mood swings. I should get some anger management counselling really but my pride will not let me. I don't want to admit I'm weak, so I'm paying the price for being weak - that's life. I still see her every now and then and I feel upset afterwards but I've got the business and the BNP to occupy me now.

My whole time is spent on BNP business and working hard to earn a small fortune. I spend most of my money on flash clothes and expensive drinks. I've been drinking a lot recently because my nerves are in shreds but I'm not going to tell anyone about this. I've got a reputation as a survivor to protect and such admissions will make me look weak. I still love Catherine and I think I've lost her for good now but it's time for work again.

I'm walking down my garden path when I see a poster stuck to a wooden fence across the road from my house. I walk over to it and I'm shocked. It reads: **"GORDON JACKSON: WANTED DEAD OR ALIVE FOR CRIMES AGAINST BRITISH NATIONALISTS!"** Above the crude text is a photograph of Jackson and his sidekick Benny Bulman. Who the hell has put this here right outside my house? My Dad will go crazy if he sees this, so I tear it down as carefully as I can. I'm going to show it to Calvin Richards when I get back home on Friday night and things are escalating again and looks like there's going to be more bloodshed.

I phone Richard Jones when I get to work and he tells me that the same posters have been put up all over Eastwood. Oh, the embarrassment! It's just another act in a long line of nuisances for me but I've probably brought this on myself, so there's no point in complaining about it. Jackson will get his comeuppance sooner rather than later according to some rumours and I can't wait for the day to come.

I met the Ku Klux Klan's Nottingham organiser at the BNP meeting a few weeks ago and he told me that they were after Jackson; that the KKK wanted him dead by any means necessary. But I think Adam and his white wizards are completely off the planet. He even had the audacity to ask me to join the KKK. I just laughed at him and walked off. We don't need an American organisation to tell us what to do here in Britain. They're all pseudo-religious crackpots anyway and the British people are not sold on religious extremism.

Some of them believe that they are the descendants of the lost thirteenth tribe of Israel. Does it not occur to them that the 'lost tribe' was Hebrew/Jewish - their hated enemy? I tell you, there's some real crackpots on the American far Right but the BNP does not seem to be riddled with them but then I've only been to one meeting so far. I'll get to know the BNP better over the coming months but for now Calvin has ordered me to keep a low profile before Jackson's trial which is just a few weeks away
- that's if the white hoods don't get him first.

I've shown Calvin the 'wanted' poster and he believes that it was put up by the KKK. How does he know about this if he's not a member of the KKK himself? I ask him about it and he explains that he went to a few meetings with Adam but left after realising how extreme their religious views are. He assures me that he's only a member of the BNP and no other group. He seems convincing but I'm not entirely sure about his 'story'. Time will tell, as always.

Calvin drives back to Nottingham and leaves me to enjoy a night out with my new BNP mates at the Hayloft pub near Eastwood. Actually, I've recruited all twenty of them from Eastwood and most of them are old school mates of mine, including Richard Jones. We've been out leafleting across Eastwood but haven't met with a very positive response from the locals. Calvin keeps urging me to set up a post office box to cover the West Nottinghamshire region, of which I'm the new organiser. I have told him I'll get round to it after Jackson's trial and he seems happy about it.

The Hayloft is packed as usual on a Friday night and I've had far too much to drink. I'd better get going home as I'm completely shattered after being at work all day, then driving home from Luton where we've been putting down some concrete floors at a new factory on the outskirts of the city. I've been trying to book a taxi without success for thirty minutes. I live just a mile away from the Hayloft but I'm really tired.

The rest of the lads are staying at the pub so I'm going to walk home instead of waiting for a taxi. I make my farewell to the lads and head off home the worse for wear. It's hard going I can tell you. I've nearly fallen over twice by the time I get to Brookhill Leys Road, just a few hundred yards from home. Still, it's all downhill from here, right to the front garden gate. This is the first time I've relaxed in months since the attack and it's a warm night late in June.

There's nobody about which should make me suspicious but I'm too drunk to care. I round the corner onto Knapp Avenue and pause to light a cigarette at the same dark entry where I thought I saw the grim reaper a few months before. I inhale the smoke deeply and feel pleased with myself when I catch a sudden glimpse of flashing steel, like a burst of starlight, and a dark figure lunges at me.

I have no time to react and then something whacks me on the forehead, I fall to my knees with a sharp pain in my head. I look up and see a skinhead running away. He stops, looks back at me and shouts: *"That's for Gordy you bastard!"* Blood is pouring down my face and I get to my feet quickly. From experience I know I have got no time for self-pity and I stumble off towards Brookhill Leys Road to get help. I decide not to go home because Dad's gone away for the weekend and I do not know if someone's waiting for me there.

I manage a few yards up the hill before leaning against a car and then I fall over. This is a nightmare. The skinhead has stabbed me in the forehead and there's a huge gash pouring out blood in the centre of my forehead just below my hairline. I put my fingers to it and feel my exposed skull, which makes me shudder and then I faint. Sometime later I'm aware of people standing around me, a police officer and a paramedic I think but I can't be sure and lose consciousness again.

I wake up at four in the morning with two CID officers standing by my bed. They ask me what I know about the skinhead who attacked me but I've never seen the man before so I can't tell them much about him other than his message was from 'Gordy'. They seem satisfied that I've been attacked by one of Jackson's men to prevent me from testifying against him. They assure me they'll pull out the stops to find him but I don't think Jackson's so careless now that he's under constant surveillance by Special Branch.

I think a 'lone wolf', a person acting on his own initiative, has carried out the attack on Jackson's behalf. Whoever he is, he's not a very good hitman, which is lucky for me. The 'hitman' probably thinks he's done enough to stop me from testifying against Jackson but he's totally wrong. I'm more determined now than ever to stay the course against Jackson and win. I want to see the great oaf sent to prison where he belongs. The thought of Jackson quaffing dirty tap water and chewing on dirty grey porridge gives me immense satisfaction. Sadly though, I realise now that I am completely ensconced in the far Right's tit-for-tat bitter rivalries. I have become vengeful and spend most of my time thinking of Jackson's demise.

I'm sat with Calvin Richards in the Hand on Heart pub in Ilkeston's Cotmanhay district in early summer 1993 just before a local council election. He starts bragging to our group which includes Laurence Johnson and Vic Scothern both former Tories, about the night he got a call from Ian Stuart in July 1990. Calvin explains with much bravado and glee that Ian Stuart ordered him to pick up two men from the KKK at a house in Heanor not far from the Red Lion pub. He was to drive them the five miles from there to Jackson's home in Hucknall. *"Did you collect them then Calvin?"* Laurence asks.

I just listen because I'm used to Calvin's 'bravado' by now having known him for three years. *"Yeah, of course I did. I drove them over to Hucknall and parked outside Jackson's house. I was pretty shocked when they pulled sub-machine guns from a holdall and cocked them ready to kill Jackson once he got home from work."* I just look at Calvin with suspicion and intrigue. I've already heard this story but the KKK men didn't have guns in the first version I heard but SLR cameras to take photos of Jackson. They were trying to unnerve him that's all but he rumbled them and drove off.

"Yeah, Jackson drove up in his white van and they got ready to shoot him but he twigged us and drove off. We chased him for a couple of miles but lost him in the town centre." Cameras become guns and a year later Calvin tells the same story to a different audience and the guns have become cameras. Houdini would have been proud of Calvin's ability to metamorphose inanimate objects at will. But then again, maybe he was telling the truth and firearms can be obtained from the right sources.

I took a few days off work after the stab in the dark to make sure

I'm well enough to face the Crown Court trial in August. It's only just turned July but I need to set things straight in my mind. My nerves are shredded, I've lost Catherine and my business partnership with Ricky is in danger because he says we're not earning enough money. I think he's greedy but I have been neglecting the business recently because of this far Right mess and money means little in my situation.

Ricky wants me to put an advertisement in the local newspaper stating that I have no more connections to the far Right. He thinks this step will help me win back Catherine and get Jackson's mob off my back. Ricky may be a few years older than me but he's got no idea about the reality of the far Right and Catherine is not interested in me now. I also think Ricky's idea will make me a laughing stock and I can't go through with it. I know he means well but the answer is NO. I think Ricky and I will be going our separate ways shortly.

Sure enough just a few days later we agree to dissolve the partnership. I've got a new contract in Leicester and another in Nottingham over the next few weeks so I'll be fine. *S R Smith Groundworks Contractor* is born and *Smith & Brooks* is no more. I prefer to be my own boss and I have never been the type to take orders from other people. I am an individual not a follower and I know my own mind and precisely what I want in life and how to get it.

I've bought myself a new Vauxhall white van for work and had my company name written on the sides in blue and red letters - true patriotic colours. A lot of people wrote me off recently but I've bounced back with a venom. At twenty-two, I've got my own business employing eleven men and business colleagues say they admire me. What could be better? But I want political power now and I want it bad enough to fight for - literally fight for. I don't want power to domineer people with but to make a real difference in society for once because all of the mainstream parties are corrupt and riddled with liars, thieves and traitors.

People are losing faith in mainstream politicians (the corrupt old gang) and the BNP is now growing at a reasonable rate. The deep recession is beginning to hurt people in their pockets and that's when governments hit trouble. It looks like Thatcher's boom is coming to an end and another boom is about to strike at the heart of British society in the form of the resurgent British National Party.

Like Jackson, I am also wanted dead or alive by his boys and the State's hired thugs as well, so I guess I'm like Bon Jovi's immortal classic, *"I walk these streets, a loaded six string on my* *back, I play for keeps, 'cause I might not make it back, I been everywhere, and I'm standing tall, I've seen a million faces an I've rocked them all, because I'm a cowboy, on a steel horse I ride and I'm **wanted, wanted dead or alive**".*

CHAPTER 7

TRIAL AND ERROR

I've waited a long time for this day. Jackson's initial trial date fixed for 13th August 1990 was scrapped to give the Crown Prosecution Service more time to prepare their case. I think a police officer was on holiday over that period so 5th September 1990 is going to be another hot day I will not forget. It's been a hellish wait but these things come to an end eventually. I'm told it's going to be a three-day trial with sentencing on Friday 'if' Jackson is convicted. He can't get away with what he's done, surely not. But after what I've experienced these last few months I do wonder what the outcome will be.

Karl Burns has been working for me for several months now and he's an excellent driver. If anyone tries to intercept us on the way to the court, I'm confident Karl will lose them with ease. I've also got a baseball bat in the car with me for self-defence if we are attacked. The country roads from Eastwood to Derby are beautiful at this time of year. Golden-yellow crops rustle and swarm in the fields either side of the road and plentiful acorn crops cluster on the overhanging oak trees from which hopefully greater oaks will grow. I love the English countryside.

It's a fine Indian summer's day and I should be sun-bathing but instead I'm riding headlong to a life-changing criminal trial in Derby. I wish I was somewhere else really, you know - a fly on Jackson's cell wall would be nice. I would be able to see him panicking about going to jail again. The good news is that Catherine and I, are an item again. I went to see her a few days ago and asked her to support me. She was hesitant at first because I was rotten to her just before we separated. I've promised her that I will treat her like my princess again from now on, so we're giving it another go.

She sat with me in the car last night, parked down a country lane not far from where we live and she looked absolutely gorgeous dressed in black. Silky black trousers and a sleek black top with a golden Christian cross hanging just above her supple pink breasts, flanked by her soft red curls. I love that girl and she must be an angel for taking me back.

I'm sat with Karl inside the court's restaurant when Jackson saunters in with one of his skinhead poodles. Our ten-mile journey to the court was uneventful but now things are going to change. Jackson's lost a couple of stones in weight, grown his hair a little longer and is wearing a tie and a smart shirt but the waxed green hunting jacket lets him down.

Still, he's made a clear attempt to smarten up his image to make a good impression to the court. His poodle goes to the bar and buys food and soft drinks for both of them. I'm sat staring at him and I am going to sit staring at him for a long as it takes to unnerve him. He's not the big-man now without his skinhead mob to do his dirty work for him. I also hope he will get aggressive with me so I can thrash him and claim self-defence but he's as cool as a cucumber, a real psychopath.

I've been told by Calvin that a Searchlight Magazine reporter is covering the entire trial for the fake anti-Fascist monthly, in reality an MI5 satellite operation. Should be interesting but things get even more interesting when the Derby Telegraph's reporter sits down with Jackson. (The reporters have been pointed out to me by DC Jim Skinner.) The reporter, Paul Linford takes out his note-book, starts talking to Jackson and then begins taking down his comments in shorthand.

What are they talking about? But every few minutes Linford turns around and looks at me and laughs with Jackson and his poodle. Just another head game then. The reporter's probably trying to wind me up so he can get a better story: **FAR RIGHT FANATICS IN PITCHED BATTLE AT COURT BEFORE TRIAL.** Any sub-editor will tell you that's too long for a headline. I'm not playing their game and just sit and stare at Jackson who cannot or will not make eye contact with me - coward!

Thirty minutes later, Linford stands up and tells Jackson: *"Well, best of luck with the trial Gordon."* They shake hands and Jackson replies: *"We'll go for drink on Friday when I'm acquitted."* He laughs but does not look at me. Linford tells him that he probably will get acquitted and then they'll go for a drink. The only drink Jackson will be getting on Friday night is prison tap water - I'm sure of it.

Jackson still can't look at me and that proves one thing to me: I've beaten him in the mind, the rest will be child's play. In walks Benny Bulman, looking every inch the shaven head psychopath but in reality he's just Jackson's runner. He stares at me and I start to rise from my chair when he sits down in a flash - Jackson laughs and for once we agree on something: Bulman is a joke! It would make a great headline if anyone knew him outside of little old Underwood in the heart of the 'teaming' Nottinghamshire greenbelt.

The loudspeaker calls everyone in the Crown versus Jackson to court one. Karl and I sit and wait for the Neanderthal boneheads to finish their fish and chips before we leave for the gladiatorial arena of the intellect, as I call it. The waiting is boring but tense. We sit reading some boring magazines on knitting and the likes - mother would be proud of me but I'm not so sure I am. Bulman is called to give evidence and strolls off with a swagger and gives me an evil look - naughty boy - I'll spank him before much longer.

Bulman is here today to give Jackson an alibi for the 20th January this year. According to Benny's testimony, Jackson was at his home in Underwood all night that night - well he must get off now then after that stunning piece of dim-witted garbage. Has it not occurred to Benny that despite being Jackson's look out man on the night of the attack, he's also listed on Blood & Honour literature as the promoter of Skrewdriver on the night. I think he must be having trouble with his glasses again.

A procession of witnesses trawl in and out of the courtroom during the day but I'm not called. And I'm not called the next day either. Patience is a virtue, seldom in a woman but never in a man - the proverb goes. Don't you believe it. I have infinite patience where it comes to matters of justice and revenge. On day three, I'm on at last.

I walk into the courtroom looking at the jury the whole time. I swear my oath on the Bible and the judge tells me I can sit down if I don't feel well enough to stand. I'm going to do this standing up because the missionary position has never done it for me. The defence barrister, arrogant non-entity Noel Philo opens his cross-examination by accusing me of being a covert member of the Ku Klux Klan. I want to laugh out loud but this is a serious accusation so I treat it seriously.

Me: "I have never been a member of the KKK. Do you have a copy of my alleged membership card?"
Philo: "NO! and I'm asking the questions here not you."
Me: "Not unless I am! and your allegation is unfounded therefore."
Philo: "My client says you are a member of the KKK. What do you say." Is this guy deaf or what!
Me: "Your client's word is not worth a tuppance sir. It is ill-concealed slander and no more. The fact that you cannot prove my alleged membership of the KKK speaks volumes for the dishonesty of your client."
Philo: "But you were wearing a Nazi armband on the night in question weren't you Mr Smith!"

(Noel Philo of KCH Barristers, Standard Hill, Nottingham)

Me: "NO! I was not. I was wearing a Nazi lapel badge with a swastika in the centre."
Philo: "So you think a small swastika badge is less offensive to people than a large swastika badge, do you?"
Me: "Yes I do. Swastikas come in all shapes and sizes and I did not see anyone complaining about my badge at the meeting."
Philo: "Mr Hill, the pub landlord says you were wearing a swastika armband that night."
Me: "He's mistaken!"

I turn and ask the judge what on earth any of this has got to do with the alleged assault on me. The judge takes my point and instructs the defence counsel to concentrate on the relevant facts. Jackson's barrister just isn't up to it, even though he's an arrogant sod who loves himself no end. Arrogance or not; he is unable to break me and at this point Jackson's defence is sunk without a trace. I look at the big thug as I walk out of the courtroom and I smile. I remember lying in pools of my blood, vomit and urine mixed with his urine on that bitter cold night. I feel very satisfied now but nothing can take away the pain of my awful memories - I will carry them with me for life.

As I walk out into the waiting room Benny is sat twenty feet away from me. I am livid and feel like hurting him but I control myself until he utters some filthy comment that I will not tolerate from anyone again in my life: *"I'm gonna kill you Smithy!"* The red mist explodes over my eyes and I'm on him in a second: *"When this trial is over Benny I'm gonna fuckin' kill you boy!"* I'm holding him by the throat. He looks at me terrified - what a hard man. The bully only learns when he gets a thrashing and Bulman has earned one. He's a very lucky boy that I'm not like Jackson. I don't need a mob to fight my battles.

The smoke hangs heavily on my lungs. I've been smoking far too much recently and I'm on my second cigarette in five minutes. It's a welcome break from the courtroom grind I can tell you. I feel exhausted and I feel like crying to release the anguish but this is no place for tears. Someone taps me on the shoulder and I turn round half expecting to look straight into the barrel of a gun and bang.

It's DC Jim Skinner. *"You'd better come back into court Simon. Bulman's changed his testimony."* Off we go to face the music. I'm called back into court and cross-examined by Jackson's barrister about my threat to kill Bulman - little creep. I deny it of course but then why should I admit it? Bulman now admits to being at the Mundy Arms on the night of the attack and acting as look out man for Jackson's mob. What a surprise.

The judge tells the court that my threat to kill Bulman cannot be proved and is immaterial - excellent. I'm discharged again to the waiting room. Jackson has testified now and DC Skinner sits with me and my eldest brother to await the jury's verdict. It's a tense time but I'm certain Jackson will go down. Silence hangs over our group like a gloomy cloud until Jackson's barrister walks by with his aide creepy Ron Birkett who just happens to be the Chairman of the Nottingham Law Society.

They stand and stare at me for a few minutes. This is obviously their last chance to break me. Don't they realise that I'm not afraid of little lawyers wearing old girlie wigs. I stand up and walk a couple of yards towards them. They both smile because they think I've bitten but I haven't - it's just counter psychology. Jim looks at me concerned but my heart is fixed on facing down these brilliantined dandies who spin lies without remorse for a 'living'.

The air is alive with electricity and I summon every inch of my willpower for this protracted head game. The little lawyer boys are looking decidedly nervous and step away - I wink at them and smile, turn around, and walk back to Jim and my brother. They look at each other and smile but when I sit down they have the look of respect on them. I'm no hard man really, but I will never be intimated by anyone ever again. I've kissed the angel of death and nothing matters anymore. I have no great love of life and no great fear of death; I live in a void between those extremes. Was it Nietzsche who said: *"When man looks into the abyss, the abyss looks into him."*

The town crier, sorry the court usher, paces into the waiting room to tell us that the jury have reached a verdict. We're off in a flash. The courtroom is packed. Jackson's in the dock where he belongs; the press gather to my left and everyone else stands silently as the judge walks in. The jury deliver a verdict of not guilty on the count of grievous bodily harm but convict Jackson of assault occasioning actual bodily harm. The QMC was 'unable' to rustle up documents that proved I suffered a fractured cheekbone, apparently they are 'lost'. I don't believe a word of it - I smell the hand of a dodgy deal done behind the scenes but I've got no proof.

Jackson is instructed to stand and the judge lectures him: *"You coldly commissioned the brutal attack on Mr Smith. You have a record of considerable violence, including sexual assault on an underage girl and you will go to prison for twenty-seven months. Take him down!"* I am happy and sad. Happy because he's going to prison but sad because I know now that I can let down the barriers and unburden my emotional pain.

The sight of Jackson descending those steps into the cells is haunting and quite surreal. He's gone now and good riddance to him. He will be quaffing prison tap water tonight just as I predicted a couple of days ago. I am deeply disgusted that Jackson has a paedophile conviction against him. So much for the British Movement's much acclaimed 'political morality'.

I just don't know what to feel the day after the trial. Last night was a blank but today has been a rollercoaster. I'm on the front page of today's Derby Evening Telegraph and my photograph is flanked on the left by Jackson's. The headline reads: **MAN IS JAILED FOR 'BULLY BOYS' ATTACK.**

I'm going to a nightclub in Derbyshire tonight and hope no one will recognise me. No such luck! Within minutes of walking into the club I'm recognised and people keep coming up to me, saying *"You're Simon Smith aren't you!"* They're not asking me, they're telling me. The ladies keep telling me that I'm "cute". Is this some big joke! Don't they realise what I've been through. Don't they realise that I nearly died. Of course they don't - they weren't there. No one was there only me and only I can truly appreciate what happened to me.

I try to get into the swing of things by dancing to some rave music but I just can't function. I feel sick and rigid. My muscles are taught, my breathing is shallow and deep and I feel dizzy. I throw a couple of whisky chasers down my throat but to no avail. I can't calm down. I'm having a panic attack and I must get out of here now. I run to the exit and throw open the doors. There's a taxi across the road, it must be for me, so I jump in and tell the driver to take me home. After a couple minutes, I realise that he's asking me where I live?

I'm lying in bed feeling dreadful and my head is spinning. I'm in bed with the blankets held tight over me and I can't understand why I'm having a panic attack in bed of all places. This is worse than a nightmare because at least with a nightmare you can sleep but I'm wide awake and the visions are horrific. The kicks are raining down on me again - the horror, the terror. I'm bleeding again heavily. I'm being sick violently. I scream at the top of my voice… ARRGH! Dad walks into my bedroom. *"Son, calm down, c'mon calm down."*

He tells me that I'll get through this bad patch and that I'm remembering what happened because of the court trial over the last few days. Neither of us realise then that I will be tormented by the same exhausting nightmare every night for the next six years. I'm on trial now because of the errors of my past but I was young and foolish like all young men. Where did I go wrong? But then I am still young and have much to learn about life and the ulterior motives of human beings.

On 7th March 2004, Alistair Bulman came to see me and offloaded some home truths. We exchanged a few points of view and agreed to put the past behind us. I am grateful to Alistair for what he told me and have found respect for him again. But what he told me was shocking and appalling but nothing surprises me about HM Government and its dirty deals. Jackson eventually mounted an appeal against his rightful conviction after serving 11 months in prison. He made a deal with Special Branch and became an informant. It did not do him much good.

In a short period, those he once terrorised turned on him and Jackson was forced out of the British Movement fearing for his miserable life. I told Alistair about Jackson's conviction for child abuse and he was genuinely shocked. He assured me had they known at the time, Jackson would have been expelled from the BM and rightly so. For years Alistair has struggled to keep alive the flame of Blood & Honour and has been a leading light in the growth of the movement across the world. I respect the fact that he has fought for his beliefs. In the end he did the right thing and turned on Jackson and came of age.

Ronald Birkett of Cartwright King solicitors, last saw Jackson in HMP Featherstone shortly before the remand prisoner died. Birkett later claimed, laughably, that he could 'not remember' if he represented Jackson at the Court of Appeal as the presenting solicitor. Birkett has rights of audience in both Magistrates and Crown courts....

Turning to me in a packed bar, and a deadly serious look on his face, Alistair said: ***"You really don't know, do you?"*** I shook my head, bemused. He explained that Jackson had won his appeal against conviction and sentence at the Court of Appeal and was awarded damages by The Home Office. My jaw dropped, my heart sank. I was cold and for a split-second returned to the Mundy Arms 14-years before.

Someone promulgated a rumour that Jackson died in a prison near Liverpool. Yet more fiction, Jackson died in South Staffordshire in October 1995. Alistair explained that Ron Birkett had instructed him to threaten to kill me outside Court 1 on 7th September 1990. Their objective was to provoke a violent response from me so as to favour Jackson's defence. I did not swallow the bait but this fact shows the depths to which lawyers like Ronald Birkett will sink to in 'defence' of their clients.

I contacted Ron Birkett but he claimed he could not remember if he represented Jackson at the Court of Appeal in 1991 – not that I was invited anyway. In Britain, victims of crime are not allowed to contest appeals, everything is done in secret behind the victim's back where dodgy deals are the norm. Nor did police inform me of the appeal. But Birkett could remember that he had not seen Jackson for 10 years! His memory functioned when it suited him.

• Gordon Jackson... Jailed   • Simon Smith... Attacked

Gordon Jackson and Simon Smith at Derby Crown Court, 7th
September 1990. Did Jackson become a Special Branch informant in
prison, persuaded to do the State's dirty work in return for an
overturned conviction and Home Office 'compensation'? No one has
rebutted the allegation with anything like credible evidence.

In truth, five men are still circulated as wanted for grievous bodily harm on me but they cannot be prosecuted now. The files were destroyed to stop me from getting at the truth because Derbyshire Police want the entire matter buried from sight of the public domain. If there's another credible explanation to offer then the police are at liberty to prove it. Derbyshire Police had a duty of care to preserve evidence in an outstanding criminal investigation but made a calculated decision to destroy the evidence. The evidence was destroyed as I got within an inch of the truth.

The CPS also destroyed files and The Home Office has refused to cooperate with me. These are unequivocal signs of an organised cover up designed to suffocate the truth about the State's sordid 'relationship' with Jackson. And his crimes are the State's crimes and one day those responsible will stand trial in the criminal courts.

Man is jailed for 'bully boys' attack

JA. 2   -8 SEP 1990

by Paul Linford

NAZI sympath-
iser Gordon
Jackson was
jailed for 27 months
for commanding a
gang of skinhead
thugs to carry out a
brutal attack on a
fellow right-winger.

The burly six-footer
coldly commissioned five
bully boys to lay into 21-
year-old Simon Smith after
a row over alleged misuse of
funds by a far-right political
group.

Maggot breeder Jackson was
convicted of assault causing actual
bodily harm after a three-day trial
at Derby Crown Court. He was
cleared of a charge of grievous
bodily harm.

The part-time punk promoter —
who is writing a book about the far

right — told the court he sympath-
ised with the views of the British
Nazi Party.

Trouble flared at Ilkeston's
Mundy Arms pub in January
during a discussion about extreme
right wing groups.

Mr Smith, of Manor Road,
Eastwood, claimed Jackson (35), of
Laughton Crescent, Hucknall,
tried to recruit him to the British
National Socialist Movement —
another name for the British Nazi
Party.

But Mr Smith refused, saying the
organisation had misused members' subscriptions.

David Smart, prosecuting, said
Jackson then demanded to know
where he had got the information
from about the funds,

When Mr Smith refused to
answer, he was dragged outside the
pub by Jackson and five skinheads
who smashed his head against a
wall and put the boot in as he fell to

the ground.

Mr Smith was taken to hospital
suffering from a fractured cheekbone, tunnel vision, cuts and
bruises and a bloodshot eye.

Jackson denied claims that he
was the Midlands commander of
the British National Socialist
Movement, but accepted he had
printed membership forms and
posters for them.

Sentencing Jackson to 27
months' imprisonment, Judge
Brian Woods told him he had
"coldly commissioned" the attack
on Smith.

Earlier Noel Philo, defending,
claimed Mr Smith had
"trumped-up" the charge against
Jackson.

He claimed Mr Smith had been
shown to be a liar by telling the
court he had not worn a swastika
armband in the pub — although
former landlord Joseph Hill stated
that he had.

Judge Woods delivered a stern
warning of "dire consequences" for
anyone tempted to carry out
reprisals as a result of the case.

And Derbyshire Police stooped to an all-time low in August and
September 2005 by claiming that the assault on me had not
happened at all. The scurrilous insinuation, defeated with ease,
was part of the 'defence' put up by Derbyshire Police solicitors,
Angela Clarke and Craig Sutherland against my civil claim for
damages on the grounds of abuse of duty of care to preserve
evidence in an outstanding criminal investigation thus abusing my
human rights.

But Andy Wright, Deputy Editor of the Derby Telegraph moved
swiftly to authenticate the article reproduced above and the tales of
Derbyshire Police were sunk, hopelessly sunk! Nonetheless,

Angela Clarke, thinking she could get away with it, continued to insist that the Derby Telegraph article did not prove the attack on me took place, which begs the question why the newspaper printed a story about a non-existent assault and a non-existent criminal trial at Derby Crown Court? Maybe the newspaper simply ran the story as a spoof for a Stephen King story-writing competition?

Once again I was put to a burden of proof over the assault, having already proved the assault happened. Derby Crown Court gave me the case number: **T19930599**. But Judge Wait QC refused my application for a certificate of conviction – what are they hiding and why? This enquiry led on to the Court of Appeal and yet more revealing information was unearthed. Gordon Roland Jackson, born 23.09.1954 had lodged an appeal shortly after his conviction. The Court of Appeal reference number is: **199004740Y2**. But typically, the result of his appeal was "unavailable" thus avoiding further embarrassing questions.

I asked Mrs Lakehal if the case text had been destroyed but was told that the outcome of the appeal was *"unavailable because we don't have access to the files."* The next day I was telephoned by a clerical officer at a London-based legal firm that holds copies of all court records. I cannot name my source because that would be a betrayal of my duty of care as a journalist to protect a confidential source. One makes these friends in the course of one's career. Not all lawyers are corrupt, just most of them.

He told me that the files were unavailable because *"when a person becomes an informant they are protected and all files relating to them are eradicated to stop the person from being located or discredited."* From the outset I alleged that Jackson was a Special Branch informant and it is now perfectly clear that he was working for the State. But the selective elimination of files is beyond regional Special Branches and the authority for this covert action can only be sanctioned by The Home Office.

The policy of the police is to deny everything and intimidate people who stand up to them and expose their lies. During a telephone call with Mrs A K Clarke, Derbyshire Police solicitor, on 15 September 2005, Mrs Clarke was adamant that, ***"We [police] have no duty of care to any member of the public."*** So why do we need a police 'service' that has no duty of care to any member of the public.

But in all honesty, the police can always rely on their equally dysfunctional counterparts in the civil and criminal courts to uphold their 'right' to misrule and deny the decent and just people of this country any form of truth and justice. Consequently, in this battle for the truth and justice, total corruption will be met with total resistance and we will persevere and win! And after years of tireless campaigning, bogged down by deliberate and cowardly obstacles and kicking down doors that had been slammed in my face, as it were, so as to hide the truth, the Department for Constitutional Affairs (DCA) released a copy of the judgment in Gordon Jackson's appeal.

The lies of Derbyshire Police were quite suddenly blown out of the water. And so much for Birkett not being able to remember if there was an appeal at which he represented Jackson as instructing solicitor to barrister Noel Philo. I was both shocked and appalled when I read this piece of contrite nonsense, in the vein so beloved of Britain's degenerated liberal Judiciary. It makes for a stunning and unnerving read, a veritable insight into the warped machinations of British 'justice' at its worst but in reality just another day in the law courts where the scum of the earth play meaningless games with the lives of others: -

ScanFile Retrieval v4.1 – Computer CA0471 – User Guest – Date/Time: 21/09/2005 11:42:37 – name: JACKSON/904740Y2 File Number: 019910823

No. 90/4740/Y2

IN THE COURT OF APPEAL

CRIMINAL DIVISION

Royal Courts of Justice

Friday, 23rd August 1991

Before:
LORD JUSTICE MUSTILL
MR JUSTICE OGNALL
And
MR JUSTICE POTTS

REGINA
V.
GORDON ROLAND JACKSON

(Computer Aided Transcript of the Stenograph Notes of Marten Walsh Cherer Limited, Pemberton House, East Harding Street, London EC4A 3AS. Telephone number 071 538 7635 shorthand writers to the Court)

MR N. PHILO appeared on behalf of the Appellant
MR D. SMART appeared on behalf of the Crown

JUDGMENT

(As approved by Judge)

MR JUSTICE POTTS: On 7th September 1990, in the Crown Court at Derby, before His Honour Judge Woods, the appellant, Gordon Roland Jackson, was convicted following a 3 day trial of an alternative count of actual bodily harm and was sentenced to 27 months' imprisonment. The Charge that he had faced on the indictment was one of inflicting grievous bodily harm contrary to section 20 of the Offences Against the Person Act 1861, and the appellant was found not guilty of that charge.

Jackson now appeals against his conviction by leave of the single judge. The facts giving rise to the charge are comparatively simple. The prosecution case was that on 20th January 1990 the complainant, a Mr Smith, was subjected to an attack by a group of at least six men following a discussion in a public house with the appellant regarding extreme right-wing political groups.

The Crown alleged that the appellant led the group of attackers and directed their assault upon Mr Smith in the public house car park. They alleged, and led evidence, that the appellant pushed Mr Smith's head against the corner of a wall and that Mr Smith was punched and kicked by other youths present. It was the Crown's case, supported by evidence, that the appellant told the youths when they should commence the attack and when they should cease it. There was evidence that, in consequence of the attack, Mr Smith's cheek bone – I use a neutral expression – was damaged and that he sustained cuts and bruises to his face.

The licensee of the public house, a Mr Hill, gave evidence that he saw a group of six youths leave the public house with the appellant at the front and the complainant in the middle. At that time he did not think that there was anything wrong.

The defence case was as follows. The appellant gave evidence to the effect that in the public house he had a conversation with Mr Smith who spoke critically of the misuse of the funds of the East Midlands branch of the British National Socialist Movement. The appellant said that he took no exception to that. He said that he left the bar and went to the toilet. There he met a Mr Bulman, and Mr Bulman, a man with whom he was acquainted, told him that there was transport at the public house to take him away.

In consequence, said the appellant, he walked across the public house yard with Mr Bulman and, when he was doing so, noticed an altercation there. It was dark. He said that he did not see any blow struck and did not see the complainant. He heard raised voices and thought that there was going to be a fight. It was none of his business and, indeed, he was discouraged, he said, from intervening by Mr Bulman. The appellant said that he called out to the group, "leave him alone."

Mr Bulman gave much the same account as the appellant. He confirmed the appellant's evidence that he and the appellant were walking across the yard whilst the altercation was in progress, but he said that the appellant did not shout or say anything to the group. Thus there was a clear issue of fact between the Crown and the defence.

When the appellant was arrested on 23rd January 1990, various documents were seized and examined. Exhibit 2 in the case was one of these documents. It was a list that had on it the name of the *complainant, Mr Smith. That list and that document features in ground 1 of the grounds of appeal against conviction. Having regard, however, to the clear conclusion that we have come to concerning ground 3, we say no more about it.*

Ground 3 is in these terms: "In reminding the jury of the evidence of the case, the learned judge properly, at page 1B, directed the jury that they would decide where the truth was to be found and that all the decisions remained theirs, but at no stage whatsoever in the summing-up did he direct the jury in the normal way that their own views as to the weight of the evidence were to have preference to his and that, where he expressed an opinion or commented on the value and weight of the evidence, they should accept that opinion or comment only if it accorded with their own views and should otherwise give priority to their own opinion and comments. This was a particularly unfortunate omission in a summing-up of the evidence in which the learned judge did not hesitate to express his own views."

It ought to be clear from the above outline that this case called for simple and clear directions as to the law that applied, followed by a succinct summary of the evidence so that the jury could judge the factual issues and reach a verdict. It is, in our view, when considering this appeal, necessary to go back to first principles. We do so by referring to the speech of Lord Hailsham, the Lord Chancellor, in R. V. Lawrence (1981) 73 Cr.App.R.1. The passage that we refer to is to be found at page 5:

> *"A direction to a jury should be custom built to make the jury understand their task in relation to a particular case. Of course it must include references to the burden of proof and the respective roles of jury and judge. But it should also include a succinct and accurate summary of the issues of fact as to which a decision is required, a correct but concise summary of the evidence and arguments on both sides, and a correct statement of the inferences which the jury are entitled to draw from their particular conclusions about the primary facts."*

This trial, as we have indicated, took place in September 1990. at that time, the suggested direction as to the functions of judge and jury in the relevant publication of The Criminal Committee of the Judicial Studies Board was in these terms:

"It is my function to direct you as to the law, that is to say to tell you what the law is. On this aspect of the case you must take what I tell you as being correct and act upon it."
And then:

"You are the sole judges of the facts here. It is for you to decide what evidence you accept and what you reject. If I seem to express a view of the facts, it is your duty to reject that view if it does not appeal to you, and if I omit to mention evidence which you think is important, you must take it into account, just as if I stress evidence which you think is unimportant, you must disregard the fact that I have stressed it."

The judicial Studies Board, in June 1991, has brought the earlier specimen directions up to date. I quote as to the suggested direction concerning functions of judge and jury:

"It is my job to tell you what the law is and how to apply it to the issues of fact that you have to decide and to remind you of the important evidence on these issues. As to the law, you must accept what I tell you. As to the facts, you alone are the judges. It is for you to decide what evidence you accept and what evidence you reject or of which you are unsure. If I appear to have a view of the evidence or of the facts with which you do not agree, reject my view. If I mention or emphasize evidence that you regard as unimportant, disregard that evidence. If I do not mention what you regard as important, follow your own view and take that evidence into account."

We respectfully commend those suggested directions to those who have to try criminal cases. We remind ourselves moreover, in R. V. Sutton, that another division of this court, on 16th March 1990, had to consider a complaint similar to that mounted in the present case. The division in question was presided over by Farquharson LJ, sitting with Garland J and Buckley J. The judgment of the court was given by the learned Lord Justice. Having considered the whole of the summing-up, the learned lord justice concluded that an adequate direction had been given. But he concluded the judgment of the court with these words:

"We are clearly of the view that the jury must have had fairly and squarely in their mind that the questions of evidence and assessment of witnesses were matters for them. In saying that, and in dismissing this appeal, I repeat with emphasis the importance none the less of judges giving clear direction, usually at the outset of the summing-up, so that the jury can fully understand what the extent and limitation of their task is in the context of the judge's direction."

We respectfully adopt those words, and we apply the principle contained in them to the present case. We now go on to consider the summing-up of the learned judge. The learned judge dealt with his function and the jury's function at two points. At page 1B in the transcript, he began his summing-up with these words:

"...... first of all, which of us does what? You have the hard work to do of sorting all the case out and deciding where the truth is to be found. All I am here to do, and it is very easy with two gentlemanly counsel conducting the case, is to keep order and to try, at the end of the case, to explain to you as briefly as I can, the relevant law and to set in front of you what is necessary for you to decide, but all the decisions remain yours."

At page 11C to E of the transcript, in the course of a passage in which the learned judge was making observations concerning the evidence, he said this:

"Does it really matter tuppance whether he [Mr. Smith] was hoisted up and taken out without his feet touching the ground, so to speak, or whether he was put in the position of knowing he had really no alternative but to go? What do you think? It is only what you think that matters but because you cannot get away from the fact that he was beaten up outside rather than inside where people could see and maybe stop what was going on, that, all of this is immaterial and, in any event, still does not help you decide the one thing you do have to decide, which is, whether or not you are sure that Jackson engineered it."

We would observe that at no point in the summing-up did the learned judge give the specimen direction to which we have referred – a simple thing to do. The jury were not told in terms that they were the sole judges of the facts. They were not told in terms that it was for them to decide what evidence to accept and what to reject. They were not told that if the learned judge expressed a view of the facts, it was their duty to reject that view if it did not appeal to them. They were not told that if the learned judge omitted to mention evidence which they thought important, they should follow their own view. They were not told that if the learned judge stressed evidence which they thought to be unimportant, they should disregard that evidence.

Following upon the directions of law, the learned judge attempted to indicate the issues to the jury by commenting on aspects of the evidence. He did so, we have to say, at times in language which was intemperate. We give but two examples. At page 4A-F of the transcript, the learned judge said this:

> "Smith, if he engineered this charge, trumped it up, to use the phrase of the defendant himself, might perhaps have recruited liars to his side all claiming to have seen either the very act done or the overture to it and thereby made his case more convincing. But he does not and we will come to that in a moment. But on this charge was there serious bodily harm done? His evidence is the continuing depression of pain, the sleeplessness, the injury which was that of the fractured cheek bone and all the other things that the doctor enumerated and which the photographs flabbily represent. I say 'flabbily' because they are taken, you will appreciate, after he is cleaned up. <u>You do not see him as he crawls away from the yard in the hope of finding somebody to take some pity on him in the bloody mess and mucus and all the roughage of being pounded by these heroic people who push off the minute they have done what they are ordered to do</u>. There is no suggestion, you see, that Smith did it himself. There is no suggestion that he is a liar in saying the group were ordered to do it and they did. No suggestion that he is a liar, <u>that the leader of this pack of animals got hold of his head and banged and banged it on the edge of the building</u>."
> [Our emphasis]

We remind ourselves that the issues in this case were whether Smith was attacked and thereby sustained injury and whether the appellant took part in that attack. At page 20E to H, the conclusion of the summing-up, the learned judge said this:

> "Now all these last few paragraphs, put down in writing, may sound very unfriendly to the defendant, but I cannot help it.

What I can do to try to redress the balance so that you are left with the two sides evenly reviewed for you to choose between in the course of your vital work, is simply to say this. It is not only Mr Jackson who denies that he made this attack, but so does the witness who has given evidence on his behalf, Mr Bulman. You cannot possibly convict in this case unless, on the vital matters, you disbelieve flatly Mr Jackson's denials and what Mr Bulman said as well, because they are both clear that there was no incidence of violence with which Mr Jackson had anything to do that night whatever."

The opening words of this passage should be noted. As he reached the conclusion of what should have been a summary of the evidence, the learned judge had perhaps been struck by the thought that his comments had gone too far. In order to redress the balance at that stage, it was incumbent upon the judge to remind the jury of the evidence of the defendant and of his witness. He failed to do this. Simply to say, as he did, "It is not only Mr Jackson who denies that he made this attack, but so does the witness who has given evidence on his behalf, Mr Bulman," was, in the circumstances, inadequate.

The learned judge's comments, of which we have given but two examples, have to be set against the wholly inadequate direction that the learned judge gave as to his function and the jury's function and the manner in which the jury were to regard any comments that he might seek to make during the summing-up. The absence of a clear direction on those matters, coupled with the approach and comments of the learned judge, as to the evidence given, was, in the view of this court, so unsatisfactory as to constitute misdirection.

We have therefore been forced to the conclusion that ground 3 is made out and that this appeal must be allowed. We reach this conclusion with regret. This was a simple case. Had the learned judge reminded himself of the essential requirements of summing-up and acted accordingly, it is unlikely that the time of this court would have been taken by the hearing of an appeal. If the judge was in doubt as to what was required of him, then he only had to go to the guidelines issued by the Judicial Studies Board to which we have referred.

We remind ourselves and respectfully commend the words of the Lord Chief Justice in the foreword to the revised specimen directions:

> *"They will often require an adaptation to the circumstances of a particular case. Above all they are not intended to offer solutions to vexed questions of law. I hope, however, that judges will find them useful and perhaps more selfishly that they will help to reduce the flow of appeals against conviction."*

There were no vexed questions of law in this case. At the conclusion of this judgment, we reiterate what we said at the start. What was required was a clear direction as to the law to be applied and a clear and succinct summary of the issues and evidence. This jury unfortunately did not have the assistance of either a clear direction on the law, as it concerned their function and the judge's, or a concise summary of the evidence.

Having regard to the view we have taken in respect of this ground of appeal, it is unnecessary for us to deal with the first ground of appeal which concerns a different matter and about which we have not heard argument.'

Jackson's entirely sound conviction was overturned because a judge spoke the truth about the evil brute and his sadistic life. Judge Brian Woods QC, spoke the truth about Jackson in summing-up to the jury and the Court of Appeal 'judges' were offended because Judge Woods forgot to conform to polite etiquette and thus a guilty man was unleashed upon society to create yet more human misery.

British courts are replete with examples of grovelling, fawning and scraping etiquette of a bygone age that has no place in modern Britain. Wigs and silks etc. etc. are nothing more than laughable costume props in a hideous theatre of insincerity and premeditated con-tricks *aka* as the 'legal profession'. And with his pockets crammed full of Home Office compensation for a crime he had committed and of which he was justly convicted, Jackson used his 'lottery winnings' to fund yet more criminal activity. In the end the State realised that Jackson had to be stopped and he met his doom in HMP Featherstone.

His Death certificate contains vital clues. The document has been redacted, i.e. sections of information have been crossed out. When a document has been tampered with in this manner it is a clear sign that certain information is being withheld for a specific reason. It is unclear what the exact reason is but it is clear that there has been an organised cover-up, designed to prevent the truth, whatever it may be, from entering the public domain. On the Death Certificate the Maiden Surname of Jackson's wife has been withheld. The occupation and usual address has been withheld. Is there any plausible reason why this person should not be identified?

Jackson's place of death is listed as '51 Oaks Drive' and this creates the image of a leafy suburb which is exactly what we expected to find when we visited Oaks Drive on the 26th September 2005. Instead, we found Oaks Drive numbered only 1-40. We asked a prison guard at 17 Oaks Drive how we could find 51 Oaks Drive, she explained that 51 Oaks Drive is in a wing of HMP Brinsford. But HMP Brinsford (pictured below) is a Young Offenders Institution and no one over the age of eighteen is detained there. Jackson was 41-years-old when he died.

On 27th September 2005, I spoke to the Governor of HMP Featherstone and was told that Jackson was in fact detained in his prison. Why is HMP Featherstone not listed on the Death Certificate as the place of death? The prison Governor thought this was an odd fact and could not explain the aberration. He explained that HMP Brinsford is opposite Oaks Drive. The signatory for the Death Certificate has also been crossed out because the General Register Office have been instructed to withhold the details!

In all honesty, most people will feel that Jackson got his just desserts and that natural justice was done. I do not agree. I was denied justice by a Criminal Justice System riddled with the moral cancer of liberalism. Judges are so out of touch with the people they are supposed to serve as public servants that multiple miscarriages of justice are inflicted on the population every year. The question is whether, we, the people who the Judiciary claim to serve are prepared to tolerate their accidental and deliberate mistakes of 'judgment'.

One dark night Jackson emerged from a public house in Hucknall and was ambushed by masked men carrying baseball bats who proceeded to smash his legs. His was left writhing in agony and unable to walk for a long time afterwards. Because he could not cope with the physical pain, he turned to drugs and drink to alleviate his suffering and this substance abuse in turn led him on the dark and unstoppable path to death. His former colleagues in the British Movement had turned on him, not for the assault on me but for selling out to become an informer

And by far the worst aspect of Jackson's reign of terror was that HMG agencies, including the police, turned a blind eye to his many crimes because he was 'useful' to them and when he was no longer useful to them he died, apparently of natural causes in one of the most appalling prisons in England. Even his death was not justice because the criminal justice system allowed him to go on the rampage and then turned a blind eye to his crimes until it was too late.

(HMP Brinsford, Young Offenders Institution)

CHAPTER 8

THE FANATICS

My business has fallen through at the height of the recession in the construction industry in 1991. It's May the same year and I am gutted. Catherine and I are getting on fine which is a real plus but I must now face the embarrassment of closing down my business interests or face bankruptcy. This is not good, not good at all but I have nowhere to escape to so reality it is. Business has been getting worse for months now and I'm sure my BNP membership has something to do with it. But then again, maybe it's just the Tories who've screwed up the economy - boom and bust no more.

I'm down to one employee now and so letting him go will help him to get on with finding a new job. My nerves have been very shaky for weeks now. I would be able to save the business if I could count on full health but I can't so that's it. Yet more frustration to deal with. I've been advised to sign myself on as being ill with the social security and I'm not looking forward to it but failed businessmen before me have faced the same dilemma.

I'll have to put up with the malicious jibes of some of the townsfolk who have been so envious of my success at a young age. But that's the point: at twenty-two I had my own business and some people didn't like it. How the British love the Eddie the Eagle 'spirit' of utter defeatism. How was that we British built the world's greatest empire, with a nation of defeatists? The answer is simple: our forebears were courageous pioneers led by a dedicated upper class. Today, the British seem to be on their knees and riddled with selfishness and cowardice.

Patriotism is like a drug to me and I'm completely addicted. I love the pomp and circumstance of Empire, no more. I'm starting to take seriously the BNP desire to rebuild certain parts of our Empire, especially in mineral rich Africa. Tyndall is a public speaker of immense inspiration and at last year's AGM I was enthused by his fervent patriotism. I'm learning more about ZOG (Zionist Occupation Government) - a phenomenon which white supremacists believe is a highly organised Jewish conspiracy to dominate the world through their control of banking and the mass media. I think the plot is farfetched really but I don't dismiss it out of hand. Paying lip service to it will help me to rise through the ranks of the BNP but I don't believe in a conspiracy by Jews to conquer the world.

It's almost compulsory to hate Jews behind the scenes but we must never speak of it openly. The BNP's national organiser Richard Edmonds, is a compulsive Jew-hater but he leads us with immense courage on rallies and demonstrations. I've only been to a couple of rallies, one in Nottingham, the other in East London, and both were very violent affairs.

I've seen the far Left Anti Nazi League and I'm not impressed. ANL is a front group for the extreme Socialist Workers Party. These neo-Marxists are dedicated to opposing the far Right with violence if necessary, and it often becomes necessary. The West Notts BNP branch now has its own post office box and a couple of hundred supporters and no more. But, we started with just three members a year ago, so I guess we've made some considerable progress. Calvin is talking about forming a mobile reaction group called the Young Templars to travel the country fighting with hardcore 'anti-Nazis' on the far Left. It's going to be a hot year and the battle will go on to the streets again.

We've pretty much agreed that I shall be a political officer from now on, organising the BNP's election campaigns and raising funds to finance our campaigns. Of course, some of the donations will go to Calvin's fighters to buy weapons with. I don't mind turning a blind eye to their 'activities' providing they bring us success. The far Left is violent and we must be violent too if we're going to survive and thrive. Looks like I'll have to get stuck in a few times though to prove myself and retain respect and that's the way it is in these political groups.

For the last six months Richard Edmonds, John Morse and John Tyndall have been encouraging us to split into two factions to wage war on the Establishment. We are going to build our organisation on the Sinn Fein/IRA model in Northern Ireland, which has been so 'successful' there. We are preparing for what the Nazi Propaganda Minister Joseph Goebbles called Total War, referring to Germany's ideological fanatical clash with Soviet Bolshevism in WWII. I've entered the big league of fanatical politics and I want to be part of this war - I want power now at any cost. I've suffered greatly in the last two years but I am harder now than ever before.

I spend my time thinking of the day when we will seize power and settle scores with our political enemies. In private, Tyndall assures us that we will eradicate the far Left by the firing squad method when we have power. Coloureds will be forcibly deported and Jews will be forced to swear an oath of allegiance to the

Crown; if they refuse they will be deported but not before their assets (merchant banks and media) are sequestered by our government.

This is frightening stuff but my business has fallen through and I'm prepared to believe Tyndall when he tells me that I'm another victim of greedy Capitalism - "Long live the nationalists!" I can hear Ian Stuart's words bubbling in my brain. Anger fuels my 'rationale' and as a person I no longer resemble the person I was two years ago. Everything has become 'deadly' serious now and tomorrow (Saturday) I will be in action against the Anti Nazi League in Nottingham. It's a chance to prove myself and I'm going to take it. Two years ago when I first got involved in the far Right I was a mere boy but now I'm a man. I lust for battle against the enemy and all I have in my life now is anger but I don't care. Someone or something has got to pay for my pain.

It's one o'clock in Nottingham city centre and the place is teeming with blissfully unaware Saturday shoppers - the perfect smokescreen for our assault on the ANL demonstrators gathered near to the Broad Marsh Shopping Centre. We walk down briskly to meet them. We're all armed with batons and steel coshes and this will be a lightning fast raid. Calvin's in charge because this is his baby; I'm here to retain respect and give the lefties a bashing.

We can see them standing fifty yards away, chanting "Nazi Scum off our streets" - we'll soon clear these Red Scum off our streets. We are a dozen strong and they are similar in number. They've spotted us and they are grabbing their wooden lollipop sticks to attack us. We rush forward, running at speed. I can feel my heart beating like crazy as we close on them. I'm picking out targets: there's an Asian guy carrying a piece of wood and I'm having him.

The clash is instant. The Asian guy swings his baton at me but misses. I sidestep and slam my baton into the side of his face and he's down on the cobblestone pavement in a flash. He's bleeding and groaning but I don't give a shit - this is war. I look to my right and Calvin has gone down. I rush forward and take a hit on my left shoulder from a white guy wearing dreadlocks. Someone screams at him, "you fucking dirty white nigger, get the bastard Simon."

Bang! I slam my cosh straight into his face and he's down. I can taste the violence and the thrill seems better than sex. Andy from Newark is kicking the shit out of some leftie on the ground. The shoppers are startled at what's happening. For them it's a normal day at the Capitalist feeding trough but not for us; we are re-enacting the merciless battles of the Russian Front, it's unfinished business. All the lefties are down when police sirens start wailing in the distance and now it's time to leg it.

It takes us two minutes to get to the waiting transports and we're away heading for Laurence Johnson's home in West Bridgford, an elite middle class district of Nottingham. Ten minutes after we've hospitalised a dozen lefties we're at Laurence's home for an election meeting. We're buoyed up at our success. We walk into the attic room and Laurence and John Peacock raise the roof with a round of applause. We cheer and shout. We're happy that we've scored a sound victory over the dirty Anti Nazi League and they're going to get even more of the same over the next few months. We are going to wipe the Red Menace off the streets of Britain, which should have been done years ago.

We intend to wipe them off the streets with serious violence and it's the only language they understand. There's no turning back for me now. The meeting gets under way and I moot an idea to raise money from our middle class members who hold dual membership of the BNP and the Tory Party. Peacock, the East Midlands organiser is not impressed but gives me permission to send out a couple of hundred begging letters. I will not be stopped by anyone. I've tasted battle with the enemy and I'm prepared to die for this Cause.

"Take me apart from my nationalist stance, take a knife to my heart without giving me a chance yeah. Shut down our papers, don't tell the truth and send us off to prison with no real proof yeah. Rock against Communism, the evils of the world they gotta be rid yeah. Rock against Capitalism, the evils of the world they've gotta be rid yeah. Long live the nationalists!" The Nationalist anthem rails through my mind.

"Seig Heil! Seig Heil! Seig Heil!" The heavy rancour is deafening. *"White power! White power! White power!"* The chorus rolls on. *"Seig Heil! Seig Heil! Seig Heil!"* The skinheads lead a deafening chorus of cheers that thunders like Thor's hammer striking clouds of lightning inspiration across the trembling hall. The venue is an old Victorian period hall in London's East End, November 1991. I've spent the late summer battling with the far Left all over England and I'm now a veteran and widely respected in the BNP. My ambition has no limits and I shall stop at nothing to become the BNP chairman.

Tyndall's an old man and his time will come to an end soon. When that happens I shall step into the breach and I've got plenty of support in the party. I'm making big impressions on the membership. My time will come. The boom from the skinheads' stamping feet is intoxicating. The whole scene is reminiscent of a fringe meeting at a Nuremberg rally in the 1930s but this is not the way to win over the majority of the electorate.

There's no Hitler here, but Tyndall's our next best thing for the moment. The skinheads in the party refer to him as the 'Fuhrer' but the rest of us, the majority, just call him the 'Chairman'. That's the way he wants it and he's right too. We can't make open shows of Nazism in Britain and get away with it in the eyes of the electorate. British voters are nowhere near as stupid as mainstream politicians think they are.

We're under constant surveillance by Special Branch and MI5. And in my case because my uncle worked in Government Service for nearly 20-years, I am watched carefully. We all have to watch our step. But this meeting is fast becoming a parade of neo-Nazism and officially we're simply Nationalists - that's the party line and I'm happy to tow it. Edmonds and Tyndall have ordered our new Stewarding Group to halt the Nazi salutes because the national media are here. (No one realises that the Stewarding Group will soon become the neo-Nazi terror group Combat 18, feared across the Western world but later corrupted by MI5 to become just another State pseudo-gang.)

The skinheads are like naughty children when they're chastised but Charlie Sargent and Eddie Whicker are tough guys to be reckoned with. After a few minutes the Nazi salutes and chants stop. We listen with fixated minds to our leaders ranting about the self-evident evils of Capitalism and multiracialism. Edmonds is very impressive and holds an audience in the palm of his hand with ease. Not surprising really: he was a school teacher until taking redundancy with a big settlement which he has used to buy the 'bunker' in Kent, now the BNP's bookshop.

It's our HQ really but we maintain the fiction for public consumption. Tyndall takes the rostrum and pounds out a speech about the influence of Zionists in the British and US governments, controlling things from behind the scenes and he meets with massive approval. *"And when some Hebrew can come here and dictate to the British government what our policy should be in Palestine, we see our government controlled by Zionism."* He must be referring to the recent visit of the Israeli premier Yitzhak Shamir to Britain to gather support for Israel's war against Islamic fundamentalism.

I don't like the Israelis or the Palestinians because theirs is a

Semitic war that has nothing to do with Britain. But if anti-Zionism draws support from the membership I'm happy to support it until Tyndall is no longer a force and the party tone can be moderated. All leaders come and go but for now I'm supporting Tyndall; he's offered to give me some professional writing instruction so I can write articles for his monthly magazine Spearhead. I want to start impressing myself on the intellectual wing of the party too. I have to do this in addition to street fighting to gain the respect I need to become the BNP's leader in a few years' time and this meeting is a good place to circulate.

Tyndall's ranting and raving about sending Britain's immigrant population back to their ancestral homelands and draws thunderous applause from everyone, me included. I know that we will only become a mainstream party if we tone down our overt racism but that's going to take years to transform - I'm a pragmatist if nothing else.

The BNP's finance officer takes the stage to launch the Dutch auction which will finance the party's General Election campaign in 1992. Laurence Johnson is going to stand for the BNP in the Erewash constituency in Derbyshire - a seat currently held by the Tories. Our campaign will begin in January 1992 to give us a few months to build up support. We need to get established in the community first.

Everyone here recognises the importance of fund raising so we all throw in crisp bank notes. Despite what the far Left say about the BNP being bankrolled by national companies, the only money I've seen going into the party is from grassroots supporters and the skinhead bands. The BNP is almost entirely financed by its members and as I've learned, the most generous donors are those who hold dual membership of the BNP and Tory Party. I think these 'turncoat' Tories are looking ahead to the days when they are no longer a great political force and we're convinced the Tories will destroy themselves eventually.

We've also hatched a plot to infiltrate some of our brightest members into the Tory Party at constituency level. But this will not begin until next summer as these things take time to organise. Still, John Tyndall is making good progress with the former Tory Defence Minister Alan Clark and the two men meet for dinner in London twice a month. Tyndall often brags about his luncheons with Clark in Spearhead; so I'm inclined to believe him. His reason for advertising this activity is to impress on the membership that he's well connected with the powers that be but that he is not corrupt as well. Strange world!

The Dutch auction has raised a few grand and the leadership is happy - Tyndall will continue to get his wages. It's time to leave now and face the police and dirty Anti Nazi League demonstrators outside the hall. We've travelled at lightning speed from Mill Hill, dodging leftie spotters the whole way, so I think our luck will hold. As I reach the doors leading out onto the main road, there are hundreds of police and left-wing demonstrators. It's an impressive scene as we stroll by their noisy ranks buoyed up by the AGM's hypnotic imagery. The lefties would love to have a pop at us but they can't get through the police ranks but tomorrow will be different on Brick Lane in the East End when they are lured into an ambush.

We're expecting a clash with ANL - the lads use the term ANAL to describe the ANL but I think that's too coarse for public consumption, so I stick to ANL - and a radical group of Asians from the local community who call themselves, The Bengali Tigers. They'd better not turn out to be little pussycats tomorrow because the shit is going to hit the fan in a big way.

Our Stewards plan to ambush the lefties as they leave through the East End's maze of streets. But tonight we're off to the West End to get some R&R. We're staying at a big house near Euston - the home of a BNP activist who's also an artist for a photography company in London. It's a big Victorian period house, like so many in the West End but it's also bloody freezing and damp in the attic room where I'm sleeping tonight. Still, a few whiskies will cure that.

It's a freezing cold Sunday morning and fog hangs around like an unwanted gatecrasher at a party. It's been freezing all night and I'm shaking like a leaf when the BNP van turns up to take us the few miles to Brick Lane. These Hugo Boss suits are pretty classy but a warm parka would be better on a day like this. I'm nervous on the way there and any man who says he's not afraid before a battle is a complete psychopath or a liar. I'm just a well-dressed political fanatic and I do not see myself as a thug. It's amazing what people can hide from themselves behind the insidious veil of ideology. Liberalism suggests that 'absolute power corrupts absolutely'. We're a long way from being that powerful yet.

We come to rest in some car park about five-hundred yards from Brick Lane and make off the war zone. My stomach is awash with spent adrenalin and I'm always like this before an action. The banter on the journey over here has been dominated by tall tales of what we're going to inflict on ANL today. I'll settle for holding my ground and getting home safely but I'll hammer anyone who tries to hurt me - for sure.

Our numbers are getting stronger by the minute and we must be close to a thousand strong now the Blood & Honour skinheads have arrived with their Celtic Cross flags, plastered in swastika badges. They are our fellow travellers really and they donate good sums to the BNP from the skinhead concerts. We don't complain and we don't allow them to hold office in the party either, just take their money. B&H refers to the BNP as the 'political wing' of British Nationalism. I'm sure they see themselves as the 'real warriors'.

We can hear the lefties marching towards us from less than a quarter of a mile away. *"Nazi scum off our streets! Nazi scum off our streets!"* Their chorus rings out and from afar they seem thousands strong. But don't they know any other chorus than *"Nazi scum off our streets?"* I respect the fact that they fight for what they believe in and we fight for what we believe in - simple as that. We are committed to destroying each other and in the end one side will triumph. They're getting closer and closer and I look around me to get a view of our numbers.

We must be just over a thousand strong - our flags flutter softly in the light wind. Our hearts are made of steel and we are completely silent. It's like a macabre scene of dreadful defiance before two armies clash on some ancient battlefield. The BNP is completely influenced by romantic militarism and some of us are hell-bent on a glorious young death in battle. It scares the shit out of me but I'm not showing it to anyone. One has to be emotionally ruthless to survive in the world of politics and I live by its rules, I did not make them.

The Muslim anti-'Nazi' League...?

The lefties come running down the street opposite our ranks about fifty yards away. We brace for battle but when they see the strength of our numbers they come to a grinding halt. Seizing the initiative we erupt into a deafening but victorious cheer. *"Hurrahhhhhh! Hurrahhhhhh! Rule Britannia! Britannia rules the waves..."* The lefties are stunned and quickly shuffle off behind their police protectors. Actually the police have a job to do to keep both sides apart and I wouldn't do their job for all the tea in Yorkshire. The police are hated by both sides here today and are frequently spat on but I don't bother with that vulgar activity - how does it further the revolution and it so common.

We're chanting immature slogans at one other for the best part of twenty minutes when Eddie Whicker comes pacing up to me. *"Fancy some action Simon?"* It's not a question. *"Damn right I do Ed. What's cookin'?"* He tells me that we're going to break through the police lines and four-feet high steel barriers and hit the Reds in the centre. The Leader Battalion formed by our national elections officer Eddie Butler, starts to gather for the lightning offensive. It's not a good strategy because once we're in the Reds' centre we'll be cut up by their flanks and the police. It's a suicide mission. I tell Whicker that we must attack on their flanks as well the moment we hit the Reds in the centre. He rushes off 'arranging' things but the police are bringing up reinforcements - they've clocked what's happening.

The air is alive with electricity like it always is on these occasions. Whicker's men are formed up now and ready to attack. Whicker looks at me, I nod and they're off. They smash straight through the police lines and barriers in seconds, we all surge forward from the centre but the police are closing in on us in a pincer movement. I can see the hopelessness of this situation and withdraw back to our lines. The police force the Leader Battalion back behind our barriers and the Reds chuckle and jibe at us.

It was never going to be a successful attack because Whicker just hadn't thought out his strategy. You cannot attack straight through the centre when your flanks are held in stalemate by superior numbers and steel barriers. Still, the minor assault shows the Reds and the police that we mean business. An hour passes without further event and the police order us to disperse - demonstration over. The Reds file off first behind the police lines and back in the direction they've come from.

We have to wait thirty minutes before we're released from the pen but we're happy because we know that the Reds will be breaking up into small groups now and two-hundred fanatics led by

Charlie Sargent are waiting to ambush them. We file off and head for some earthy East End pubs. Two hours later Sargent's men start bringing back reports of a bloodbath. They claim to have stabbed and slashed a few Reds but I wasn't there so I can't confirm their story. I'm sure though they've done some serious damage to the Reds though. It's been an eventful weekend down in London and I'm more committed to the Cause now than ever. I'm fanatical and hungry for action. The General Election campaign will start our major offensive against the State on every level - this is total war!

CHAPTER 9

TOTAL WAR

We've spent months leafleting in the Erewash constituency, without any sort of trouble. The lefties have been out looking for us on midweek nights but we've outfoxed them by not visiting the same area twice. They will be annoyed about this but Class War is threatening a 'disturbance' at the election count tonight in Long Eaton and I think it's just hot air from the far Left. Riot police are outside the doors at the sports centre and Special Branch officers are active inside. No surprise really when we're around. How do I know Special Branch officers are here? I've just had an interesting conversation with my old 'mate' Frank Bailey.

Frank: "You fully recovered from the attack now then Simon?"
Me: "One-hundred per cent Frank."
Frank: "I'm glad. I really am."
Me: "Well thanks for that Frank." And I start to walk off.
Frank: "Not so fast Simon. I would like a word."
Me: "I'm all ears." I'll humour him.
Frank: "I've investigated corrupt politicians from all parties in the past, you know." He must be referring to Labour's PPC Sean Stafford who's under investigation for fraud and signing off council accounts from his prison cell.
Me: "So, what's your point Frank?" Frank: "I think you [BNP] will do well tonight. Better than one per cent, anyway." He chuckles.
Me: "I certainly hope so."
Frank: "We don't want any trouble tonight, Simon."
Me: "Keep the Red trash at bay outside, and you won't get any. Deal?"
Frank: "Done. The BNP will win eventually you know, Simon.
"Me: "Yes, I know! And God help our enemies when we do."

I wink at him and walk into the hall where the count is going on. Frank smiles wryly as I turn away and he will never get the better of me. But, I felt warmth in his voice tonight - he must be *human, all too human* after all. Laurence Johnson is talking to an old guy with a blue rosette - Tory so I'm going to see what's happening. The 'Tory' is no less than the Tory candidate's father. He wants some of our literature to read and tells me that if he likes what he sees, he will 'arrange' for some donations to come our way. I like this man but I'm not so sure his daughter Angela Knight would appreciate his "empathy" with BNP politics but then most of these Tories are raging hypocrites.

(Angela Knight, former Conservative MP, Erewash)

What this old man does not realise is that our national infiltration of the Tory Party has begun. Headed by Eddie Butler in London, over three-hundred activists have been selected to join the Tory Party in two waves but they will also remain members of the BNP. The second wave will join after tonight's 'election results'. Very cunning really. I don't like Eddie Butler but I respect him as a strategist. He's improved the BNP's election results all over London. He intends to join the Monday Club in time, a Tory pressure group on the far right of the party, from where he will oversee the implementation of our plan.

His contacts in the Bloomsbury Forum, a BNP pressure group consisting of middle class Fascists in the Oswald Mosley genre are supplying the funds for this venture. Lady Jane Birdwood is a significant benefactor in the BF and a long-term Fascist. I'm not supposed to tell anyone about this strategy, so it's just between you and me, right!

The results are coming in and surprise, surprise - the Tories (quasi-nationalists) have won. Angela Knight is the new MP for the Erewash Constituency. Laurence has taken the rostrum now and the 'childish' candidates from the other parties have walked off. We've won 2.7 per cent of the vote, nearly a thousand ticks for the BNP. The other candidates are pissed off but a few of the 'Tories' come over to congratulate us. Strange that! A Fifth Column is at work in John Major's governing party and he doesn't even realise it.

We're playing the State at its own game and winning. Tyndall always says that the National Front was destroyed by Thatcher adopting anti-immigrant rhetoric at the 1979 General Election and the covert infiltration of the NF by Special Branch and MI5 agents. They're going to get a taste of their own medicine now. Tyndall is motivated to destroy the Tory Party out of revenge but for the rest of us; we need to crush the Tories so the BNP can become the new Right in Britain. It will take years to achieve but I'm in for the long haul and we will win.

We're off to a BNP paper sale on Brick Lane again. We're expecting a clash with the Anti Nazi League and Red Action. The latter group is full of hardcore Reds looking for a serious fight. But we've got the Combat 18 stewarding group to match anything they've got. The situation report from Calvin is that C18 and Red Action have arranged a 'meet' in the East End after the paper sale. It's freezing cold yet again and a light fog clings grimly to London's streets. I much prefer London in summertime but these things have a mind of their own. Tyndall is pushing us to eradicate the "Red Scum" over the next two years. He intends us to crush all Red opposition on the streets of Britain by winter 1994.

It's a tall order but I've got bigger things on my mind now that I've been promoted. East and West Midlands have become one region in BNP organisational terms. It has always been my intention to unite the two regions and climb the greasy promotion pole. My perseverance has paid off and the new Midlands organiser John Peacock, has made me his second-in-command. My new title is Midlands Elections Officer and I'm preparing big things for the region. November 1992 has been a good month for me and I've just turned twenty-four. We're about four-hundred strong and the Asian community on Brick Lane is pretty scared today. Most of the Lane's shops are Asian owned and they've decided to stay open for the day. Which is good for us because we need cans of pop, chocolate and cigarettes. No one is offensive to the Asians because our battle lines have been drawn for later in the morning and we do not need unnecessary police diversions.

The ANL lot are noisy and full of their usual boring slogans that make no difference to anyone anymore other than their own small band of hardcore fanatics. We taunt and shout at them in turn and generally wind them up. Their very presence stood before us is offensive to us, so we don't need much winding up. The police are ordering us to disperse first today which is good for us because we need time to prepare for the ultra-militant Red Action, also allied to the IRA. They are traitors, particularly when innocent Britons are being murdered by the IRA and today Red Action will pay.

The East End pub is awash with BNP activists and Combat 18 led by Charlie Sargent and Eddie Whicker fresh from their dealings with the Loyalist Paramilitaries in Ulster. C18 has been fostering links of "mutual interest" with the Loyalists in an attempt to secure weapons. First they've got to supply the Loyalists with some weapons. They're being used that much is clear, and I do not like either side in the Ulster sectarian conflict - they're terrorists. If C18 wants weapons then why don't they buy them from the criminal underworld and use them for their own 'activities'? Poor leadership is the answer but Tyndall seems to have little control over the monster he's created earlier this year. The official line is that C18 is not connected to the BNP. It's a replay of Sinn Fein/IRA all over again only this time it's BNP/C18.

The Nottingham BNP organiser Calvin Richards is also a member of C18, having merged his Young Templars with Sargent's bigger organisation earlier this summer. Richard Edmonds walks over to me and shakes my hand. He tells everyone in earshot that I've got a great future in the BNP. He congratulates me on my recent promotion and the fact that I have raised thousands for the BNP's coffers from Tories in the Midlands. I'm starting to get noticed in the party which is good for my ambitions. But first, I've got to prove myself as Midlands Elections Officer.

Calvin walks over and tells me that the Reds are getting closer. Our spotters are tracking them and we've invested in two-way radios to stay in touch. It's been a sound decision to invest in the radios - our operational efficiency is vastly improved and it makes us look professional to new recruits who are scared witless on these occasions.

I don't get the butterflies in the stomach now before battle. Calvin's recounting some past glory when the windows come crashing in and a grubby house brick lands on the bar just two feet away. It's Red Action's calling card. ***"OUT! OUT! NOW!"*** Sargent screams and we bolt for the doors. There's a mad rush to get at the Reds but we're soon through the doors and onto the forecourt. Skinheads are hurling pint pots left on the tables outside at the Red Action boys.

I look to my left and Calvin is leading a group of C18 boys into action against the Reds' vanguard. I order our BNP boys to race up the adjoining street to catch the Reds in a pincer movement. We're tooled up with knives, bottles and batons - the usual accoutrements for these 'occasions'. We're round the street now and can see the Reds racing towards us. Their only hope of escape is to smash through our lines but C18 is racing up fast behind them to close the trap. And despite their treachery Red Action can certainly fight and Calvin is engaged in one of the best fist fights I have seen, no quarter given, nothing between to the two men.

The Reds are rushing at us screaming and shouting, holding their weapons aloft like phallic symbols. The air is tense with expectation and we rush at them and clash and it's immediate: Bang, kick, smash, thump, whack, thud - the sounds of battle are deafening in this intense arena of close quarters combat and stomach-turning screams echo eerily across the East End.

My heart is thumping with exertion as I smash and whack at the Reds, stepping back to avoid the odd baseball bat and iron bar. This is the hottest street battle I've been in so far and it's so surreal that I expect Jack The Ripper to leap out of the freezing fog any time now. But we're doing enough ripping of our own without him. The Reds are getting thrashed badly. Blood spoils the pavements everywhere and mixes with the damp from the morning mist, macabre.

It's like a scene from a medieval battle and human-beings are cutting each other down in scenes reminiscent of battles from the Middle Ages. Injured combatants from both sides lie writhing in agony on the road and a few are out stone-cold. It's sickening really, very sickening. This is the worst thing I've ever seen in my life and God knows if I will ever feel good about anything or anyone ever again.

I turn to my left and watch with a mixture of grim fascination and repugnance as a gang of skinheads smash a Red's head onto a car bonnet. Bang! Bang! Bang! The bonnet is dented in several places and blood pours from the man's head. This is not a pretty place to be but I'm here of my own volition. I 'volunteered' for this battle, I was not press ganged. The hype and bravado is one thing but the harsh reality is something very different.

I begin to withdraw at the sound of police sirens. Obviously

Metropolitan riot police and capture means an instant prison remand at HMP Brixton with its many black inmates - not for me. We've hammered Red Action and taught them a lesson they will never forget. We run off and make for the pub when I see several skinheads holding a young Red against a wooden fence.

"Someone stab the bastard! Someone stab the bastard!" They scream. I draw my knife and walk over to them. The young Red is blubbering with fear. *"Please, Please don't do it mate."* He begs me. I return to the Mundy Arms in 1990 and this is the first daymare I've had since then. The strength in my hand collapses at the sight of this young man trapped like a defenceless rabbit.

He's crying and begging for mercy in his coarse Mancunian accent. I empathise with him: he's two-hundred miles from home and expecting to die on a cold London street. Not today sunshine, I decide and throw the knife over the fence into the undergrowth, which I guess will make his mother very happy. But it's survival time now and the moralising must wait until later. The police sirens wail and bring me back to reality and I run like hell for the pub to meet the waiting transports. I'm running down the street trying my best not to slip on the damp paving stones and blood. I'm panicking and this whole 'episode' for want of a better term is bloody disgusting!

A police riot van draws up a few yards ahead and several plods jump out of the back holding plastic shields and carrying batons. I slow down and start to walk. I'm not wearing any badges in case I get stopped by the police - a dead giveaway. I'm wearing a smart tweed jacket, sky blue shirt and an expensive red silk tie. I walk by the plods and shake my head muttering *"fuckin' skinheads are a menace"* and one of the plods with a black moustache smiles at me and I walk straight by them. I walk for a few yards and look back to see the police arresting the skinheads who've been holding down the young Mancunian and I run like hell again. I'm turning the corner now and the pub is in sight - freedom! A sports car comes screaming along the road in front of me and nearly decapitates me - I've not come this far just to be mown down by some Capitalist yuppie, at the last.

I cross the road, the smell of burnt rubber stings my nostrils and I can see the BNP van a hundred yards away. But there's a ruckus coming from the offside of the pub and I'm going to take a look at what's happening. I walk a few yards around the corner of the pub, weaving through the forecourt tables and I'm there. A dozen skinheads are pelting pint glasses at two hippies, who I estimate are in their early twenties. The scene before me is absolutely horrific. Both of them have long hair, and one has purple or dark red streaks, I can't be sure it's such a mess. I can't even tell whether they're male or female. Shards of glass protrude from their bodies and the whitewashed brick course they're leaning on is just a mess of bloody graffiti. Time has disappeared and I've entered a nightmare of my own making - everything is slow and horribly real.

The skinheads are pelting them with pint glasses and the two bodies do not move with any signs of life except the occasional involuntary shudder as a shard of glass hits a nerve. A siren wails close by but it seems an eternity away to me. Steam rises from the bodies and blood spills onto the pavement. One of them is wearing green tights - must be a girl - and they are 'decorated' with flashes of fresh red blood. I can't stop myself from being sick, it rushes through my teeth. I'm not so battle hardened as I thought but I've never seen anything like this in the BNP or at any other time in my young life.

The hippie furthest away from me has lost an eye and it hangs down on the victim's right cheekbone, like a worm trying to eat a blue and white egg. The one closer to me, wearing green tights, has a huge gash in 'her' left cheek. She's still alive because I can see her tongue slithering through streams of blood and her teeth are visible but blood soaked. There are hundreds of shards of glass sticking out of their bodies like a porcupine's needles dripping with crimson fluid. A siren wails very close now and the skinheads run off. Self-preservation awakens me from my dire fascination and I bolt off for the van. The whole 'episode' has lasted no more than five minutes but it seems longer, much longer. I will never forget haunting those images, never for as long as I live!

I jump into the back of the van and Richard Edmonds greets me with: *"We gave them a fucking good thrashing today Simon!"* I look at him with a blank expression and manage a false but unconvincing grin, gallows humour. Inside I am experiencing purgatory. I should have stayed and helped the hippies but what could I do and I'm not a doctor - I don't even have First Aid training. But I left them bleeding to death. I hope they don't die, we men are wretched things.

God forgive me, please God above forgive me. What have I become? What has happened to me? Why am I living like this? I'm arguing with myself, you know. I still have a conscience and what I've seen today is not right - it is not right! I hang my head low and do not speak to anyone. My face feels drained of life and I imagine that I'm white like a ghost and not like a racial supremacist. I'm in emotional and mental agony but I'm not cut to shreds like the hippies but I've been there in the past, you know. I feel like crying and imagine I will never stop if I start. A man sat beside me in his thirties pats me on the shoulder and says: *"It's war, you know! It's horrible but we have a race and nation to save."*

So that makes it alright does it. Hide behind an ideology and you're abnegated of any wrong in life. NO, NO, NO! Innocent people should not be caught in the crossfire but history is replete with examples of millions of slaughtered innocents in wars. So, this is war and I don't think my life will ever be the same again. The van pulls off and the men seem to be happy with their work against Red Action but then they are not innocents and the hippies were innocent. I witnessed their destruction and did nothing and I suppose that makes me just as bad as the skinheads who cut them to pieces.

I'm lying in bed and I cannot get close to Catherine. I feel dirty and unworthy of her love. I call her 'my last contact with normality most of the time. I don't think she really loves me anymore but stays with me because she's a loyal woman. I can't tell her what happened today. I'm too ashamed and I also think she will dump me right away. I didn't throw any glasses at the hippies myself but I'm just as responsible as the skinheads who did because I helped to organise the battle with Red Action. I'll just have to live with myself but the sight and sound of the scene won't leave me alone all night. Catherine knows something is wrong but I tell her that I'm tired and she offers to go home. I'm glad. I don't need her trying to pin me down.

I wake up every hour or so gasping for breath. Panic attacks - panic attacks me, I should say. I think about leaving the BNP but I've only just been promoted. It's the skinheads who behave like this not the ordinary rank and file of the BNP. Tyndall should remove the skinheads from the BNP. It was skinheads who almost killed me nearly three years ago. They're a menace. They're just cowardly thugs, pack animals we call them in the BNP. I'm blaming them for everything because they're vile.

I will stay put in the BNP and campaign to clean up our public image. No more street battles for me now. John Peacock has told me to be very much aware of my public image from now on and I'm going to take his advice. A senior elections officer cannot go around fighting in street battles - leave the brainless thugs to that. Catherine has been on at me for months now to stop fighting and concentrate on writing for BNP publications instead. I've proved myself on the streets so the street war is over for me now. I have plenty of respect. A more studious approach to the BNP will suit me fine now.

Calvin is planning a spectacular to 'greet' the opening of Spike Lee's Malcolm X film premier at Nottingham cinemas in December 1992. I've told him that I don't want to know anything about it now that I'm a political officer. It's the only way to save my BNP career and my relationship with Catherine, not to mention my sanity. I must adopt a more studious approach to BNP politics from now on. The fighting I will leave to the thugs in Combat 18. It's a cop out, you know but I'm happy about it. I still can't clear the cut up hippies from my mind and I think like ghosts they're guiding me away from violence. Sounds weird but that's life for you.

I'm going to the News House pub in Nottingham city centre tonight to meet Calvin and the rest of the boys. I must keep up with things because I've not been active so much since the hippies incident. Calvin strolls in with Dean and plants a copy of today's Nottingham Evening Post on the bar next to my glass of whisky. *"What's this then, Calvin?"* I'm intrigued. *"It's the latest sign of our growing strength."* He tells me with a broad smile. I unfold the paper and on the front page the banner headline screams: **BOMB SCARE - HUNDREDS EVACUATED FROM CITY CIMEMAS.**

Calvin tells me how they decided to use a bomb hoax to disrupt the premier of Malcolm X at Nottingham's three cinemas. One of the boys made up a codeword to convince the police that he was serious - XK7. I've no idea what it stands for and I don't care anymore. At least no one was injured. The fact that they were disrupted by the hoax tells me that they should not be watching films about black racists who hate white people.

Malcolm X was nothing but a vile street pimp and a drug dealer before he converted to Islam - so why should Hollywood make a movie about such a man? Selling drugs and destroying young white girls is nothing to be proud of. It's beyond me, so I don't feel too bad about the hoax. Calvin explains that C18 is about to launch a series of attacks on the homes of far Left activists across the country.

He's been gathering intelligence on the far Left from his interception of their letters at Royal Mail sorting offices. Calvin's been a postman since the late 1980's and claims he first stumbled on the idea when he was sorting mail one day in 1989. He claims a manila envelope was badly ripped and he happened to notice that the package contained Anti Nazi League leaflets and instructions to activists to mobilise for a paper sale in Nottingham.

Anyone who knows Calvin does not believe his story but he may be telling the truth. He's got a dozen of his mates at sorting offices all over Nottingham intercepting the mail of our far Left enemies. I'm not bothered though because we're able to stay one step ahead of the opposition.

I've got to organise for the Derbyshire County Council elections in May next year and a big BNP march through London in April to oppose the IRA that could turn out to be very hot. It's going to be another eventful year but I hope to God that I can avoid anymore battles in the East End. I've told Catherine that I feel like a coward for not getting involved in the street battles now but she tells me to keep my nose clean and keep rising through the ranks until I become leader. I'm going to achieve some special things in 1993, that much I can say.

CHAPTER 10

CONDITION RED

Coventry City Council proposes to open a sex offenders rehabilitation unit on the outskirts of the city, close to a private housing estate where hundreds of young children, live and play. This is absolute madness and just another insane act of the liberal kiss-em-n-cure-em mafia that has infected every aspect of the British criminal justice system. From social workers to probation officers, liberals are making excuses for the criminally minded and the insane.

"They're victims of society too you know." I'm constantly told by liberals when debating them on crime and punishment. According to liberals, every murderer and rapist the world over can be rehabilitated by 'understanding' and anti-psychotic drugs. They're about as mad as their patients in our eyes. The day unit for paedophiles will not go ahead at any cost even if it means direct action. Where the State cannot protect children we will do the job for them.

It's a cold day and late winter 1993 has been tough for all of us. We've been all over England recently striking up support for the BNP. Ten of us have travelled from Nottingham down to Coventry. We're not expecting any opposition from the Reds or ANL. They have been ordered not oppose us on this one. This is a 'populist' issue, closing down a planned sex offenders unit. The leaders of the far Left know that they will be deeply 'unpopular' if they turn up today to support a paedophile unit and it's a public relations disaster waiting to happen for them.

We are unopposed and we are going to make a big impact. We're about two-hundred strong - all from the Midlands. No C18 boys today because we're not expecting trouble and despite this fact, Charlie Sargent has fallen out with Tyndall. Like I said, I'm keeping my nose clean. Our union flags flutter impressively in the morning wind and passing motorists are hooting their horns in support. Every two in three cars gives us a supporting hoot. We've put together a makeshift banner about ten feet across by five feet deep. In large red letters on a white background our simple but effective message reads: **HANG CHILD MURDERERS! NO PAEDOPHILE UNIT IN COVENTRY!**

I look around and I'm proud of these men and women who've

turned up today. This is a good cause to fight for and a welcome break from the horrors of the last three years, for me anyway. Peacock is in overall command and I'm his 2IC. Things are going very well for the Midlands region now that we've unified under a single command. I'm Calvin's boss now and I don't think he likes it. But when I see one of our activists wearing a Nazi armband I ask Calvin to get him to remove it - I don't order him - this is not the army.

After thirty minutes of displaying our flags and banners we're off into the estate which consists of newly constructed houses. We've got a few thousand leaflets to deliver today. The banner headline in red letters reads: **THE DEAD AND THE LIVING. HANG CHILD MURDERERS!** The leaflet depicts a poor young boy who was abducted, sexually abused and then murdered by some evil monster who liberals call 'victims'. It's hideous to think paedophiles are victims of society. When we get in power the prisons will be emptied of these evil monsters. We intend to hang them and the law not being applied retrospectively in this country does not matter to us. We will simply alter the law. With a majority in Parliament who is going to stop us?

I'm on the megaphone chanting *"HANG CHILD MURDERERS. STOP THE SEX CENTRE!"* I like using the megaphone and I guess it gives me a chance to exercise my big mouth. I find it very relaxing too inasmuch that I burn off stress rapidly. Better than being up to me knees in human remains. We're getting a positive response from nearly everyone and we have hundreds of signatories for our petition to stop the centre. I'm feeling very positive about all of this and what a difference it makes not fighting.

I'm wearing my smart grey double-breasted suit that I bought from French Connection a couple of years ago. It's a timeless classic and the women love it. I'm still a narcissist even though I have scars on my face to remind me of Jackson's outrage. I still dream of the event every night but I've started taking sedatives prescribed by my GP at night to blank out the images and I'm experiencing some relief.

Some big mouth guy down on the estate is shouting *"You're all fucking Nazi scum. Fuck off home Hitler boys."* He's irritating and he's getting louder with it. I drown him out on my megaphone with volleys of *"Pervert lover! Pervert Lover!"* He is livid and lashes out at Calvin. I lose my self-control and run down the street to confront him. Calvin ignores him and walks off but I'm sick of these pretentious lefties with filthy mouths who think they own the moral high ground. I ask him why he supports the pervert centre being opened. He tells me that he doesn't. *"Then sign our petition man or you're a pervert yourself."* He lunges at me, throwing a careless right hook, which misses my chin by an inch or so. I sidestep him to the right and hit him with three hard punches which would down a normal man but this guy's still standing.

I hit him again and again and again. He falls back onto his car and I grab his head and slam it into his passenger window several times. But he's strong and I can't get enough strength behind my blows to put his head through the window. My anger has erupted again. Every time someone gets aggressive with me I see red in the shape of Gordon Jackson and his skinhead mob. My rage is awful and this guy is in the wrong place with the wrong person at the right time.

I'm about to let him go when his crazy wife comes screaming out of the front door, her nails glinting like an eagle's talons and tears into my face. Fucking hell! Bang! The guy hits me with an uppercut and I'm dazed. The wife tears at my left eye socket and blood starts to pour down my face. She's trying to rip my eye out and he's knocking twelve shades of crimson out of me at the same time. It's such a serious matter but I find it hilarious when they start arguing about who should try and smash my head through their own car window. It's a mad, bad world at times and amusing too.

Too late - here comes the seventh cavalry in the shape of Ady, a local skinhead. He's rushing up the drive with a flagpole draping our national colours before him. He's like a lancer on heat. The leftie has no time to react and Ady drops him with the flagpole thrust straight into his abdomen. The leftie is in agony on the tarmac being comforted by the wife from hell and we run like hell to catch up with the others. Blood is pouring from my eye socket where the wailing banshee has tried to surgically 'remove' my left eye. I've got a two inch gash down my left cheekbone caused by her talons. I'd better get a tetanus jab on Monday - never know what's she been doing before she attacked me the dirty leftie bitch has probably been tearing up the Alsatian's fresh steak with her bare teeth. But inside I respect her for fighting for the man she loves but then again maybe he's just not insured and poverty hurts more than punches.

Apart from the attack of Edwina Scissor hands, the activity has gone well. We've collected over a thousand signatures for our petition to close down the proposed paedophile unit. Over the next few days Combat 18 telephone Coventry City Council and threaten to bomb the unit if it's opened. The Council cannot get insurance cover, so the proposal is scrapped. Round one to us and the children of Coventry can go on playing free from molestation by evil perverts, 'courtesy' of **BNP/C18**. The State, as always, failed the parents of young children in protecting their babes and so the policy of ***"by any means necessary"*** does get results.

I've got an election campaign to fight and can do without today's anti-IRA march in West London. It's just a stupid diversion from the real political business of winning elections and will lead to violence and bad publicity. When will Tyndall learn that these confrontational marches achieve nothing other than very poor publicity. Now, hold a march through London to ensure the Bulger killers are never released and you're talking big support and little opposition from the Reds. It's all about tactics but Tyndall simply refuses to evolve.

As it is we're three-thousand strong for today's 'event'. The journey down here has been uneventful apart from a failed ambush by Red Action at M1 junction 25 near Leicester. Their bag of flour has achieved nothing and the rain has washed it away. But their attempted ambush shows we're expected in London - no surprise there really. We've been swilling down some brandy on the way so we're tanked up and ready for action. I'm chosen as a flag bearer and I'm delegated to the front of the march where it will be white hot and we're definitely on **'Condition Red'** today.

The drummers assemble at the front; behind them are Tyndall, Morse, Butler, Edmonds and Tony *'The Mad Bomber'* Lecomber, being our national leadership. I'm behind them with fifty other flag bearers and behind us is a solid phalanx of British nationalists. We're an impressive sight as we march off and the drummers rap-tap, rap-tap their beat to instil discipline, order and inspiration in the march. The April shower has stopped and the air is mild but damp and very tense.

The streets seem deserted and quiet - too quiet. I've got a bad feeling about this one but that's usual on big marches. Our march progresses and there's no one around except the BNP, the police and the press. We press on for a few hundred yards more. What on earth is this going to achieve? I'm asking myself when I spot three ranks deep of riot police a hundred yards ahead. So, the police are not going to let us march onto Hyde Park after all - again, this is no surprise, just deliberate obstruction. The police have perfected the art of messing us around and generally harassing us on demonstrations to provoke a violent backlash that the press can report on.

Some skinny little Superintendent swaggers out from the ranks of blue and orders us to halt. Tyndall orders us to march on and a pitched battle is now unavoidable. We're closing on them with fifty yards to go and on we go in seemingly unstoppable motion. The air is humming with electric aggression and the Combat 18 contingent have come up from the back with the Ulster Loyalists, ready for the inevitable heated clash.

The press photographers have whistled off to the right and stand in a pack snapping away. It's like a battle scene from the English Civil War. Tyndall orders us to halt twenty yards from the police lines and the ensuing crush from the back of our lines pushes us a further five yards on. These Met riot police love themselves and stand there with complete arrogance and contempt for us in their 'defence' of the IRA. Their pathetic little round shields will be no good against our spears today in the shape of fifty brass spiked flag poles. We're like pike men in Cromwell's New Model Army.

The Superintendent walks forward to talk to Tyndall and the two men are locked in heated debate. Tyndall keeps on saying *"NO! NO! NO! We will not disperse."* The Super' walks off completely infuriated and for once the police have not got their own way which delights us no end. The paparazzi sense the mood and start pushing their SLR cameras in the skinheads' faces. The tension is mounting and it's almost as if a nuclear bomb is about to explode. Whack, Whack, Whack. The skinheads are smashing at the snappers, ripping away a couple of expensive SLRs which they kick back into the ranks of the filthy gutter press.

The snappers rush forward to get the best shots and two of them are seized by the skinheads, roughed up and thrown against some steel railings over to my right. The Super' orders his men to advance and the police rush at us screaming like Amer Indians. We lower our flagpoles and advance two feet, they crash into our spears and their first wave is crushed like a broken egg. It's like a turkey shoot and the police are sitting ducks for our spears. We ram them into their padded torsos and plastic shields and they retreat dragging a couple of injured fellows with them.

The Super' orders them to attack two rows deep this time and they're off like stallions bolting from starting traps, pelting towards us screaming and shouting in some inane tongue I don't understand. I rush forward with the rest of the spearmen and ram them in a terrific clash of arms. My spear hits a copper's plastic shield and knocks him over. Two more coppers advance in through the spears and one whacks me on the arm with his bloody truncheon - bastard! I stand back and ram my flagpole straight into his padded abdomen and he keels over onto the tarmac. We hate the police with a venom. They're nothing more than the State's storm troopers; just glorified thugs in uniforms, long overdue a bloody good thrashing.

The third wave of riot police comes crashing down on us and this time they make a break in our lines but C18 rushes straight for them and kicks them out and back into their own ranks. *"HURRAH! HURRAH! HURRAH!"* A deafening roar from our young lions fills the air as the police retreat. Behind their shattered lines the mounted division is forming up ready to press their next attack. Our Schiltrons have held out against the police infantry style attack but they mean to beat us now with mounted horse.

I only wish we had thousands more men today on this march in London - we could storm Parliament and seize power - another Munich Putsch in reality - our longed for Revolution incarnate. Our boys start hurling bottles and stones at the police and they lock their shields together for protection. Bottles bounce off their shields like stones skimming off thick ice. Crash! A bottle explodes on a copper's helmet and knocks him to the floor. Another huge cheer goes up from our ranks and the press scuttle off behind the police riot vans for protection like pathetic little cowards.

The mounted police are in position now, their yellow jackets glowing like small luminous suns. We're ready for them. It's going to be like William Wallace's defeat of the English at Stirling in the thirteenth century. *"C'mon ya bastards! Fucking c'mon ya bastards!"* The insults pour out and the police start rattling their batons against their shields. We brace for their imminent assault, our nerves tingling with fear and excitement. Their ranks part to let the cavalry through and they file up about fifty strong no more than thirty yards away.

A police helicopter chatters overhead its rotors clapping like an overexcited seal. Sirens are wailing along Hyde Park Corner and their moan cuts at the heart. The sky is black with rain clouds and it seems like the end of the world is upon us. Police reinforcements are pouring in behind the riot vans but these coppers don't have shields or protective clothing. I shout to our flag bearers to bring down the mounted officers first if we're to stand a chance of victory. *"Aim for their chests. Aim for their chests!"* I shout to my fellow patriots.

Everyone is wearing worried expressions and some of our newer boys are petrified. I've never faced a cavalry charge before either but I'm not giving in to this. If they want war, then let's give it to them and hard. We outnumber them three to one. We're better armed, prepared to die for the Cause and our three-thousand strong square will not be broken by fifty mounted officers and a few hundred coppers with sticks and transparent plastic bin lids.

I pray to the Gods for deliverance from evil and beseech them to let me enter the house of the fallen if I die today. We're ready then. My chest is so taught and tense I can barely breath. The intense mood of anticipation is akin to the splitting of the atom. The arrogant little Super' comes strutting out through the police ranks and orders us to disperse one last time and behind him the cavalry comes forward. He shouts at Tyndall, telling him that the entire BNP leadership will be arrested and charged with public order offences - they'll spend years in prison.

Tyndall, who's been sent down before for public order offences, turns to face us and orders us to... 'disperse'. *"You must be fucking joking."* Someone shouts back from our ranks. *"Fuck it. Let's take 'em."* Most of the lads agree but Tyndall has enough support in the party to get his own way. We stand down and in a second we have lost the initiative. I have to say that we should have fought them. We'd have beaten them after an hour or so but it would have been a bloodthirsty business and many people would have been injured, possibly killed. The C18 lads say they will never march with the BNP again after this calamity. We had victory in our grasp and Tyndall snatched it away from us. He lost his nerve and thought only of his own future, disregarding the wishes of his subordinates.

Not only does he like to provoke these big battles, he can't cope with the heat at the front now. He's too old for the job - he's in his sixties and a younger man must now take over. Many people in the Midlands want me to challenge Tyndall for the leadership in 1995 and I'm thinking about it very seriously now. Tyndall has lost my respect. If we had won today a clear message would have reverberated throughout the land. Where the NUM and the miners failed the BNP succeeded and beat the police. The working classes would have fallen in behind us: Revolution is the only solution! Tyndall's on his way out now, that much is certain.

Deflated but with our heads held high we march off past the police and we look at each other with grudging respect. Some of the coppers look at us and wink and smile - hope they're not gay. But I've seen more than a few coppers turn their ties around to reveal a BNP badge on the back before now but only in London strangely enough. We're being escorted to our coaches now and then we'll be escorted out of London by police outriders. I feel so disappointed. I would have ordered the lads to stand fast against the police charge, if I was the BNP leader. *"The times are a changing"* as Dylan sang and not for the better either....

We're back on the coach to take us 'home' to immigrant-infested Nottingham and heading up to Hyde Park through very heavy traffic. It's slow going and we chug and chug along like an old tank thirsting for fuel. We're at the traffic lights and Hyde Park is directly ahead, we were so close and yet so far away. We're turning right and the North Yorkshire Coach behind us is turning left. Why are they splitting us up?

We turn the corner and the police outrider pulls away. Oh shit, what's happening. I'm stood up looking to my right when hundreds of Anti Nazi League thugs come charging at the bus. I tell the driver to pull off now but he can't move for traffic. Calvin stands up and tells everyone to get down and brace themselves for action. This is definitely 'Condition Red'. They're just five yards away now and eggs and all kinds of filth are clamming up on the windows. The din outside is like being inside a metal dustbin while people smash at it with iron bars.

The back window on the coach comes smashing in onto the back seat and shards of glass fly in every direction, like a fragmentation grenade exploding. I can see Reds at the back trying to climb in but a couple of the lads smash their hands with batons. They let go. *"Oh shit. They've got a grenade. Grenaddde!"* Someone shouts in a terrified voice. My heart skips several beats and I imagine the carnage in this confined space. Everything is still and haunting... A small black canister drops through the smashed window, lands on the back seats, rolls off and comes to rest three seats back from the window. *"Get down!"* There's a deafening BANGGG! WHOOSHHH!

A cloud of smoke erupts from the canister - CS Gas. *"Gas! Gas! Gas! Gas! Gas!"* Calvin screams and we hit the deck and crawl under the seats with whatever clothing covering our mouths. I can hear the windows being blasted through and fresh air seeps into the coach with thousands of shards of glass ricocheting off everything. We're choking and spluttering and some of the lads at the back are being sick.

The gas is clearing now but my eyes are watering like a fountain. I decide to look up and see what's happening outside. The window is shattered but not broken and most of the other windows are destroyed. A steel ball bearing comes whistling through the window about a foot above my head and lands in the luggage rack on the other side of the bus. I'm back under the seat in a flash, heart pumping like crazy. That was bloody close - too close for comfort. Blood drips from my nose where I've been caught by flying glass. We're getting massacred.

Our coach driver has seized the initiative now and is moving us forward by ramming the cars in front of us, hooting his horn the whole time. We're making headway but the Reds are still smashing and hacking at the coach with iron bars and baseball bats. The cars ahead are starting to move out of the way and we're leaving the Reds behind us. I run up to the back of the coach and see the Reds running after us about fifty yards away but they've had their fun now.

The driver makes off for safety and what a bizarre sight we must be driving through central London in a coach that resembles an old tin can that looks like it has been used for a kids football game. We eventually come to rest at Paddington Police Station, where the driver needs to report the incident for insurance purposes. The police led us deliberately into this ambush - revenge for their necessary beating at Hyde Park.

When Laurence Johnson booked the coach from a company in Heanor, he told them that we were the Historical Review Society, travelling to London for an intellectual seminar. Lesson over for today - *"No dark sarcasms in the classroom."* I'm sat at home with a bottle of sherry and I'm treating it none too gently. My nerves are popping with excitement and the 'thrill' of London town is buzzing in my head. Phew! What a day. I feel numb and just want to sleep, so I'm off to bed now but there's not much rest for the wicked in this world; I've got an election campaign to get on with tomorrow in rural Derbyshire.

"I believe in Adolf Hitler and his solutions. There is bound to be a racial war in Europe - it is only a matter of time and we in Britain are the frontrunners when it comes to fanatical Fascism. The Rest of Europe, particularly the Germans, look up to Combat 18. We will soon be ready for the big racial conflict. There has never been more support for Fascism in Britain than now." - Charlie Sargent, Combat 18 leader, 1993.

(Charlie Sargent and his henchman Martin Cross are serving life sentences for the murder of a rival C18 member 'Catford' Chris Castle, on the 10th February 1997 in London. Mr Castle was lured to a meeting of 'financial reconciliation' with Sargent, whereupon the two hardcore Nazis stabbed him to death.)

(Charlie Sargent, former leader of Combat 18, later an MI5 agent)

CHAPTER 11

TWILIGHT

Cotmanhay is a small working class district of Ilkeston and predominantly white - 99.9%. We have established sound local support and we expect to improve on our general election result in proportionate terms. In Erewash we secured 2.7% of the vote and Cotmanhay is a prime area in the constituency for us. We're standing only one candidate at the Derbyshire County Council elections to maximise our strength on the ground in one area. If the result is strong, the effect of our result will cause greater controversy in the local press - a domino effect.

We've been campaigning hard for the last few weeks and for the first time I've persuaded our activists to knock on doors and canvass the electors' views instead of just pushing leaflets through their doors. Our canvassing shows around 12% support and rising. Whether this figure will be reflected in the actual result in May is another matter. Canvassing returns are notoriously inaccurate as canvassers often inflate their returns to make matters look better than they are.

We've been pounding these streets for weeks now and Cotmanhay is a rough area, known locally as the 'Bronx'. A vast council estate dominates the top end of Cotmanhay and the lower end is predominantly private housing for the lower middle classes. It's rumoured locally that there are more guns in Cotmanhay than in the British army. A huge guy offered to sell me a Uzi sub-machine gun recently for a thousand quid and a thousand rounds of ammo thrown in. I don't have much need for a canon like this but some of the lads have expressed an interest in buying one. As usual I turn a blind eye to such activities - I couldn't stop them even if I wanted to and I don't want to because this is war. Let's be clear about this now: we have adopted a twin-track approach of contesting elections and procuring weapons to launch a shooting war against the State.

I'm a political officer like Gerry Adams in Ulster and fighting elections is my business but I'll fight as well when I have to but I prefer not to. Scott has been driving me round in his car all day while I use the megaphone to whip up support for the BNP. Our candidate John Leather is a bit of a loner but he's willing to stand up for his views. We respect him for that but I've instructed him to stay away from the press until election night because he's a loose cannon with his mouth. We don't need any embarrassing hiccups now.

People seem startled to see the union flag draped from a car window and me belting out *"vote BNP - the only solution"* as we drive by but it seems to me that the British have been forced to feel ashamed of our national flag lest it offends some ethnic minority. I don't give a damn whether ethnic minorities like our flag or not - if they don't, they can always leave the country which is fine by me. We get waves of support from a few people but most people look at us as if we're aliens and I'm not even wearing my green head today.

Scott pulls up outside his Ilkeston home and we go in to prepare the details of tonight's meeting at the Hand on Heart pub in Cotmanhay. The landlord Mick, who's a twitchy and itchy sort of bloke, has kindly agreed to let us use the meeting hall upstairs which can hold around two-hundred people at maximum. Mick the Twitch is a good sort really but he should leave off the Coke for awhile and I don't mean cola either. His head staccatos back and forth like a pigeon eating seed. His nervous system is more fucked up than mine and that's saying something and I don't even use Coke - can't afford the stuff at 38p a can.

We've got an hour before the lads start to arrive from Nottingham and Blood & Honour is sending around fifty skinheads as well - they'll be useful as cannon fodder. Calvin's bringing over his Templars and Edmonds is coming up from London with a small team of observers. I wonder if they're coming to spy on me - see how I handle this new assignment. This is my first time as officer commanding an entire election campaign, organising a meeting and liaising with the heavy mob to deal with any aggro should the lefties turn up.

I've got Calvin on the phone and he's telling me that the Anti Nazi League is forming up on Ilkeston Market place for a small demo. Big deal. Scott drives me to the Hand on Heart to set up the meeting hall upstairs. Not only am I the officer commanding but I'm an interior designer as well now. The chairs are set out, the flags are flying from the walls behind the stage and all is well... until Mick the Twitch shouts upstairs: *"Fuckin' hell the lefties are here."*

I bolt down the stairs fast and look through the pub windows at streams of Anti Nazi League activists plodding along with their little yellow lollipops bearing the same old anti Nazi slogans. I tell Mick to stop panicking and shut up. If they knew we were holding a meeting here the pub would have been attacked by now. I send two spotters to track the Reds. They're back in minutes and tell me that they're heading for Cotmanhay Community Centre where they intend to hold a demonstration against the BNP.

Bloody idiots! Don't they understand anything about strategy? They're now sitting ducks and we are definitely going to attack them in force. I rush out of the back door with a couple of heavies and head for the Working Mens Club a hundred yards away. Edmonds is parked outside the club and I report to him what's happening with the Reds. *"I'm preparing an assault against them right now Richard."* I smile. *"You are not to take any offensive action tonight. Avoid trouble and avoid bad headlines Simon."* His words fall on deaf ears and I tell him to *"bollocks - we're not having another Hyde Park fiasco here"*.

This is my patch and after the West End debacle, I'm not taking orders from old men who can't handle the heat. Not to mention the fact that If I don't order an assault, I'm finished in this area. The local youths will not respect me if I allow a hundred lefties to march into their town and take over. It's not going to happen anyway because our local supporters are mobbing up already for an assault. It's my job to direct them. Everyone is assembled in the Working Mens Club.

I stand up and explain what is at risk here - not that they need telling - and we are finished in this town if we lose here tonight. *"The destiny of the British National Party and indeed the continued Britishness of the people of this area is at stake. Win here and the Anti Nazi League and their inner-city ethnic supporters will never step foot in Ilkeston again. This is our land and no one, no one is going to take it from us!"* HURRAH! They greet my little ad lib speech and brush past me and make for the doors leading out onto the street. Well, it's nice to be loved, isn't it especially in dangerous times.

I instruct Calvin to load the vans with his leader battalion. They will attack the Reds head on. Ten men in each van and a driver apiece. They're tooled up with every form of unpleasant weapon you can imagine: bike chains, baseball bats and batons. A local lad tells me that two men with pump action shotguns (shooters) are waiting in a car at the top of the estate should we need them but I certainly hope not. Our main phalanx marches off for the community centre. We've already sent a twenty-strong detachment on foot to harass the Reds and fool them into thinking we're not so strong. I take my place with two heavies stood beside me for protection at the end of Cotmanhay Road with a clear view of the intended battle ground. I lift my hand, the signal to Trev to launch the mobile attack from our vans.

Two white vans come screaming out of the estate, drive straight over the grass verge and screech to a halt a few yards from the Reds. Our boys are out in a flash and attack the Reds at their centre with a ferocious assault. I can see the Reds going down but their flanks are closing on our leader battalion now. Time to spring the trap.

I order both of our flanks - each fifty strong - to attack the Reds from behind on their flanks. *"GO! GO! GO!"* I shout at them and they rush headlong to glory screaming and cheering like Woolf's Green Jackets at Quebec during the Indian Wars. The Reds are being crushed and their lines are scattered all over the car park and the adjoining grassy knoll. Sirens are wailing in the distance and it's time for me to retire - job done. We've held the field and battered the Reds quite badly but this is war and I have no emotion or pity for any of them. They know the score and they know that if they turn up in Cotmanhay again, they'll get slaughtered.

I jump into a waiting car and head off back to a prearranged RV in Nottingham where we debrief and celebrate minus twelve of our number who've been arrested. Calvin is among the arrested and he's not going to be happy about it if his bosses at the Royal Mail find out. Still, it's been a good night in military strategic terms but the headlines in the local press the next day are awful. Edmonds was right about that but there's good and bad in every argument. The election result is ferried to me the next morning by Laurence Johnson and we've scored 6.7%, a three-hundred per cent increase in proportionate terms of our previous showing a year before. We're delighted but not ecstatic. I think the battle of Cotmanhay lost us a couple of hundred votes, so I'm considering my position as they say. Many people were disinclined to vote for the BNP because of the endemic violence that follows us everywhere. But a few hundred voters didn't care about the violence and saw the Anti Nazi League as 'invaders'.

The leadership in London congratulate me on a *"sound result"* but no mention is made of the fact that I disobeyed Richard Edmonds' direct order not to attack. Privately, I'm told, Tyndall is furious with me but can't discipline me because I have got too much support in the Midlands and he does not want to destroy the party's unity. Tyndall will wait for his moment and then strike at me in some obscure way. I'm sure of this but for now it's time to bask in the 'glory' of increased support.

I don't feel like celebrating though. My thoughts are becoming ever more mechanical by the day and I don't like being such a cold person. Everyone and his dog seems to be criticising my 'bad attitude' and Catherine is their cheerleader. Our relationship is virtually non-existent now anyway. Everyone in my family seems to be telling me how to lead my life. I'm not having them dictate my beliefs - I'm free to choose my own path - this is a democracy, isn't it? The fact that Britain is not a democracy is the reason why I am in the BNP!

My personal life is a mess though and there's no point in trying to deny it. I have no friends outside of the BNP and feel like I'm part of a cult or something else that's freaky to other people. Catherine complains that I never take her out anymore and she's right I don't. I just can't relate to 'ordinary people' anymore and I don't like their false Capitalist world of greed and indulgence. I can't say that I am happy. How could I be, living a life of constant conflict and bloodshed and misery everywhere.

It's all very well for me to go on climbing the greasy pole of promotion in the BNP but I have no life outside of the party. I've become a true political animal. I'm depressed when I'm not on BNP activities because that's the only 'excitement' in my life now but it's not joy or happiness. It was a different story four years ago when I first got involved with the far Right. I had a good job and plenty of money to spend on fashion labels and great nights out on the town.

But even then I felt as though I was in a void and needed something bigger in my life. I certainly got something bigger but I'm not sure this is what I wanted. The BNP has taken over my life now and without it I am nothing. Going out? I feel like a hermit crawling from his cave to find out that the world he once knew has left him behind. I've got nothing now but the BNP, so I'm sticking with it.

I've started to read philosophy at my local library in Nottingham. It's a pretty singular philosophy though because I'm only interested in the insights of Friedrich Nietzsche - Germany's great philosopher. I'm reading *Human, All Too Human* at the moment and I'm being confronted by the concept of the wanderer and his shadow. Nietzsche postulates that man is like a wanderer basically blundering through life trying to understand his environment and the whole time he is followed or pursued by his shadow the higher-self of Hindu mysticism, what we call the soul.

At the end of life Nietzsche says that a man's soul must confront his creator (God?) and be able to look him in the eyes but that God is dead and we have killed him - a strange paradox. In fact, every man and woman is God-like in Nietzsche's world; so when we look into the eyes of the creator we look at ourselves. If we can look into the eyes of the creator without averting our eyes then the creator knows we lived a good life and we can enter paradise. But if we flinch, the creator knows we've been bad and we're sent to hell.

Will I be able to look my creator in the eyes without flinching I wonder? I've done many good things in my life but I've done some pretty bad things too and I'm worried about the afterlife now. In my line of business, death is an ever present hunter. I spend my days looking over my shoulder for a Red assassin or a snatch by Special Branch or maybe the plods will lock me up and frame me on a trumped charge, one of their favourite tricks. I don't believe for one minute that police officers suddenly become impeccable human-beings the moment they draw a warrant card and most of them are lying crooks.

They're wanderers too… and I've seen enough dirty tricks from the agents of the State to last me a lifetime. I wish I was somewhere else right now, I can tell you. I'm starting to confront the realities of my miserable life now and it's not pleasant, I can tell you but I will face my reality with courage, that's all I can do. I've never run away from a battle in my life and I'm not going to start now.

After three-and-a-half years my compensation has finally come through. I've got twenty-thousand pounds to spend and the BNP is getting none of it. I'm turning over a new leaf and I'm going to spend this money on rebuilding my life. The first thing I'm going to do is get my own flat. I've been living with Mum for the last two years and she's sick of me being around her in my petulant BNP moods. Can't blame her really - she doesn't need my aggression in the house. Catherine wants me to move back to Eastwood but I'm not going back there. I couldn't wait to get out of there two years ago. Small towns are usually surrounded by beautiful countryside which I really miss but small town people are very nosey and I don't want everyone knowing my business.

I've decided to move to Ilkeston instead. Some new private flats have just been built near Cotmanhay and I figure I'll be safe among my own kind. There's plenty of support for the BNP in the area and the locals don't know me very well which is good. I sense that Ilkeston is going to become a hotbed of support for the BNP in future years and I want to be in at the start. Even so, I want more of a life away from the BNP now. I need to rebalance things.

Catherine is livid that I'm not going back to Eastwood but at least she's only got a couple of miles to drive to see me now. I honestly don't think we'll be together for very much longer. There's no passion or lust when we make love anymore. Twilight is upon us and night is falling. We still have meaningful conversations but I just don't like her constant Catholic lecturing which is really her mother's voice speaking not her own. I'll be truthful with you: I do not like Catholicism which I see as cruel and obsessed with original sin. I will never convert to that dreadful pseudo-religion, in reality just a money-making racket for the Vatican bank in Rome.

Catherine's mother wants any children we have to be raised as Catholics, she tells me one night in June 1993. *"Tell your mother that she can go to hell! I hate Catholicism Catherine. Get out now!"* I virtually chase her out of the door and she runs away crying. I don't feel good about it but there's only so much a man can take. I love spirituality but I abhor all religions because they breed slaves in my opinion. Religion tells adherents to believe or go to hell and I don't take orders, religious or otherwise from anyone anymore. Like Nietzsche, I'm a free spirit in a world of slaves who are hooked on good and evil. *Reading Beyond Good and Evil* has liberated me from the world of spurious 'religious moral values' - it's immature to divide the world into good and evil, isn't it? Like Nietzsche, I believe that **'this world is a will to power and nothing besides.'** Life, as far as I'm concerned is a huge game of bluff.

The money is good and makes some repair for the wrongs of Jackson's criminal beating. I'm out and about buying clothes and fancy shoes. I love shopping again and the nihilist void of the market place makes me happy again for awhile. Maybe I don't hate Capitalism after all. Maybe I should just make it my slave. Shopping for new clothes is certainly a lot better than being in a BNP bloodbath. The only sadness I feel today is Catherine's loss. We have split up after five years together but I will never forget my first love and maybe she'll be my last - who knows. I'm not too bothered at the moment though because I've got money to burn and places to go. I am buying my way out of trouble or maybe I'm buying my way into trouble. Catherine gave me an ultimatum to leave the BNP or lose her for good.

I told her years ago never to make me choose between her and the BNP - she could only take second place. I don't like being told what to do. I refused to leave the BNP just like that, so she finished with me. Well, that's life but I will miss many things about her. I'm not averse to leaving the BNP at all to be honest with you. But I know too many things about certain things and leaving just like that would arouse suspicions. I have to leave the BNP on my own terms and my worsening health is the perfect excuse but I need a few months more yet to decide whether I'm going to leave.

Having all this money has reminded me of the good things in life that I have missed. I think for now I will spend less time with the BNP and only attend the big events where my face will be missed if I'm not around. It's time for me to take things easy for awhile because my nerves are in tatters. I'm taking tranquillisers at night and anti-depressants in the day - not to mention the booze binges. I'm just trying to blot out the horrors of the past - I'm only human after all.

There's nothing remarkable about the 26th September 1993, other than it seems that summer has finally gone. It's been cloudy and grey for days now. I'm walking along Eastwood's high street feeling as dull as the weather when Richard Jones comes racing along the street; his face is fraught with emotion. *"Simon, haven't you heard the news."* He blurts out. *"Calm down Rich. What's happened mate?"* I'm holding his arm. *"It's Ian Stuart... he's dead. Killed in a 'car crash' a couple of days ago. I can't believe it Sime... I can't believe it."*

He's really cut up and I can't quite take it all in either. A young lad from a neighbouring town Brinsley has been killed in the same 'accident'. I tell Bones that it was no 'accident' in my opinion. *"They were assassinated by MI5 or Mossad. He was becoming too powerful across Europe and the US, mate."* He looks stunned. *"We'll never be able to prove it Sime."* He retorts. *"True. But one day we will have our revenge on the State and all its agents, I promise you that!"*

I've no proof that Ian Stuart was killed by MI5 or Mossad (Israeli Intelligence Service) but these rumours are flying around in the aftermath of his death. Calvin tells me that nearly everyone he's spoken to in the far Right thinks the same thing. They're promising revenge but I'm more concerned with helping Ian Stuart to have a great send off at his funeral in the North of England in a few days' time.

I liked Ian Stuart despite his 'fearsome' reputation. He was respectful to me and helped me immensely unlike that evil brute Jackson. I will miss him no end too and the entire worldwide far Right is in mourning tonight and probably for many more years to come. Car accidents and accidents of all types have long been favoured human disposal methods of Intelligence Services across the world - why should it be unreasonable that Ian was murdered by the State? I'm convinced that he was but I'm sure the State will say I'm being paranoid or maybe I will be bought a new car. I guess we'll never know but someone or something is going to have to pay for this outrage. The far Right has its neo-messiah to replace Hitler now and our resolve is stronger than ever.

We send a Celtic Cross shaped wreath of white carnations to Ian's funeral being held somewhere in Lancashire, from Nottingham BNP but his family have requested a private funeral for family members only and a few chosen followers including Steve Jones from Eastwood. The Anti Nazi League has threatened 'action' against the funeral if thousands of neo-Nazis turn up to send Ian off to Valhalla. I sympathise with his family's wishes and write a eulogy for him that is published in the Ilkeston Advertiser the following week.

Good thing we didn't turn up at Ian's funeral really: there would have been a massacre of the far Left and a few more funerals on their side, I dare say. Nonetheless, the war will get even more bitter from now on but to be truthful with you, I'm getting very tired of this unending war that seems to be going nowhere. People are dying and getting seriously injured all over the country and these things are only going to get worse. The far Right is now locked in a bloody war for survival and I'm right in the thick of it - I must be stupid or just plain lost. Tyndall simply cannot evolve and change tactics so what chance do we have?

What happened to his policy of cleaning up the party image and every attempt I make to modernise the party is shouted down by the Tyndall faction who are lost in the 1950s and post-modern Fascism is the only ideology they understand. One cannot talk to Tyndall about these matters and address the need for a change in policy to take the middle ground of moderate nationalism to bring the masses on side. I am convinced that Tyndall is like a kamikaze pilot, hell-bent on taking down the entire movement with him in a divine wind. His refusal to change defies all rational argument and my heart is sick of violence and confrontational marches that achieve nothing.

This is not the way forward and I am almost ready to leave the BNP. Many activists are leaving the party because of Tyndall but leaving the party simply means he will stay on as leader. In the end I may have to follow the same route and it would be a great waste of years of hard work. Tyndall has nothing to offer the party anymore other than great oratory but even that is becoming tiresome to veterans like me who have heard it all before. I have to make one final attempt to modernise the BNP or resign if I fail. Most people in the BNP just do not understand the need to modernise and why we need to do so and that is the greatest obstacle facing me. I suppose in many ways the time is not right yet and someone else will have to finish the job when I am gone.

With socio-economic conditions ripe for the rise of the far Right as happens so often across history, we are wasting out golden opportunity because Tyndall is a dinosaur. He writes repeatedly in Spearhead – or 'borehead' as most activists call it now – that Combat 18 and Charlie Sargent are in the employ of MI5 and uses there latest glossy magazine as evidence to prove his point. If C18 has been infiltrated by MI5 agents in a classic disruptive action operation then Tyndall is to blame. He created C18 and after he lost his nerve at the battle of Hyde Park Corner it was inevitable that C18 would find new paymasters.

Since leaving the BNP over the fiasco C18 have become even more violent than before and have started attacking leading BNP activists. Tyndall insists this is evidence of C18 being *"nothing more than a creature of MI5"* but refuses to accept the blame for this strategic failure but that is typical of Tyndall and now our own creature has been turned against us and we are watching our backs, ever conscious of a stab in the back from **MI5/C18**.

CHAPTER 12

A WAKE UP CALL

Derek Beacon has won the BNP's first council seat in London's Docklands. Tower Hamlets will go down in history as the beginning of the BNP's socio-political revolution through the ballot box. At last, we have made a big breakthrough on the political scene. Yes, it's only one council seat but the media has written us off so many times as a nasty little party full of no hopers that this victory is all the sweeter.

The whole party is alive with enthusiasm and hope and the collective party mood is positively infectious. I need a lift to my spirits and after nearly four years in the BNP, I am starting to think that we have a chance of winning again. I hope it won't be another four years before we win another election. We've taken a heavy toll recently what with Ian's death and another Skinhead band Violent Storm has been wiped out.

On the morning of Friday the 13th 1992, the lads from Violent Storm made their way along the M4 motorway to the airport near Bristol; the car they were travelling in suddenly went out of control when the tyre blew out and slid into a ditch. Paul Casey, Brian and Darren Sheeley and their friend Jason Oakes all were killed. Billy who was driving was the only survivor who staggered from the wreck.

One of our men in London had his eye gouged out by men who tricked their way into his flat by impersonating local council workers. Alf Waite is recovering from his injuries but tells an interesting story of his attack: his assailants were looking for BNP membership records, which he had access to. Very suspicious and the rumour mill says that pseudo-gang Combat 18 carried out the attack.

And a telephone operator at our Kent HQ has suffered burns to his hands and face after a letter bomb exploded when he was opening it. Again Tyndall levels the blame at the MI5/C18 nexus and warns every activist of senior rank to upgrade their security. This war is getting vicious and deadly. And of course there's the usual litany of street warfare casualties all over the country and increased racial attacks wherever the BNP is strong. This is a very depressing and worrying time for me. I'm concerned about my safety and tell the Cotmanhay BNP members about my concerns. A couple of evenings later a young man in his early twenties comes to see me at my flat near Cotmanhay.

He's about 6.2 and has a huge stature like a Roman God. I know this man vaguely from the earlier battle of Cotmanhay but I know him only as Marc. He's wearing a long grey trench coat and looks like a 1930s mobster but I like him nonetheless. He opens his trench coat and tucked into a large pocket inside is a sawn-off shotgun. He whips it out and breaks the barrel - two red and brass cartridges gleam menacingly under the focused spotlights.

Fucking hell it's loaded! This guy means business. *"I've been assigned to protect you Simon, right!"* He's not asking me. *"No problem, Marc!"* I reply trying not to look nervous but I am. *"I will call on you every night and check you're OK. We'll also keep an eye out in the day, just in case anyone tries anything nasty."* I don't ask who 'we' are but I have a good idea and it's not a good idea to ask too many questions in this game.

Sure enough, Marc calls on my flat every night with his steel nostrils tucked into his trench coat. He knocks on the window, asks me if I'm alright, and opens his coat to show me the shotgun. He smiles slowly, his fresh blue eyes glinting like polished steel, and then he walks over to the Hand on Heart pub where he sits keeping an eye on me all night. This is not the first time I've been given armed protection either. When I lived at Eastwood, a man sat outside my house in a car for hours on end carrying a pump action shotgun.

It seems that someone wants me alive. Am I that important to them? I'll never know but someone is taking the effort to save my life even when I'm reckless with it. Maybe it's the Gods at work, and only the Gods will ever know, I suppose. I've got a bad feeling about this new flat I'm living in. I just can't rationalise it but instinct is telling me to get out and quickly. I've developed a nose for imminent danger these last few dark years and have to leave this property and quickly.

This year's AGM in London is going to be a big event to celebrate our Tower Hamlets election success in October. But why do these meetings always have to be in winter when it's bloody freezing. I love November though for its star-studded night skies and it's my birthday in a couple of day's time. I'm going to be staying with Arthur Flinders in Lewisham for the next couple of days. I'm told he's trustworthy but I've never met him, so I'm on my guard. I've bought a beautiful three-piece grey-green suit for the occasion and I feel great again.

The train draws up at Welling station in Kent and I'm off to the BNP HQ. It's a converted end terrace house bought by Richard Edmonds with his settlement from a London school where he worked as a teacher for over a decade. I walk up to the building and see the scars of the Anti Nazi League's demonstration a few weeks before. The building is pockmarked like a spotty face where bottles and bricks have impacted on the masonry.

Jim White, a tall Scotsman with ginger hair greets me at the door and opens the steel shutter to let me in. They know I'm coming. The place stinks of sweat and new books, nicotine stains seem to drip from the whitewashed walls. It's all quite gloomy and tatty and the windows are boarded up - a bunker mentality prevails among the HQ staff. Good God and they let the national media conduct interviews here! I'm not impressed in the slightest. I've been in the front half of this building before which is used as a bookshop. The walls are draped with blue cloth and BNP literature is everywhere.

Arthur Flinders is a telephone operator at the 'bunker' and deals with book orders and enquiries from our membership. He's quite jovial and large but his eyes are very suspicious and considered. I think this man is more than he appears. My first thought is that he's a far Left plant (instinct at work) but Jim has told me that he's 'safe'. We'll see. Maybe I'm being paranoid but that's doesn't mean it's not happening just because I'm being paranoid.

There are two types of paranoia as far as I'm concerned: The first type keeps you alert and alive on the battlefield of life; the second type is when you imagine that everyone's out to get you. Not far from the truth then, in my game. I chuckle to myself with a wry gallows humour - the very same humour Catherine hated so much. I miss her like crazy now. I've lost her for this but I've got nothing else now, so I'm going to make the best of what I've got.

Two Americans from the Southern States come strolling in through the back door. Dean is Greek American and Don, well, he's just American. Dean is short with black curly hair and a moustache that makes him look like Groucho Marx - better not mention that. Likening a neo-Nazi to a Jewish person can be a death sentence in this game. Don is fat and balding and speaks very little. Dean is a frenetic livewire and cannot stop bragging about this, that and the other.

"Oh everything's so much bigger and better in the States, mannn." A typical loudmouth Yank, in my eyes. They're both

connected to the KKK and that turns me off right away. I don't like pseudo-Christian fanaticism. I don't like religion full stop but political fanaticism is fine by me - lessons in subjectivity, hey? I've been given the task to chaperone these Rednecks to the AGM somewhere in London. Just my bloody luck! We'll probably have to stop off several times *en route* to feed Don's bulging burger habit - 'everything's so much bigger and better in the States'.

We're ploughing through the streets of South London in some district I've never been to before. I know that we have to take security precautions but this is getting ridiculous. I've phoned Arthur several times now and the redirection points he's given me have just led me round and round in circles until we've reached a point close to Lewisham. I can see the block of flats now where Arthur lives and I'm getting paranoid again. Is someone watching us from those windows over there?

Is someone following us - a sniper at work, maybe? A Special Branch snatch squad with the Rednecks as bait? Oh, fuck this! I've had enough now and tell the Rednecks that we've been sold a red herring by HQ. They seem stunned and can't take it in. *"Someone does not want you to get to the meeting and I'm your decoy."* I tell them, really pissed off. *"I don't think that's the case."* Dean tells me. What does he know about the BNP and its little schemes.

Don tells me to follow my instinct and he's not the dimwit now that he appears to be. *"We've been set up Simon - that's clear. Follow your gut instinct man."* I'm getting to like Don. And he should know about his gut instinct, yeah. *"We're going back to the 'bunker' to thrash this out."* It's an order. I've travelled over a hundred miles to get to the AGM and instead I'm walking two white hoods around London. I'm not a happy man and sparks are going to fly when I get to the bunker. Someone had better have a bloody good explanation for this.

I walk in and confront Jim White straight away. *"What the fuck is going on here today, Jim? I'm a senior leader in the party and should be at the AGM, not walking two white wizards around town."* He knows I'm ready to bite him. *"Well, Arthur says he gave you the correct directions but you got lost."* It's a weak response. *"Lost, lost. Arthur can get fucking lost for all I care. He gave me directions which sent me round and round in circles until we ended up near his flat at Lewisham. He is dodgy Jim. I'm telling you that, not asking you."*

Jim's face is ashen. *"Tyndall trusts him. So that's good enough for me."* I smell the hand of Tyndall at work here. Maybe he hasn't forgiven me for the battle of Cotmanhay. Arthur's upstairs the whole time this is happening. Obviously hiding his guilty conscience or planting another recording device. I'm going to stay at his flat tonight as planned and get the measure of this little sneak - see what his real agenda is.

Dean, ever the over-anxious prat, has volunteered to be interviewed by Channel 4's Alex Thompson in the bookshop. I sit in the back and listen to him raving and ranting about America's inner-city race problems. This is the BNP's AGM and Channel 4 get to interview an American. The 51st State of the USA whistles through my brain. I'm wasting my time with these people. I've sacrificed everything for the BNP and this is how I'm treated. Well, I'm going to get to the bottom of this. Something tells me 'Arthur' is a spy for Searchlight magazine. I can't explain this feeling but it's similar to the one I had a few months ago in Ilkeston.

A young woman claiming to be an 'avid follower of the far Right' says she wants to get active in the BNP. She flaunts her sexuality at everyone including me but I don't do honeytraps - they always lead you to a nasty sting. I suspected she was press or police. No one listens to me on this one - they're infatuated. So I do some digging and find out that she's the old flame of an old army mate of mine, who I went to school with and she's also a Detective Constable in Derbyshire police. She never came out with us again. I passed her a message through her ex-boyfriend to stay away. She did as she was told. I learned later that she got hitched to my old army mate.

The pub in Paddington is full of BNP and Blood & Honour supporters who've been to the AGM. It's not a remarkable place by any standard. Mirror tiles reflect back at me from every angle my growing dismay with the far Right. Skinheads with swastika tattoos on their forearms, wearing Fred Perry T-shirts and boots half way up their legs. The usual assortment of Nazi badges mingled with BNP motifs seem to drip from every shirt and coat in the room. I'm starting to think that I'm back at the Mundy Arms in Ilkeston.

We've won an election recently but in terms of the party's collective thuggish mentality we've progressed not an inch in four years. True, Combat 18 has been expelled from the BNP but that was only because Tyndall couldn't get his own way. Stamping out violence had nothing to do with his decision. And when I look at myself I think that I've become little better than the rest of them, even though I wear smart suits and ties. I'm sick of this completely unwholesome garbage.

I look at Tyndall as he walks into the pub escorted by a few heavies and he reminds me of some sad old dictator who can't exist without violence and discord in his life. It's a frightening thought that I might become like him in thirty years' time. He's on the usual handshake tour now and the grovellers and the fawners are all over him like a bad rash. He walks over and shakes my hand, telling me that he's pleased to see me. Like hell he is. *"What did you think of today's show then Simon?"* He asks me with an ill-concealed smirk on his face. *"I don't know. I wasn't there."* He smirks in response, sad old man.

I walk straight past him and with a few steps I'm out of the pub and heading for a nearby taxi rank. I take off my BNP badge and throw it in the gutter where it belongs with the rest of the garbage. The taxi winds through London's wet back streets after a downpour and I'm soon at Arthur's flat in Lewisham and Dean's there too. He rants and raves about the evils of multi-racialism as though he was some sort of saint. Arthur and I, just look at each other and smile.

Arthur is definitely a Red infiltrator in my eyes but I don't give a stuff anymore - I've had it with the BNP and I think Arthur knows that somehow. He's a very watchful man and his eyes take in everything with the speed and sharpness of an eagle hunting its prey. Dean starts banging his drum about the *"filthy Hispanic scum who are invading the US. Yeah. We go down to the border some weekends and shoot the fuckers as they're coming in across the border. You should come over and join us sometime Simon."* Why on earth does this prick think that I would want to shoot Hispanics. They've got just as much right to live in Texas as the Yanks. After all, the US seized Texas from the Mexicans by force of arms in the 19th Century.

"It's just like hunting Simon. You should come over too Arthur. We'd have a great time." He rattles on. He's one hell of a sick sonofabitch. *"I can't afford the air fare."* I tell him as I head for the bathroom with Arthur's laughter ringing in my ears. I wash my face with freezing cold water and stare blankly into the mirror. My eyes, once so young and blue, are now tired and grey. I notice for the first time also that I have more than a few grey hairs. Smart suit or not, at twenty-five I look haggard.

I've sacrificed my construction business, my lovely Catherine and over four years of my life for the far Right and this is what I'm left with - nothing! Most of this has been my own fault but I know now that I have wasted a vital part of my life and my youth has been lost forever. How different it was back then when I was but a boy at twenty-one. I was prepared to listen to anything older men told me of the way the real world is - their world. They quickly impressed their ideas on me and here I am. I feel like an old man, worn out mentally and emotionally starved of love. I can't remember the last time I had any true love in my life.

I'm drifting off back to the summer of 1989 just before I got involved with the far Right. I'm sitting back with Catherine lapping up the summer sun in a fallow cornfield. The verdant green grass swims and rushes in the light wind and the scene is blissful and very innocent. Swallows rise and fall like empires in great sweeping strokes, and we're surrounded by the innate beauty of lush Moorgreen; the same countryside that inspired the famous novelist D H Lawrence.

It's almost like we're held in the comforting soft bosom of our earth mother, basking in the glory of our fleeting youth. Everything makes sense here. There's love and peace aplenty and the crops of happiness seem abundant and ripe. Catherine unbuttons her pink and purple floral blouse, to reveal her firm pink breasts and she lies down in the frothing grass. Her red mane seems to me like a sunburst full of hope and love - my sun Goddess incarnate. I lift my head from the sink and stare again into the pale reflection of my former life. How mighty are the fallen, I rebuke myself. Tears pour from my eyes and tip tap gently into the sink. The full horror of my life is unfolding before me. Bricks and bottles crash down on the pavement where I am. Knives and batons crunch and cut into skin and bone. I want to be sick but can't allow it to happen.

I see the mangled faces of the hippies just two years ago, haunting me, beseeching me for help. I think of comrades dead and buried, others mentally destroyed by the whirlwind of extremist violence we've been subjected to. None of this makes any sense to me now. I've reached the crossroads and there's no turning back, never look back. I steady myself, dry my eyes and make off for the 'living' room.

There's a dispute going on now in the Midlands BNP for who controls the region's bank account. Men and money, hey! My cynicism has no boundary now. My colleagues disgust me as they fight and scrape for every penny. Peacock wants the money to go on fighting his meaningless election campaigns which rarely achieve more than 2% of the vote. Peacock, along with Tyndall, Edmonds and Morse is a dinosaur and refuses to conform to the modern age of voter reality. People aren't interested in compulsory repatriation and any suggestion of adopting a softer face of moderate nationalism is met with cries of derision from the leadership. Voluntary repatriation is a vote winner because people see the policy as not being cruel and extreme like forced repatriation is.

Tyndall treats these moderate notions with a gasp of incredulity and lambastes the BNP leadership by telling us: *"Give me the credit of knowing how to run a nationalist political party. I've been in this game for over 30 years now..."* Well, Tyndall knows it all so what's the point of hanging around for years more of wasted 'activities' in the name of a Cause that means nothing to me anymore. Where once the BNP meant everything, today it leaves me cold and despondent.

I resigned my position as Midlands Elections Officer a few days ago in January, and February promises eventual release from the BNP. The greedy fools who want the money I've raised all these years from the Tories can have it. I am sure they will squander it and then be incapable of raising more thousands to squander. Laurence Johnson is busy grovelling up to Tyndall now that I've resigned. He knows that I will never challenge Tyndall for the leadership.

I'm setting in motion the steps for my permanent departure from the BNP. It will take a few months but it will be worth it. I resigned on health grounds because I did not want my enemies to have the satisfaction of thinking they'd forced me to go. I will use the same pretext to leave the party completely in a few months time. My GP says I am suffering from severe stress and must avoid anymore conflict. Nothing untrue about that. I'm going to keep my head down and not make any waves. I won't have to now that I'm the West Notts organiser again - the branch exists in name only. I've decided to go on taking the BNP's publications just to make things look good. I hardly read them at all now - just the same old drivel about immigrants being the root of all social ills. I swallowed that claptrap once but not anymore. I have an empty diary for BNP meetings and it's staying that way but the dramas are not over yet.

CHAPTER 13

PAYBACK TIME

After five years away from the party, Calvin Richards has invited me to a BNP meeting at The Mill public house near Langley Mill in Derbyshire, at the end of February but I'm not really interested. He's says a *"great young leader"* has taken over the leadership of the BNP. Nick Griffin is a Cambridge graduate and promises radical reforms of the BNP's public image, internal organisation and an end to far Right violence, which is precisely what I tried do before resigning. That would be very welcome for many people if it's true. Nick Griffin seems to be quite the peacemaker or at least he's marketing himself as one now. Calvin's got me intrigued but I won't make any hasty decisions just yet. Nonetheless, I think the Griffin thing might be worth taking a look at soon.

Late February arrives and I'm reading module one of my journalism diploma. The text instructs the trainee journalist to 'write about what you know'. So, here I am writing about what I know, in the most honest way that I know. And I know quite a bit about the far Right and maybe that's a starting point for me. We'll see. It's the meeting tomorrow and I've got nothing special planned for Monday night. I explain to my girl that I'm going to the BNP meeting to see what Griffin's BNP is like. I have no agenda to further and I am strictly apolitical. I phone Calvin and tell him that I will be going to the meeting after all because I'm intrigued by Griffin's 'new BNP'. *"You won't be disappointed Simon. See you there."* He tells me in a warm voice but then the BNP has never been hot on warmth.

I mount the stairs from the public bar downstairs and walk into the large meeting room. Tables are laid out for the speakers, BNP literature adorns them, and union flags hang from the wall behind. I look around anxiously and see Calvin at the end of the room. He's sat with a cabal of new faces I've not seen before, and I'm more nervous now than ever. I walk over to him and he greets me with warmth and a strong handshake. *"Good to see you Calvin."*

He introduces me to his close colleagues from Nottingham BNP. The old faces are no more and a fresh crop of recruits has come into the BNP. I turn and walk over to the bar to get a beer and I'm confronted with a vision of sheer despondency, for me that is. Along the wall leading up to the bar there are dozens of skinheads, probably 70 in total. I didn't see them when I first walked in because their position is offset to the left from the main door.

(Stigger posing as the 'replacement' to Ian Stuart)

They're wearing the same old swastika badges and Blood & Honour literature adorns their tables. Skull and crossbones SS rings are on open sale for £7 and National Front leaflets are strewn between piles of leaflets advertising skinhead bands. So much for the 'new BNP', I'm thinking, but I've not heard Griffin speak yet, so I'll make up my mind about all of this later. I turn away from the bar and Stigger and Sisco come walking through the main door and sit with the skinheads.

These two far Right 'musicians' are adored on the far Right, much like Ian Stuart was when I started out on this journey in 1989. Stigger seems to have filled Ian's Doc Marten boots as the skinheads' young avatar. Stigger's real name is Steven Calladine. He was my class mate at Eastwood Comprehensive School for three years and I know him pretty well. Sisco, works with Calvin at Royal Mail but I don't know him too well, other than the fact that his first name is Mick.

I've been living In Eastwood again for some months now and

Tommy Swift told me recently that Stigger is the new leader of Combat 18 in the UK. Tommy's not been involved with the far Right since he was knocked out by a C18 baton in London a couple of years ago. The same old diet of violence and internecine warfare scars the far Right today just as it did years ago during my active years.

There does not seem to be much difference now, than when I was a young fanatic in the early 1990s. It's depressing and sickening and I'm not getting involved in this madness again. I sit down with Calvin and sip rapidly at my drink. I'm very apprehensive and when I look at the skinheads I see visions of 1990 again. What on earth am I doing here?

Griffin takes the platform and speaks to us about the need to change the BNP's public image but retain the core belief in race and nation. *"It's all about presentation, presentation,"* he tells us with a smirk. He's no great speaker, not like Tyndall was but the flock love him but not as much as he loves himself, I dare say. I'm disappointed with his appearance though. He's wearing a single breasted dark blue suit, black shoes and a white Fred Perry T-shirt, open at his neck to reveal three large love bites. 'Presentation, presentation' - be damned, I think.

Griffin waffles on about Britain pulling out of the Balkans war and draws thunderous applause. I go along with it, to make it look good. He then postulates his belief that voluntary repatriation works better with voters and gives the BNP a softer image more conducive to mainstream politics than the fringes. I was promoting this policy throughout the early 1990s and Griffin has simply jumped on the bandwagon. The BNP has made no breakthrough in British politics since the council seat win at Millwall in October 1993. But Griffin intends to change this with sweeping reforms.

"We can't forcibly deport all of our coloured immigrants, even though we want to, because America would bomb Britain. We've seen US hegemony at work in the Balkans recently, so we must be coy about our policies." He's clearly forgotten the fact that American does not attack any nation that can really fight back and prefers backward Middle East states to bully into accepting the Capitalist/Zionist nexus or face destruction. Griffin's impractical speech closes and again he's applauded by his adoring supporters.

Calvin has promised to introduce me to Griffin and makes off in the young demagogue's direction. They chat for a few minutes and then both of them walk over to me. Griffin greets me with a smile and a handshake. Even though I've not met him before tonight he tells me, *"It's good to have you back Simon."* I'm still seen as safe in the far Right because after five years in the wilderness I've kept my mouth shut and just got on with my life and not embarrassed anyone with public indiscretions.

Griffin is smarmy and completely self-infatuated, on first impression. He brags about his years at Cambridge University. He explains that he started out studying law but switched to modern history after year one because he found law quite boring. But he sees nothing wrong in allowing the BNP membership to think he's a law graduate. The newspapers I've read recently also refer to him as a law graduate. He smirks and cajoles at the same time and turns my stomach but I try not to show my disgust.

Griffin is impressed with the fact that I'm a trainee journalist. *"Would you like to work for us in our media relations department?"* He asks me out of the blue. I tell him that I'm not qualified yet but he retorts that I've got five years experience in the *"old BNP"* under my belt and that I was always known as a 'moderniser' back then. *"You won't be able to use your own name though - you will never work in the mainstream media if you use your own name."* I don't think he's asking me a question for one minute. I explain to him that I will use my own name if I'm going to become his press officer because I've got nothing to hide. I'm known from the old BNP as Simon Smith, so I really would make myself look stupid if I turned up again as Fred Johnson, would I not?

Griffin introduces me to Dr Stuart Russell, the BNP's senior media relations officer based in Nottinghamshire. Dr Russell prefers to call himself *"Dr Phil Edwards for BNP business."* I ask him which name he prefers in private and he retorts that his girlfriend has several names for him. I'm determined to pin him down on the pseudonym issue and press him further even though he's clearly uncomfortable with this line of questioning. We begin an interesting and enlightening conversation:

Me: "Nick tells me that you're the BNP's media monitor and that he'd like me to work as a press officer under your 'tutelage'. What do you envisage as my role?"
Russell: "The media monitoring unit is responsible for scanning the national media and challenging smears about the BNP. We're not going to tolerate anymore Nazi smears against us."
Me: "You mean the old smear about us being neo-Nazis?"
Russell: "That's pretty much what it entails but we also have to point out that the party has changed its image and got rid of the skinhead element under Nick's leadership." I have to do my best

not to burst out laughing at this point.

Me: "So what about all the skinheads here tonight then Doc? Why, are they here?"

Russell: "Well," he mumbles, "they're nothing to do with the BNP. They're from Blood & Honour and the NF. We didn't invite them but the local organiser could not get any help with obtaining a venue, so he approached Benny Bulman who helped us to get this place tonight. So, we have to allow them in or there would be trouble, you know!"

Me: "Yes, I understand what you're saying and I know how hard it can be to get a venue for a BNP meeting."

Russell: "Yeah, sure, I mean they're not connected to the BNP, Simon. I can assure you of this!"

(Dr Stuart Russell, right, resigned his position in the BNP in late 2007 after a serious bust-up with Nick Griffin)

Me: "OK Doc, but tell me why it is that you use an assumed name for your work as a press officer in the BNP. Is it to protect your livelihood?"

Russell: "Well, all famous writers use pen names and I have a position in life to protect, you know."

Me: "Well, we all have positions to protect Doc, but not all of us use false names for the obvious reason that the press latch onto the fact and destroy our reputation as a 'respectable' party. Got something to hide, you know. Moreover, you're not a famous writer, are you?" He's rattled now.

Russell: "Well, I know that but I'm going to be and it's agreed with Nick that I use the pseudonym Dr Phil Edwards or I don't work in the party at all. I can't have people where I live finding out about my association with the BNP until we're a major power - strong enough not to be opposed. It's that simple!"

Me: "So Doc, do you want me to release press statements using my own name?"

Russell: "Yes, if you want to but I advise you to use a pseudonym instead. It's much safer, you know!"

Me: "I don't agree with you on the pseudonym matter Doc, and I think it just makes the party look shady. I'll use my own name because I have nothing to hide."

Russell: "Well, I've got nothing to hide either. I just want to protect my anonymity for a while." How odd for someone who wants to be a 'famous writer'.

Me: "I understand what you're saying Doc and I'll do my best for the party on the terms that you've set out. You have my word!"

Russell: "I look forward to working with you, Simon." He extends his right hand and we shake on it - job done.

I turn to my right and walk straight into Sisco. *"Not seen you for years Simon. You gettin' involved again now?"* I tell him that I've accepted Nick's offer to work as a press officer but only on a trial period, see how I get on. I ask him what he thinks of the BNP's new public image. *"It's a con but a good con to fool the public but you'd better believe that we're going to deal with these corrupt politicians when we get in power. Hang the bastards - all of them, I say!"* He's deadly serious as well and a great many electors would probably agree with his sentiments after years lies and betrayal by the mainstream political crooks.

The BNP has not changed its core belief in practising violence and manipulating the ballot box as a means to win power. Sisco waxes on for another ten minutes, talking about buying shotguns and crossbows for the revolution - heard this somewhere before, me thinks. Was it back in the early 1990s, when Tyndall led the BNP and 'young fools' like me swallowed his diatribe of violence and race hate? Yes, of course it was and in today's BNP nothing has changed other than a slicker media image - 'just a con to fool the public'.

But I can see that Griffin is making the BNP a force to be reckoned with and he's heading in my direction again now. *"Simon, before you go, can I ask you to come up with some leaflet designs to explain the BNP's strong stance against drug dealing and the like."* He's a real smoothie this one. *"Yes, of course I will Nick. I'll send them to your PO Box in Wales, yes?"* He tells me 'that's fine' and we shake hands again and I make for the exit quickly, resisting the desire to spit or vomit. Griffin has simply used all of the ideas that I was promoting in the early 1990s and markets them as his own.

I'm sat at home now, mulling over the night's happenings. I'm very clear about the 'new' BNP and immediately realise that there's no such thing yet. There's just a violent BNP and 'old' or 'new' doesn't come into it but Griffin is trying to clean-up the party and I think he should be given a chance. I'm thinking of what to do now that I'm in, so to speak. I'm not really sure what I'm going to do but I'm going to do it. I think getting closer to Griffin and understanding his strategy would be the best thing. Any unpleasant details I pick up on the way about the covert BNP, I can use for an exposé with the media if Griffin betrays his promise to reform the party.

I've got 'five years under my belt' in the 'old' BNP and people still trust me. I start thinking I might write a book about my old life in the BNP but these are early days yet. I have done nothing but design leaflets for months now and Nick has told me that I will not be allowed to work for the BNP in public until I complete my journalism diploma successfully. I've been out with Calvin and some of his skinhead boys in Langley Mill and Ripley but have not seen anything of a violent nature. Tommy Swift tells me that Combat 18 is stockpiling weapons for a race war and they have weapons dumps around Cotmanhay and Underwood on the Notts/Derbys border but it's probably just hot air again from boys who want to be big men. The problem with the far Right is that too many of its activists talk about revolution instead of getting on with it.

The nearest thing I've seen to violence thus far is some members of Calvin's team carrying concealed weapons in Langley Mill in preparation for a clash with the far Left. Carrying the odd knife and baton is nothing new in the BNP but then you know that by now. The BNP is targeting populist issues of crime and asylum to make headway with the electorate and concentrating on community politics. The strategy is succeeding and this is reflected by the fact that the BNP now has thousands more members and supporters across the whole of the UK.

Griffin and his team are preparing for the 2001 General Election in which the party is fielding about thirty candidates. Not a huge showing but Griffin believes that concentrating party resources in small areas will produce big results for the party and he's not wrong either. Across Lancashire and parts of Yorkshire the BNP is making waves and I've never seen so many BNP supporters who believe that total victory is nigh. Most of this new ebullience is borne of Griffin's infectious optimism and excellent organisational skills. He is not a great orator by any means but he is a first class organiser and I understand why the Political Establishment fear him and they should, for now at least.

Griffin is standing in Oldham where there has been significant racial tension in recent months between disgruntled white youths upset at attacks on them and the violent Asian gangs pumped up on radical Islam. Post 9/11 it is not difficult to whip-up contempt for Islam and the radical Muslims are simply playing into the hands of the BNP. I do not believe that the BNP is entirely to blame for this tension. There is good and bad on both sides of this unfortunate racial divide. The real blames rests at the doors of successive Labour and Government governments. At least I'm not being asked to do any fighting this time round. I just have to make press releases to the media distancing the BNP from any racial violence. Griffin has steered the BNP away from confrontational marches and demonstrations to avoid bad publicity.

But I am sure that the BNP is whipping up racial hostility in Northern towns to make electoral gains. The strategy is quite simple: incite racial tensions, get Muslims out on the streets attacking whites and the police, distance the BNP from the violence and blame it all on the NF and C18. When the dust has settled, the BNP creams off support from white voters terrified of more 'Asian riots'. I've not seen any clear evidence of this so far from within the party's nucleus but I think it's happening this way. I have a clear perception of these matters but I'm not going to get closer to Griffin until I'm a qualified journalist, so I'm going to put everything into my journalism studies and get them completed as soon as possible. I also need to get a decent job at the end of this. I'm not taking a journalism course just to impress the BNP leadership.

CHAPTER 14

ALL TOO EASY

(Asian mob on the rampage in Bradford attacking the police)

The brimming racial tension has spilled over into mass race riots across Northern England since the BNP's strong showing at the General Election in Oldham and Burnley. Bradford has experienced unprecedented race riots and the BNP and NF are being accused of inciting the violence by the media but not by the police who know the radical Muslims are as much to blame. The largely defunct Anti Nazi League has played a significant role also in provoking the Bradford riot, inciting Asian Muslims to go on an anti-Establishment rampage. The evening news carries pictures of young white men being stabbed and beaten by gangs of young Asians.

All this dire conflict has earned the BNP massive media attention and won over thousands of terrified white voters. I sense that the BNP is now on the verge of a serious political breakthrough and it will come soon - very soon. The BNP is now recruiting at an unprecedented rate and the entire party apparatus is finding it difficult to cope with enquiries from the general public and the world's intrigued media. CNN have been pestering Griffin for an interview but Simon Darby steps into the breach instead. Whether the BNP can become a party of national government is something for posterity to record and I cannot predict this. First the party has to break into mainstream politics and that is going to be a very difficult business because mass organisation requires ample supplies of money which the BNP does not have at this time.

I'm sat at my laptop computer searching the internet for a new firewall program to secure my personal data when I'm online. It's a quiet Saturday evening at my Nottingham home in late July 2001, and the sky outside is fifty grey shades of dullness but forty miles away there's a storm rising. My mobile phone hums into life to break the pattern of boredom I've had recently. I look at the caller display and see that it's Nick Griffin calling me, so I open the line immediately:

Griffin: "Hi Simon, it's Nick here. Will you issue press releases to the West Midlands media distancing us from any racial trouble in Stoke. Target the BBC in particular for maximum effect."
Me: "I thought that was Doc's job."
Griffin: "He's busy with other things and anyway you're qualified now, so it's time to step into the limelight, so to speak. D'you want it?"
Me: "Yeah, sure thing. So, what's cooking in Stoke then, Nick?"
Griffin: "There's some trouble brewing in the Asian Muslim community after someone from the National Front issued a warning that they are going to march in the town next weekend to wind up the Muslims there."
Me: "The NF never learn do they, Nick?"
Griffin: "Well..." He pauses to laugh, "It's useful for us to conjure up the image of an impending NF march to get the Pakis out on the streets attacking the police and white communities. Then when the dust's settled we move in as the white messiahs. Only the BNP can save British whites from Muslim violence - you know how it goes, Simon. 'Creeping Islamification' and all that stuff." Now there's a new term.
Me: "Sounds like a good strategy."
Griffin: "It's worked well 'elsewhere' for us; in fact it's all too easy. We can always make capital out of the NF, you know. So, just say to the media that we do not hold marches or demonstrations and it's very important for us to distance ourselves from the coming violence. Let the Pakis take the blame - they're the ones rioting, Simon."

Me: "Well, that's true Nick. Consider it done."
Griffin: "Thanks Simon. Speak soon."

The BNP use mobile telephone and email communications because these methods are invariably ultra-fast and very difficult to track. Particularly so if emails are PGP encrypted which is standard military grade encryption software used on most personal computers today. Islamic Fundamentalists have used the same software to communicate details of their attacks on Western targets and caused the CIA and MI6 serious difficulties cracking their codes. The BNP's website advertises a PGP hotkey for enquirers who want their emails to be secure.

I sent out several emails to the West Midlands media distancing the BNP from the racial riot that exploded in Stoke just two hours after Griffin phoned me. Young Muslims, fearing their communities were about to come under attack from the far Right hit the streets and pelted the police with bricks, bottles and petrol bombs. Earlier in the year, when race riots flared in Oldham and Burnley, the NF had issued warnings to the media warning of its intention to march in those areas.

This is not standard practice at all, as anyone involved in the planning of a march or demonstration will tell you. In fact, when planning to hold a march or a demonstration; the chief representative of an organisation has to make a formal application to a police Chief Constable, not the regional or national media, who simply report on these matters. For me, this is concrete evidence of what I suspected all along. That someone in the BNP is issuing press releases claiming that the NF is going to march in a particular area torn by racial tensions, then sit back and wait for the inevitable.

It also strikes me that someone in the Muslim communities in these towns should realise the connection between race riots and increased support for the BNP. No matter what the provocation, there can be no justification for rioting - it achieves nothing lasting in the long-term. Communities talking to each other will bring understanding. But extreme elements on both sides seek to further their cause by inciting racial and religious divisions. Working for the BNP again has proved to be a stressful experience and I do wonder if it's worth the hassle?

The stress of all this has caused a big argument with my girl and she asked me to leave. I can't tell her what I'm really doing in the BNP and the pressure of leading a double life has caused tension between us. I'm staying with a friend Dean Lambert for now but my laptop is locked in the house I share with my girlfriend. I must get hold of my laptop - it contains vital information pertaining to my work in the BNP and Griffin has just asked me to open a broadcast forum on the BNP's website. I'm to work with Simon Darby the BNP's Information Technology Director, who brags that he can 'hack into anything'.

Simon Darby, with on the surface 'respectability' he has risen through the BNP ranks with ease. His tactic has been to befriend Griffin to expedite promotion, a grovelling yes man. Behind the smokescreen of decency and 'tolerance', Darby is a vicious and hateful racist but he is in essence a physical coward with his eyes on the leadership. When the time comes he will stab Griffin in the back for his own personal gain.

I've never met Simon Darby but that's the norm in the BNP these days. Using emails and mobile phones saves time travelling to meet one another. I'm going to have to phone Darby though and explain the situation to him. This is going to make me look a real arse but that's life and I will pay my girl more attention in future. That way she won't be difficult about letting me have my laptop when I need it.

I've tried telephoning my girl one last time and done a bit of grovelling but to no avail. She's a real tough cookie when she wants to be. I sense she wants me to feel the pinch of the doghouse for a while. I best get my dogfood out then and start eating quickly because now it's time to speak to Darby and I'm not looking forward to it either. I feel a complete prat. It's just before ten in the morning, it's the end of August and the sunshine is warm and bright. Simon Darby's mobile is switched on and he's not going to like me phoning him so early on a Sunday morning. Dringggg, Dringggg, here we go…

Me: "Hello Simon. Sorry to phone you so early mate. It's Simon Smith in Nottingham. I've got a problem with the radio recordings for the website."

Darby: "It's a bit early but fire away now. I'm still in bed you know!" I can hear a girl giggling in the background - must be his lover.

Me: "Sorry Simon but it's important. I've had an argument with my girl and she's thrown me out of the house. I can't get my laptop with the radio recordings on its hard drive." We're supposed to be going to a digital telecommunications exhibition in London on Wednesday.

Darby: "Is there no way you can pacify her by being nice to her, even if you don't mean it?"

Me: "You don't know her like I do, Simon. When she makes up her mind on something she is very formidable, mate. I've tried being nice to her but it didn't work. She won't let me in." I feel so pathetic now, banished like a little schoolboy.

Darby: "Well, if we're going to work together Simon, you need your pc sharpish, mate!"

Me: "I've done everything I can think of."

Darby: "Why don't you go round and spray some CS gas through her letterbox then. That'll get the bitch out and then you can get your laptop." He obviously doesn't know that I am asthmatic.

Me: "Are you for real, mate?"

Darby: "You bet I am! It wouldn't be the first time something like this has happened."

Me: "You must be fucking sick to suggest such a thing. I would never do anything like that to her. I love the woman for God's sake!"

Darby: "It's up to you mate but I'm not joking. You need to get those files quick sharp!" He laughs.

Me: "Fuck you Darby!" Oh shit, I've blown it now.

Darby: "Only my girlfriend is allowed to do that. We have a strong anti-gay policy in the BNP, you know."

Darby and his lover break out into fits of immature laughter as he ends the call and I feel truly sick to the core of my stomach. I have made a big mistake. I have lost my cool with one the BNP's top brass and may have endangered everything. I just couldn't help it though. Advising me to spray CS gas at my girlfriend just because she's got sick of my inattention and moodiness, is sick and evil. Here's a BNP leader, widely respected throughout the party, 'advising' me to mount a CS gas attack on the person I love. No one ever spoke like this when I was a BNP advocate in the early 1990s. I had arguments with Catherine back then but if anything Calvin would advise me to treat her better because she tolerated my BNP work. Calvin would never have dreamt of 'advising' me to CS gas Catherine.

What type of people are these new breed of jackals in the BNP today? Dr Russell cannot even use his own name for BNP activities; Griffin is not concerned about playing dangerous games with the lives of others; Darby's a woman hater; Tony Lecomber has been in prison twice, once for trying to bomb the London office of the left-wing Morning Star and the second time for assaulting a Jewish school teacher on the London Underground and Calvin runs Nottingham BNP like his private army, advising new members to join through his post office box lest they be 'spied on by MI5 and Special Branch'.

Thank God I am no longer part of this sorry mess. But then I realise that I am part of this sorry mess. I don't support the BNP anymore but I am involved in uncovering the darker side of its activities. My argument with Darby, a record of which will be on Griffin's answering machine by now, is the perfect excuse to take some time out. Griffin will be livid with me. He's asked me to design a weekly newspaper for the BNP website and record radio broadcasts for a new media venture the party is launching in January 2002.

He will not understand that Darby provoked me because I believe that he's of the same mindset. Insulting one of his top men is a no, no. Griffin is a pragmatist and anything goes to get the job done in my opinion. The job of bringing him power and success, no matter what the consequences for anyone else. Chairman Griffin is a fully subscribed member of the Self Preservation Society and heading for its presidency fast.

So, I'm going to take some time off. I'm sending Chairman Griffin an email explaining my decision to take some time away from the BNP to save my relationship with my girl. Which is true anyway. But during this time away I'm going to take a serious look at Griffin's political background in the far Right; from the National Front and the International Third Position to the BNP. No stone will be left uncovered.

It's January 2002 and things are stable with my girl again. Well, stable in the sense that we've decided to go our separate ways and she's going back to her family who live in Johannesburg, Republic of South Africa. I'm not happy about it but this BNP thing has become very important to me and I've been neglecting her again. So, I'm sitting at my pc searching for information on Griffin's background and just take a look at what I've found.

Writing in Nick Griffin's glossy election address in 1999, Tony Lecomber wrote: 'Nick Griffin is putting forward a positive vision of the future and a blueprint to make it happen. The tone is upbeat, the confidence is infectious.' But Lecomber made no mention of Griffin's criminal conviction for incitement of racial hatred in 1997. There would be very significant developments though in the Griffin/Lecomber nexus when Lecomber later resigned from the BNP after being caught out trying to incite Griffin's bodyguard Joe Owens to assassinate senior politicians in what he called a *"suicide mission"* and rejected Lecomber's warped overture.

In the same publication Mike Newland wrote: 'Nearly everyone accepts the necessity of making the radical alterations needed to every part of the party, which should have been undertaken many years ago. John Tyndall now accepts this too, albeit without any enthusiasm. Unfortunately, his acceptance has come decades too late.' Mike Newland was later expelled from the party after accusing Griffin of financial impropriety in making payments to his cronies who were not even members of the BNP.

Newland, the BNP's former national press officer, challenged the new leader over alleged misappropriation of party funds. Newland alleged that Griffin made illegal payments to his cronies in direct contravention of the BNP's constitution. Newland was rewarded for his loyalty to Griffin with expulsion from the BNP over his gerrymandering 'slurs' against him. The BNP deputy chairman Sharon Edwards and her husband, Birmingham Organiser Steve Edwards, also accused Griffin of mishandling BNP funds and both were expelled from the party.

The Edwards alleged that Griffin made illegal payments to unnamed party officials in contravention of the BNP's constitution. Both were subsequently expelled from the party. Although, Griffin later made a seemingly magnanimous gesture by inviting them to return to BNP work if they toed the line. In effect, keep your mouth shut about my financial dealings or else! Another blatant threat dressed up behind baseless gestures. **The hallmark of Griffin's 'leadership' has been to expel anyone in the party who dares to criticise him let alone challenge him for the leadership. Is this democracy in action?**

In the August 1999 edition of Spearhead, John Morse wrote: *'Nick's words would seem to be whatever flavoured chewing gum for the ears that he calculates his audience of the moment might prefer. It's all done for effect. To this writer, as to anyone else who has had the tiresome spectacle of Nick Griffin before their eyes for enough years, Nick's auricular spearmint has long acquired a monotonous taste of cow dung.'* Morse published his article in response to what he saw as Griffin's complete rewriting of his political past. A view augmented by the International Third Position, which Griffin led for several years, was amazed at his political gymnastics, as it reported in its email newsletter during Griffin's challenge for the BNP leadership in summer 1999.

It read: **'He has been a conservative, a revolutionary nationalist, a radical National Socialist, a Third Positionist, a friend of the bootboys and the skinhead scene, a man committed to respectable politics and electioneering, a moderniser. Which is he in reality? Perhaps he has been all of these quite sincerely - in which case his judgement is abysmal; or perhaps he has been none of them sincerely - which speaks for itself.'**

Griffin left the National Front in 1991, claiming the party was *"bedevilled by religious cranks. It was with great sadness that I made the decision to leave."* So why did he then impetuously launch an even more bizarre political group with the same pseudo-religious cranks pumping policy directives in the International Third Position? The ITP professed support for Colonel Gaddaffi, the Ayatollah Khomeini and black nationalist Louis Farrakhan, leader of the Nation of Islam in the US.

The answer may be found in Griffin's sponsored trip to Tripoli in 1988, courtesy of the Libyan regime, in the hope of securing funding there. Griffin, Patrick Harrington and Derek Holland, the NF's representatives secured no funding and did not get to see Gaddaffi. Instead they were 'magnanimously' offered 5,000 copies of Gaddaffi's ridiculous Green Book - a manual describing how to start a revolution in the Arab world. But allegations still persist that Griffin was an MI6 operative, recruited at Cambridge, and his ITP, just another state sponsored honey-trap.

Today Griffin speaks of the need for "community-based" politics to build respectability in the eyes of voters. But this was not always the case. Several years ago he wrote in The Rune magazine which he edited: **"The electors of Millwall did not back a Post-Modernist Rightist Party, but what they perceived to be a strong, disciplined organisation with the ability to back up its** *slogan 'Defend Rights For Whites' with well-directed boots and fists. When the crunch comes, power is the product of force and will, not of rational debate."*

Is this what Griffin means when he says the BNP does not hold demonstrations because they are provocative and confrontational? But Griffin set about preparing for the 2001 General Election with great zeal, declaring: *"This then is our task - to build a responsible and powerful nationalist movement which can unite town and country, and bring together the rank-and-file of the old right with the voters of the old left. We are going to create a fusion of racial nationalism and social justice. And when that is done, we are going to win!"*

You never know which side of his personality you are going to talk to next when dealing with Chairman Griffin. Will it be the 'radical National Socialist' or the 'respectable moderniser'. Maybe he's not too sure himself and sure only of the fact that he has to tell each particular audience what he thinks they want to hear – in effect, the BNP's version of Tony Blair. And then I stumbled on something that was very shocking indeed. An issue which could be fatal to a BNP leader's career: homoerotic allegations against Griffin from his former NF boss Martin Webster, a self-confessed practising homosexual.

Webster claims their sensational 'affair' began in 1976 and continued throughout the period Griffin was studying at Cambridge University. It lasted four years in total, according to Webster, during which time Griffin stayed with Webster four or five times a year. Webster says that Griffin should not be condemned for his bi-sexuality but for his 'rampant hypocrisy and the rewriting of his political past'. Webster further stated, *"Griffin should have had the common sense to let sleeping dogs lie. But they misconstrued my silence as a sign that I was tongue-tied with embarrassment and that they could get away with saying what they liked - a big mistake. In Griffin's case, homophobic claptrap descended into a vicious mania."*

But Griffin sprang back immediately to deny Webster's allegations when the exposé broke in the Sunday Times on 5th September 1999. *"It's all a pack of lies from a spiteful old man,"* he told the 'paper of record'. Adding, *"I've got four children and I've been married for 14 years."* Griffin issued no formal writ for libel against the Sunday Times and made no complaint to the Press Complaints Commission either. Considering the damage that persistent slanders and innuendoes about his sexuality could inflict on his political career, Griffin's unnatural silence speaks volumes for the credence of Webster's allegations. Only the two protagonists will ever know the full truth of this matter.

In October 2009 following his disastrous performance on BBC Question Time, a ridiculed Griffin was forced to defend himself against the gay slur once again saying that two men kissing *"was a bit creepy"*. He told The Times newspaper that Webster had once offered him gay sex in the 1970s but Griffin rejected the 'proposal' out of hand. He claimed the incident was traumatic but not enough to expose Webster as being homosexual thus ending his career in the National Front. On the contrary, Griffin merely calculated that by leaving Webster in place his own career would be advanced and the truth was irrelevant.

(Webster, centre, with Griffin on right at NF rally in Fulham in 1981)

CHAPTER 15

THE EDITOR'S CHAIR

Griffin's political career is a real eye-opener for sure and is akin to that of a politicised shaman constantly changing shape than a statesman in waiting. Griffin's real problem is that he lacks gravitas and class and as such suffers from poor focus. But I've said it before and I'll say it again: I'm not entirely convinced that all of the allegations made against Griffin by his former colleagues have complete validity but who would know him better than them? I remain open-minded on the these matters and prefer to think of Griffin as a mere opportunistic chancer looking for his next meal ticket and he's found it in the BNP and intends to retire at 55-years-old on the back of the money he has made from the party.

Getting a national to publish my BNP exposé shouldn't be too difficult. The media interest in the BNP is going to be significant in a few weeks time. It's time to get involved again. First, I have to come up with a credible explanation to give Griffin for my prolonged leave of absence, so to speak. I've been thinking of applying for a job at the Press Association's office in Wetherby, West Yorkshire. So, why don't I tell Griffin that I've been working abroad for PA News for the last few weeks. He told me to get a job with a major media organisation a few months ago and pass information to him on the media's anti-BNP activities.

We agreed then, that if I was successful in this venture, I would send him an email stating: *'Alpha one, in position. Receiving, over.'* It was my suggestion and he agreed to it and Griffin is desperate to get inside information on the covert activities of the national media and their smear campaigns against the BNP. I've sent him the email and I've just got wait and see if he replies to it or even if he remembers our agreement but I am sure he does and being an opportunist he will not sulk on my insulting Simon Darby and instead seize the chance to get constructive intelligence. I have little trust in the media and know only too well that the mainstream press in the past have had a policy of either deny reference in terms of the BNP or outright hatchet attacks dressed up as 'investigative' journalism.

It's late February 2002 and Griffin has not replied to the email I sent him two weeks ago and I wonder if he has forgotten our agreement. Maybe he's not interested anymore and Simon Darby has won the day over our revealing telephone conversation. There's no point in worrying about these things - I've got to find out the truth of it now. It will be March in a couple of days time. I'm resending my original email to Griffin and hope he replies but no reply lands in my inbox and nothing the next day as well. Looks like the game's over so I've taken my girl to Heathrow and sent her off to South Africa. I'm upset at losing her but there's hope yet because she told me to 'sort myself out and get my priorities straight' before she went and we might just have a second-chance; or maybe that's a fourth or fifth, I honestly can't remember and it doesn't matter now.

I'm staying with Dean Lambert at his flat in the Wollaton area of Nottingham. And Dean has rattled on several times about a PC Richard Hardy stationed just 100-yards up the road from where we are living. At local resident meetings designed to combat crime in the community, PC Hardy has been asking Dean what he knows about vigilante 'attacks' on career criminals in the area. Dean seems to think that PC Hardy might suspect that I am living at his flat and planning something big in terms of the BNP. I think Dean is simply angling to make some money out of me if the media pay well for publishing my work.

True to form, Dean who has flirted with the BNP for several years, asks for a percentage of my earnings from the media for letting me stay in his home and keeping quiet about my intention to expose Griffin and the party hierarchy in the press before the forthcoming elections. This is clearly soft blackmail camouflaged as a 'reward' for a friend who has helped me to nail the Griffin clique and expose the New BNP as a sham. What Dean does not realise is that the 'New BNP' is not entirely a sham and the party has recruited a great many decent people who want t change the party's image to win greater appeal at the ballot box. It is the small clique around Griffin who are deceiving people and therefore operating a sham to cover their tracks.

Dean cannot be trusted I realise because he is only interested in making money and there are higher objectives at stake in this investigation. I look at Dean in his wistful mood and can almost see the pound signs clocking up in his greedy little eyes. I turn away and look over into the dark woods, making out noises from squirrels and birds resting up for the night when a familiar electronic noise interrupts my musing at Dean's motives. An email has just landed in my inbox but I'm enjoying the wood scene so much. Over to the west, the last violent red streaks of the sun are burning like medusa's helmet in the sky. The scene looks quite ominous really, almost like a storm rising. It reminds me of the night before the Second World War broke out. Hitler is stood on his balcony at the Berghof in Bavaria, surrounded by his flunkies, watching the sun setting.

A leading Nazi occultist, steps forward to advise her Fuhrer that 'the blood red sky is a bad omen' - 'it threatens a massive war and disaster for Germany' (and the rest of the world.) Hitler steps forward, points at the sunset and tells his flunkies: *"So be it. Better war now than later. Better to face destiny now no matter what."* I turn and look at the computer screen. I hope it's from my girl because she's not been in contact with me since she went home a few days ago. I'm getting a real taste for dogfood now and the accommodation's not too bad either. I click on the symbol and there before my eyes is Griffin's call sign: *'Receiving Alpha one. Over.'* This is the sign to phone him on his mobile. So, he hasn't forgotten about me after all.

I reach for my mobile, scroll through the menu and hit the send button. He doesn't answer. I call again. He doesn't answer again. Am I being set up here, I wonder. Dringggg, Dringggg, it's Nick Griffin. He explains that he was on the other line when I called. He tells me that he's a 'tolerant' man but he won't tolerate me upsetting his advisory council members again. *"No matter what the provocation,"* he says, *"you should report such matters to me and I will deal with them, OK!"* I mutter some feeble reply affirming that I understand him. I tell him what I've been up to with PA News and he's impressed. I tell him that I've got a few weeks back in the UK before being transferred to Israel to report on the conflict there from Haifa. *"Better you than me, Simon. Don't much fancy taking a Jewish bullet up my arse, don't know about you."*

He chuckles and we laugh together. *"Don't much fancy it myself Nick but I need to make a living like everyone else. Got any work for me."* He explains that I have got to toe the line this time or he will not 'trust' me ever again. No problem there then. *"How do you fancy sitting in the editor's chair for a while?"* Sounds interesting, so I ask him to explain and he tells me that he wants me to edit the BNP's national newspaper, *The Voice Of Freedom*, to cover staff shortages due to the intensive election campaign. A breakthrough at last. I'm not passing over this opportunity. *"Yeah, no problem, Nick. What does it entail?"* I'm trying to sound clueless. *"I will send you a stream of emails detailing the content of the newspaper, layout and house style etc and which stories to use from activists across the country. Right."* I tell him *"no problem"* and he promises to start sending the emails within a few minutes.

He wants my current address, so I give him my old address in Carlton, Nottingham, which I still have access to because my girlfriend's house will not be sold for a few months yet, so I've got something to play with until then. He promises to send me the disk containing the VOF files the next day. Brilliant. Now we're talking. Everything's back on track. Sure enough the disc arrives the next day with instructions on how to layout the newspaper. I sign for the recorded delivery to show 'I'm at home' and head off back to Dean's flat and with him driving who in the BNP could suspect that I am on anything other than party business.

Griffin has sent me over a dozen emails containing stories on every subject imaginable but one in particular sticks out. It's a story about the growing success of the anti-immigrant Pim Fortuyn List in Holland. And Griffin's instruction reads: *"Make a big thing of the List's electoral success but don't forget to warn readers that Fortuyn is a poofter. Don't make too big a thing of it though because his party has done well over there."* Pim Fortuyn was later assassinated by a lone Marxist gunman as his party stood on the verge of a fundamental breakthrough in Dutch politics.

It was a classic case of good old political hypocrisy. Criticise the leader's manifest homosexuality but his nationalist politics are acceptable. 'There's nowt so queer as folk', as they say and Griffin is ever the opportunist looking for a bandwagon. And this is a good opportunity for me to make headway in the BNP again, so I say nothing and just confirm that I shall as asked. I'm busy designing VOF when Griffin calls me and asks me to design two more newspapers; regionals to support local election campaigns in the North of England.

These regional newspapers are to be called *White Worker* for the Sunderland region and the *Real Oldhamer* for Oldham, where the BNP is now deeply embedded and strong. I advise Griffin to change the name of the Sunderland rag to British Worker, to diminish the racial aspect of the suggested title. He says that I'm *"learning fast"* [patronising twat] and in position for a real promotion with part-time income if I do well. Sounds good to me, so I'm going to do the best I can on these new newspapers.

I have to decide whether to launch my BNP exposé this April or to wait longer and I see how much further I can get. But after two years, I'm tired of all this skulduggery and want a new start after this. I've also decided to write a book about my entire BNP expe-rience and this project will take a few months to complete professionally. It's going to be April now or nothing. I've got other subjects of an apolitical nature to move onto after this is over. Some research work abroad is on offer and I'll need to get out of the country for a while after this is done. The far Right looks upon so-called 'traitors' with vengeful disdain, to put it mildly and some of the hotheads will try to exact revenge.

(Wollaton Hall, Nottingham, where I met the Sunday Times to put the finishing touches to the plan to expose Griffin's 'New' BNP)

Tony 'Mad Bomber' Lecomber has just telephoned me 'demanding' to know when the newspapers will be ready for publication. What's he worrying about. The disks don't have to be at Tony Hancock's printing offices south of London for another three days yet. It's early April and the weather is not so bad for the time of year. I've been sat editing poor grammar and spelling mistakes for the last few days and I need some physical exercise. I've put on weight recently and need to shed a few pounds quickly, so I'm off for a long walk in the extensive grounds of Wollaton Park.

The leaves rustle in the soft spring breeze and it's quite mild outside today. It's so good to be out of the office getting some fresh air. The sky is blue and cold looking and I can't help but think of my girl thousands of miles away in Johannesburg lapping up the sunshine. She's not been in contact with me yet and I'm starting to think she never will. It's been six weeks now, so I guess that's the end of that one. I feel glum when I think of her and just how difficult it was to let her go at Heathrow but that's life and things have changed rapidly since then.

The telephone rings again and it's Tony Lecomber. *"Look Simon, I really need that disc mate. We can't be late for the printer. Thousands of people are waiting on those newspapers."* He's really pissed off. *"I've just posted them by recorded delivery Tony."* He's not satisfied. *"I'm sure you have copies, don't you and if so I'm coming over to Nottingham tonight to get them."*

That's all I need at this time; the 'Mad Bomber' checking me out on my own turf. Think of something, think of something. My mind is racing. *"I've made copies Tony but as for coming over to Nottingham, I'm about to drive over to the Wetherby office in Yorkshire. Can't help you mate, on that one."* He sounds furious and I'm sure that he suspects something. Why is he being so pushy about coming over to Nottingham?

It's four in the afternoon and he's wants to drive over from Essex. It's a five hour round journey, probably longer. There's more to this than him wanting the discs I'm sure of it. I suddenly become mildly concerned for my safety and spin around 360 degrees to see if anyone is following me. No one but an old man and his dog. I'm sure Mutley the dog is not a BNP spy, too clever by half.

I enjoy my reinvigorating walk along the beautiful footpaths of Wollaton Park; the only decent scenery Nottingham has got left after decades of building ugly tower blocks. Sat in the Victorian Garden at the rear of Wollaton Hall it becomes clear to me that my time in the BNP is almost at an end and there will be no going back after this. I am making a complete break with the past and feel relieved but also saddened because the BNP could have become a real power under the right leadership.

Tony Lecomber telephones again the next morning to tell me that he's received the disk but there is no file on it. *"What!"* I exclaim in disbelief. I ask him if he's got a standard cdrw drive in his pc and he says not. I explain to him that he needs a cdrw drive to read a cdrw disk. This man is the BNP's national organiser, by the way and do my utmost not to give him sting of my sharp tongue for being such a clown. He has a bit of a petulant strop but says he will go over to a colleague's house in London and try to get it copied there.

He phones a couple of hours later to tell me that he's got the disk copied and it's on the way to the printers. No wonder the BNP fails to make progress on all fronts with people like Lecomber at the top. Griffin has sends me an email thanking me for my work on the newspapers and that I can have the job of editor on VOF if I want it and to let him know of my response ASAP. I'm not replying just though until I've got things finalised with a national to take my BNP exposé. The time has now come to spring the trap on Griffin's real BNP and I am sure it is going to make for some colourful fireworks when he learns that I have played him at his own game – check mate.

(Nick Griffin in his previous 'incarnation' as a white power fanatic)

Griffin has changed his mind so many times on personal and political beliefs it is a wonder anyone can take him seriously. He is the archetypal political shape shifter and will wear any face he calculates will draw support to him.

CHAPTER 16

DANGEROUS CONFESSIONS

(Wapping, London, HQ of News International)

Two long and arduous years working in the BNP collating information on its surreptitious activities are coming to an end. It has not been a pleasant *tour-de-force* but then I knew that Griffin and his clique were deeply unpleasant people. The beginning of April 2002 is ringing like an herald to action for and there's no time to lose now. It is time to strike before the BNP romps to victory at the May local council elections across England. My timing has to be perfect because a mistake at this stage could prove costly for everyone concerned. I must admit to feeling nervous and apprehensive. What is life going to be like after this? But I know that I'm doing the right thing.

The BNP's covert plots and schemes have to be brought into the public domain. This is not about revenge for me and nor am I motivated by malice or money. I believe that I am working for a greater good; something much bigger than me, at any rate. Maybe, I still feel guilty after all these years about leaving the hippies in such a horrible state of human-tragedy. Their faces have been present in my mind for most of the last two weeks. I didn't hurt them personally, but I left them bleeding and that was immoral and unjust. When I was broken and bleeding in 1990 a nurse came to my rescue. Some things never rest until they're finally dealt with and I know that some of these fanatics are extremely dangerous and not the least bit committed to democracy. Only violence and intimidation floats their boat.

Royal Mail junior manager, John 'Calvin' Richards and his fellow conspirators at the Post Office have been intercepting the mail of their far Left political enemies for over a decade at several Nottingham sorting offices. They have launched violent attacks on Anti Nazi League supporters and scanned the mail of Nottingham South MP Alan Simpson, a venal little man.

The objective was to establish his connections with the far Left, if any. Richards' team claim they have established that Simpson was in contact with Ross Bradshaw, the Information Officer for Nottinghamshire County Council. Calvin claims that Bradshaw is a Searchlight operative and a member of the Anti Nazi League, and that he needs to "taken care of." Bradshaw was the manager of Mushroom Bookstore in Nottingham, when it was attacked by Blood & Honour in the mid-1990s. Calvin Richards helped Blood & Honour skinheads to organise their attack on the premises.

My objective is to portray to the public the BNP's real policies and schemes from behind the scenes, helping the media to educate the public about Griffin's plans to win power. Mindful of this immense responsibility, I have contacted the world-famous Insight team at The Sunday Times in London. I've sent them an anonymous email, purporting to be a freelance journalist called 'Dave', and only the name issue is untrue. I do not want to pepper my real name around the media until I have secured a firm response. It's always best to take precautions in the murky world of politics and journalism.

It's been forty minutes now since I sent the email and my mobile strums to life. The voice is that of a young man and he tells me that he's the Insight team editor, Stephen Grey. He assures me that he's very interested in my story and invites me down to London tonight for a secret meeting at a London hotel. I have to be in London for 6pm. I'm convinced of Grey's sincerity even though I've not met him before. I've nothing to lose really and I've leapt out into the void many times before now. I've already said 'yes' and my word is my oath. Opportunities in highbrow journalism do not come any bigger than the world renowned London Sunday Times and they reputedly the 'paper of record'.

I did not expect such a prompt response, so my timing must be right after all. We'll have to wait and see. The Sunday Times…hhhmmm - my mind wanders. Dame Fortune seems to be smiling on me. It seems that my moment has arrived and I have no intention of letting it slip - like the scorpion, I must strike now! I'm rushing around in a flap looking for pertinent documents and my laptop. Then, I remember that I've got a meeting with the news editor of the Sunday Mercury based in Birmingham - another BNP story. Bob Haywood's *en route* to Nottingham, so I'd better get my things together and get over to the other house at Carlton to meet him, then the train to London.

Bob Haywood arrives at midday, right on time - I like punctuality. We discuss the finer points of the BNP story relating to his region and after ninety minutes we're done. He's kind enough to offer me a lift to the railway station. Saved me a taxi fare anyway. We're driving through Nottingham when he tells me not to worry about far Right reprisals, *"Thirty fags a day will kill you sooner than them."* He's not a smoker and maybe he's dropping an ambivalent quip here. I hope he's right and wrong at once.

I'm stood in Nottingham train station, sweating feverishly with nervous excitement. I grab my tickets from the ticket booth and a thrilling tremor of excitement races up my spine. This is it, after years preparing my story, I'm hours away now from the end, so it seems. The train jerks forward, the tanoy announces our departure and there's no turning back - never look back but I always do. Nottingham Station is fast disappearing and with it too my past, seemingly. I feel relieved and in some part unburdened. The journey from Nottingham to London usually takes around two hours but this journey seems timeless. The train snakes its way southwards to confront my destiny.

Beautiful green English countryside rolls by as I take intervals to look away from the laptop screen. The spring sun, now quite warm, bathes the verdant landscape in golden-green light; ripples of gold seem to pour through the rough brown plough lines, riddled across the essential rural environment. My greatest fear is not the far Right's possible reprisals but rather that the notoriously inefficient British rail system may not get me to the capital on time for the meeting with Stephen Grey. I begin to ponder on my early experiences of the BNP in Ilkeston and Eastwood. I remember vividly in flashback scenario, every boot blasted into my broken face on 20th January 1990. I can still see Jackson's grinning face staring at me from the witness box at Derby Crown Court.

I raise my right hand to my forehead and feel eagerly at the slim furrow caused by the assassin's blade in the summer of 1990. The hit designed to kill me, to stop me testifying against Jackson - how mighty are the fallen indeed. Anger rises in the pit of my stomach, quickly replaced by determination to succeed no matter what. Any doubts I have about going through with this exposé are now banished from trace. There is no way I'm turning back now unless the train takes a wrong turn, which is not so implausible on British railways, particularly under New Labour.

The train winds on and picks up speed a few miles from Luton as we pass through the Hertfordshire countryside I think of my Tomlin ancestors who once lived in the county. What would my grandmother Margaret Tomlin make of all this skulduggery but then she was no stranger to secrets, so I suppose it is in my bloodline. I'm preparing the points of my story to present to Stephen Grey. Daydreaming over and cornfields out of sight we arrive at London St Pancras railway station with just forty minutes to spare before our meeting. I bolt from the train and run across the platform taking care not to knock over fellow commuters. The rat race is no place for mice though and I plough ahead regardless.

It's like chopping through a dense jungle. Ugh! Ugh! I moan as people tread on my feet. The taxi rank is in sight but my phone is ringing, better answer it. *"Hello!"* I'm trying not to sound gruff. *"Simon, it's Tony Lecomber."* Oh, just what I need. Have I been rumbled or what. *"What can I do for you Tony."* Cool as a cucumber but I'm bubbling inside. *"You've changed a couple of fonts on page one of VOF."* Big deal. *"I okayed it with Nick first, OK!"* Get stuffed now, I'm thinking. *"Wish you'd have told me first."* He moans. *"You know now don't you, BYE!"*

I leap forward and nearly fall over. Not a good idea when carrying an expensive laptop and a data mine of very useful information. Steady as she goes and I'm in the cab. I shout instructions to the driver and he rolls off, all of fifty yards, straight into a traffic jam. Will I ever get there, I wonder, more frustrated than I've been for years. Tony Lecomber phones me to ask about font changes at a crucial stage – I've heard it all.

But he wasn't to know how crucial this moment is for me which is a good thing for my personal safety. He thinks I'm now in Wetherby anyway. The taxi chugs along the straight road - damn Romans - I could do with a winding road right now so I can get through the traffic quicker. It's slow going but we arrive with ten minutes to spare before the tense meeting. I jump out of the taxi, slot the driver his fare and make off quickly for the hotel reception. The hotel staff know I'm coming under an assumed name which makes me a little paranoid. Guess you've got to book in under some name or other. I take the escalator to the fifth floor and enter the room with ease. I search every corner, every nook and cranny for surveillance devices.

(Stephen Grey, former Insight team editor, now a freelance writer on the Afghan war)

Probably, just being paranoid but with the national media you never know and it's best to be on guard at all times. I open my case and power on the laptop when my mobile rings again and its Stephen Grey. He's bringing a colleague with him but they're going to be forty minutes late because of a delay at the Wapping office. I get paranoid again but quickly decide that it's now or never. No point in being too suspicious; after all, this is why I came to London. Stephen Grey walks into my hotel room and introduces me his colleague Edin Hamzic.

The mood is slightly tense at first as we find our away around each other. We get down to business and discuss the nature of the information about the BNP's covert activities the Sunday Times may want to publish. It's hard going as we thrash out shared details and concerns but after a few hours we reach an agreement and set a date for another meeting in London in a few days' time. Edin leaves my hotel room at midnight and informs me that he will collect me at eleven in the morning. We're going out for lunch to iron out a few creases and I have a contract to sign....

The train journey home was a time of fitful emotions for me but essentially I felt relieved the job was done. I wondered what my former BNP colleagues might have in store for me when the exposé is published but there's no point in extrapolating these things until you're half mad with worry. That just hands an easy victory to the opposition. They get a kick out of making people fret and tremble. And I tend to save my trembling for exceptionally cold mornings and what those 'thirty fags a day' could be doing to my lungs, so I've cut down to twenty a day.

Soon, the story will be in the public domain and I will have to deal with the fall out, if there's going to be any and I'm sure there will be because I know how the BNP boys react to whistleblowers. I realise I am putting my safety at risk and maybe even my life but journalists sometimes have to do these things to get the story out - always the story. Stories, like promiscuous whores, tend to love you and leave you very quickly in the media business and one has to be media savvy to survive.

I've taken many more risks for the BNP during the five years I served. The street warfare and the ensuing carnage almost erased my will to live in later years but I fought on and built a new life. Taking a few risks now for the greater good makes me feel good and that's what I care about. I am passionate and committed to everything that I want to do and no half measures ever. People have a right to know what's happening inside the 'real' BNP and that Griffin is not to be trusted.

I've travelled to London again to sign an affidavit at News International's Wapping fortress. We've agreed on the outstanding points of the final copy and everything is ready for publication on 21st April 2002. The article will run between Hitler's birthday and St George's Day in England. And my identity is not to be disclosed to Griffin and company prior to publication.

Both of these dates are celebrated across the far Right, usually with much drinking and some fighting. It is hoped that the emotive impact of the story will be much greater between these dates even though Hamzic denies this is the reason it is perfectly clear to me what they are doing. Richards mail interception racket will be compromised without recovery. Griffin will be seen in a whole new light and hopefully the BNP will realise what a charlatan they have for a 'leader'. I've already told anyone who will listen that the BNP will win several seats. We'll see.

I'm back at the hotel in West London and waiting nervously for Edin's call to confirm that he's about to speak to the BNP leadership and Richards concerning my allegations against them. My heart is pumping like crazy as the tumult approaches. A flood of emotions wash over me in these minutes and I feel close to breaking down after so long but I have to be strong to survive this, so I regain control immediately. I know the far Right will declare war on me for betraying 'secrets' to the Establishment. They work on the 'ethos' of 'those who work for the enemy are the enemy'. That's settled then. But for me this experience is the 'mother of all releases'. My phone rings, it's Edin Hamzic…Edin: *"Hi Simon, it's Edin. Just to let you know that I am about to phone Griffin and Richards. Speak to you later, mate."* I reply slowly, "OK, Ed!" and replace the receiver and there's total silence here, deafening silence.

The Euston Plaza Hotel now renamed the Hilton London Euston. I was booked in under the name of Mr David Williams by The Sunday Times using one of their travel companies that exist only on paper. News International use several front companies that do not exist in reality. The bogus companies are used to cover the tracks of journalists working for Rupert Murdoch's UK-based newspapers….

Waiting for Edin's next call is a time full of profound intrigue, as I wonder at the response he will get from Richards and Griffin. I'm just sat waiting for the telecommunications express train, destined for my future, no stops, just a radically different life from now on. I wait as patiently as I'm able to given the tension but there's nothing I can do to expedite this situation now. I'm smoking heavily to calm my shredded nerves. Forty minutes later the phone crackles into life with the sweet melody of Beethoven's triumphal fifth…

Edin: "Simon, it's Ed. It went better than I expected, mate. Griffin was quite helpful and referred me on to Richards, who phoned me back after taking legal advice [quick lawyer] and he denied everything. He even swore on his life."
Me: "By that token, Richards should be dead soon then, Ed. Swearing on one's life whilst lying is a very dangerous thing."
Edin: "Mmmmmh?" Ed sighs.
Me: "They know it's me then that's put out these allegations?"
Edin: "Nope! And I did not tell them about you as we agreed… just said you [Griffin and Richards] will have to read about it in the paper on Sunday and that was it."
Me: "OK, Ed. Thanks for letting me know. Speak soon."

I slept much more peacefully last night and was not troubled by the nightmare of the previous night. I'm travelling back to Nottingham in the full knowledge that I have done the right thing and my heart feels easier and lighter than it has for years - that's got to be a good thing. I'm going to spend today packing my belongings together. I'm moving to a new flat before relocating abroad. The day passes without event and I begin to feel relaxed again. It's all done and dusted. The shadows are drawing in and night is falling fast and an eerie intuition clouds my *raison d'être*. If the BNP boys have twigged that I'm behind the Sunday Times story, then 'something' should be incoming fairly soon….

Page 1 of 1

From: "GRIBIN" <griffin@gribin.freeserve.co.uk>
To: <simon@britmedia.fsworld.co.uk>
Sent: 21 April 2002 02:42am
Subject: The Sunday Times

Simon,

You poor, sad, mixed up, lying fucker!

Nick

It's nearly 10pm and it's dark out there — very dark. My mobile vibrates and it's a private number. I answer and the caller shouts, *"You're fucking dead, Smithy!"* I am not surprised in the slightest and log the call and save the details for a complaint to the police. Tonight is going to be a strange time. They haven't got the faintest idea where I'm staying. I can't sleep though with the excitement of looking for The Sunday Times article on the internet. It's 2.42am on 21st April when my email alert goes off. It's from Nick Griffin and he's broken his media friendly face for once.

Choice language from a 'sophisticated' and apparently media savvy Cambridge graduate who likes to pass himself off as a law graduate when in fact he took modern history having studied law only briefly. And it's a good thing that I'm a tough cookie too because I've seen with my own eyes that Griffin gets a big kick out of destroying people. But then I guess he's festering inside anyway what with all of his hatred eating at him day after day. I know Griffin a damned sight better than he thinks I do and I have rattled him no doubt. Later in the morning I scan the BNP website for any mention of me and find a rather turgid headline that does mentions me:

'The sad fantasy of Simon Smith

SIMON SMITH was a member of the BNP in 1992, and rejoined for one year in 2000. He has not been a member since, and has fallen out with almost every-one in the BNP with whom he has come into contact. He volunteered via email at one stage last year to do media work for the party, but having discussed setting up an internet paper, he sent several hysterical emails saying that as a result of a break up with a woman he was not going to be able to do anything.

Known to those BNP members in the Nottinghamshire area with whom he has had contact as intelligent but unstable, Smith became particularly notorious for his loathing of [John] Calvin Richards. Hence Calvin has become the focus for his fantasies about the BNP, which are utterly without foundation.

We should also point out that Mr Richards works at a sorting office on the other side of the city, which would not be responsible for the handling of mail addressed to Labour MP, Alan Simpson.

If it wasn't for his clear attempt to have BNP postmen sacked, we'd feel sorry for him, particularly if the Sunday Times was telling the truth when it assured us that his request for a large sum of money in exchange for the story was turned down. All those lies for nothing..."

A few years ago they would have had me believing this

codswallop as well. So, it's time now for a few salient facts to rebut the BNP's fairy tales. The details below are perfectly correct and can be verified by any lawful enquiry with the appropriate named organisations. But the BNP under Griffin has never been particularly interested in verifying evidence to prove one side of a story or another. It's all about what they can persuade the party's members to believe.

(1) I joined the BNP on the 20th January 1990 at the Mundy Arms public house in Ilkeston, whereupon I was attacked by British Movement thugs led by Gordon Jackson. The Ilkeston Advertiser carried a story reporting the incident on 25th January 1990.The Derby Evening Telegraph covered the entire trial of Gordon Jackson at Derby Crown Court from 5th September 1990. But according to the BNP these incidents never happened.

(2) I remained on good terms with John Calvin Richards until the day of the Sunday Times article, speaking to him just a few days before it was published, while he was out on his mail deliveries near to my Nottingham home. When I first met Richards in January 1990, he was working at the Canning Circus sorting office, close to Nottingham city centre. Before Nottingham's sorting offices were reorganised, Canning Circus was the central sorting office covering the Nottingham South constituency where Alan Simpson is the Member of Parliament.

(3) Calvin Richards worked at the Bilborough sorting office in Nottingham, until spring 1999. Richards claimed that he was intercepting letters destined for Alan Simpson MP and showed me copies of the letters bearing the House of Commons portcullis emblem. The Bilborough sorting office sorted my own mail (Wollaton Village) situated in the Nottingham South constituency.
   Richards' employment records at the Royal Mail will prove these points beyond refutation. Finally, Richards moved to the Westdale Lane sorting office in spring 1999 to be closer to his fiancé Susan who wanted them to live together nearby, hence his reason for the move. Richards owned a house just two-hundred yards from the same sorting office at the time.

(4) Nick Griffin did not join the BNP until late 1995 – a fact he openly admits – several months after I did not renew my membership of the party in January the same year. How on earth

can Griffin say that I was only a member of the BNP in 1992 and 2000? BNP membership records for the period covering the early 1990s were denied to Griffin by a bitter John Tyndall, following the former leader's sacking in September 1999.

(5) I did not become a BNP member again until January 2002, and only then to impress Griffin to gain his further trust. My last BNP membership card is reproduced faithfully below and please note the closing date. Once again, Griffin and his henchman have deliberately misinformed the public just to save face. Moreover, Simon Darby, the author of the BNP 'denial' did not join the BNP until 1996, having spent years in the National Democrats beforehand.

BRITISH NATIONAL PARTY
Membership Card 2002

THIS IS TO CERTIFY THAT

Mr. Simon R. Smith, Member No. 8422.
is a fully paid up member of the party until
the 31st December 2002

(6) Griffin admitted to the Sunday Times that he asked me to work as his press officer. Furthermore, he waxed lyrical about the Stoke riots issue to Edin Hamzic, saying he 'knew about the trouble in advance because of all the football fights and so on.' The race riot that erupted in Stoke in July 2001 had nothing to do with 'football fights' and was caused by 'someone' from the National Front threatening a march through the town the following weekend. Over to you Nick Griffin and associated liars.

Nottinghamshire Police Special Branch officers visited me a few days after The Sunday Times exposé. They advised me that I had made myself a target for far Right reprisals and gave me some security advice, which included urgent relocation abroad. Within a short time of this meeting I decided to move abroad under my own steam and did not ask Special Branch to relocate me

Sunday Times - Pg 12 - 21 April 2002

Andrew Moore

nside knowledge: John Calvin Richards, left, is accused of intercepting mail to help the BNP plot political campaigns

Far-right post workers 'read mail of opponents'

Edin Hamzic

THE British National party has been intercepting its political opponents' mail for more than 10 years, says a whistleblower inside the far-right group.

Simon Smith, the party's press officer and former election organiser, has spoken out ahead of next month's local elections in which the BNP is forecast to make gains.

Smith described how mail was intercepted, read and copied by party supporters at post office sorting offices, including one in Nottingham. Letters to Alan Simpson, Labour MP for Nottingham South, were among those opened.

Smith also says the BNP stirred up last summer's race riots in the north and the Midlands. He claims that party supporters bought weapons for a "race war" and plotted to make a bomb.

The revelations are likely to spark fury at Westminster and damage the BNP's prospects in May's council elections. The party, which is to field 68 candidates in what it calls its "biggest push ever", is targeting towns affected by rioting, including 13 of the 15 wards in Burnley and five in Oldham.

The BNP, which opposes immigration and is anti-Islamic, wants seats in areas where it won a significant share of the vote at the general election. In Oldham West and Royton, Nick Griffin, the BNP leader, was third to Michael Meacher, the Labour minister.

In an affidavit Smith says that John Calvin Richards, the party's Nottingham organiser and a Royal Mail employee, along with a dozen colleagues intercepted political opponents' mail. Richards denies this.

Smith said: "Calvin told me how he started intercepting mail by accident in 1989 and how his team at Westdale Lane sorting office regularly open and read mail going to anti-fascist and left-wing groups."

Smith also alleged that Richards, a martial arts instructor and long-standing right-wing activist, stole letters and parcels addressed to Simpson.

Smith said: "I remember being at his house and seeing numerous manila envelopes addressed to Anti-Nazi League supporters and also Alan Simpson, who they particularly despised."

Last week Simpson said: "I am not surprised the BNP has identified me as a lifelong opponent of extreme right-wing politics, but I am shocked to learn they have been so organised as to infiltrate the post office and tamper with mail for so long."

According to Smith, intelligence gathered by opening letters was used to help the BNP identify targets for political and physical attacks.

Last night Richards denied intercepting mail or being involved in any other criminal activities. He said: "No, I can swear on my life . . . I don't know where Alan Simpson lives and [at] the offices I worked at I do not come across Simpson's mail at all."

Smith also described what he said was the role of the BNP — which claims about 8,000 members — in provoking last year's riots. He said that in July, only days after violence in Oldham and Burnley, he was asked by Griffin to put out press releases denying the BNP's involvement in riots in Stoke-on-Trent — before violence had begun.

Smith said: "Griffin told me it was very useful for us to conjure up the image of a National Front demonstration to get the Pakis out on the streets. It terrifies the whites and then we come in as the white messiahs."

During the Stoke rioting the police were attacked by Asian youths who took to the streets amid rumours of a planned National Front march — which did not materialise.

Griffin, who graduated from Cambridge with a boxing blue, became BNP leader in 1999. He tried to rebuild the party's image as a mainstream group rather than a collection of neo-Nazi cranks.

Smith also revealed plots by the BNP to buy firearms and crossbows to be used in a "race war" and said he saw Richards buy at least one handgun, although it later turned out to have been disabled.

According to Smith, Richards and his group carried out a bomb hoax in Nottingham in 1992. They claimed that explosive devices were in cinemas and nearly 1,000 people were evacuated. The scares were intended to disturb a premiere of the film Malcolm X.

Griffin last night dismissed Smith's allegations as a "left-wing trick". He added: "We have repeatedly complained about our mail being interfered with and we've never interfered with anybody else's mail."

Griffin also denied any BNP involvement in the Stoke riots — but admitted knowing about them in advance "because of all the football fights and so on". He added: "Most definitely we had nothing to do with the Stoke riots."

Additional reporting: Will Iredale

Just after the Derby Telegraph published a two-page spread in the newspaper under the headline *'my terrifying days in the BNP'* on 14 November 2002, I had another chilling encounter with the ghosts of yesteryear. Sat on a bus travelling into Nottingham to catch a train to Derby to make a connection with the Edinburgh train via York, I had a chance meeting with an old school friend from my hometown. Marco Radulovic, whose brother Milan is the Labour leader of Broxtowe Borough Council, sat beside me and explained he was *en route* to Bournemouth in Dorset via Derby Railway Station.

Marco was a former activist in the ultra-left Class War organisation that by then, according to former MI5 officer David Shayler had been heavily infiltrated by the spooks. We laughed and joked about old times, old enemies meeting up in a time of peace and swapping stories about violent protests between our respective parties. Nothing particularly revealing on both sides until we actually boarded the same train for Derby to make our respective connections to York and Bournemouth. Marco and several of my schoolmates had joined far Left organisations in adulthood and I could never quite get used to the idea of perceiving them as the enemy even though they were.

No sooner had we pulled off from Nottingham and begun the twenty-minute train journey to Derby, Marco mentioned Ian Stuart and realising it was still a sore subject in the far Right he said, *"Yeah, that was a bad job with Ian Stuart and it should not end like that for anyone."* Marco had turned his back on Class War and left the area to begin a new life and we had a great deal in common. We both agreed that they were *"bad days"* and I thought that was it but he was keen to offload more information. He kept looking around the carriage, clearly not wanting anyone to eavesdrop on our tryst. I could see he was agitated and working up to something momentous so I let him continue.

He visibly had confession on his mind and explained that he had become a born-again Christian in the years since he left Eastwood and put Class War behind him. Part of the spiritual resurrection for born again Christians entails purging the soul of sins. Speaking clearly and slowly but in a low tone he said, *"Sime, I was at a meeting in Derby on the night Ian Stuart got hit, it was no accident, I know you know that anyhow. Well, I say meeting, it had almost finished and we were getting the drinks in while still discussing tactics and future operations against your lot, when these two blokes came in at the end and told us they had just taken out Ian Stuart and everyone in the car as well."* I cold chill ran down my spine and I knew Marco from years ago and saw no reason to doubt him because he was genuinely upset.

"So who were these guys Marco?" I asked him in feverish anticipation but he refused to tell me, saying *"it's more than my life's worth and I can't go that far, I'm just trying to put you in the picture about that night."* But I was not content to drop it because he had put me on a horse, as it were, and I had to ride it for all it was worth. I asked him if anything else was said and he replied, *"yeah sure, quite a bit but don't go repeating this to anyone you don't trust, in fact, don't talk to anyone about it,"* I nodded my consent and he continued. *"These guys who I can't name said they had chiselled the tyres of Ian Stuart's car whilst it was parked outside the pub they were rehearsing at, to weaken the tyres. They said there was a special way of doin' it and they knew how to do it and had done it before."*

I was more deeply intrigued than shocked and asked what was the purpose of chiselling the tyres because surely that would cause the tyres to explode in their faces, dangerous work, if you can get it. Marco, looked at me with bloodshot eyes, black bags under both and sweat leaking from his pores, he went on, *"No, I don't know how it's done, they said they knew how to take the chisel down to within a whisker without causing it to blow. They said it would only then take a few miles before the car tyres blew out and cause the car to roll over at speed and crash."*

Puzzled and wondering if his story was true and I had no reason to doubt him after all these years, I formed the impression that these *"men"* would have to be trained to carry out an operation of this nature and practise the method time and again to get it right. I asked Marco if the Class War activists at the meeting took these two men seriously and he said, *"someone said to them 'don't be fucking stupid, if Ian Stuart's dead, then MI5 killed him not us OK!' and that was the official line. That's how the rumour was spread into the far Right that MI5 had killed him."*

His revelation was starting to make some sense to me at last and with Derby Railway Station just minutes away and our going to separate ends of the country, I had to ask for more information quickly. *"Look Marco, we go back years yeah to primary school, I'm not looking for revenge against you or anyone in Class War, so tell me quickly what else you can, please, it's ultra important."* He lowered his head and then looked up at me and spoke in a tone just a decibel above a whisper.

"They told the bloke to get fucked and that they had done Stuart, and they'd even followed his car all the way on to the A52 and were behind it when the front tyre blew out and the car rolled

over and crashed. They said they'd just come back from the job and were sure everyone in the car was dead." At that we both got off the train and his Bournemouth train was due out any minute and was already boarding.

I caught the Edinburgh train to York twenty long minutes later and spent several days there musing on what Marco had told me. In the finest city in the whole of England where history leaps from every wall and dark alleyway I reasoned that I may have stumbled on the possible cause of Ian Stuart's murder. I thought long and hard about keeping Marco's confession secret for the rest of my days and spoke to no one about it until 2008 when I told Richard Jones what I had been told and he said *"who knows for sure what happened but it wouldn't surprise me at all if that's what happened."*

To this day, in April 2010, I have not been able to verify Marco's revelation. In the end I thought it best to make the details of what I knew public for Ian Stuart's sake because he if was murdered in this manner then the public had a right to know. In the far Right the accepted version is that MI5 killed Ian Stuart because he was becoming a major threat to the Establishment and indeed he was. Another, theory doing the rounds is that Ian Stuart was killed not by Class War in the foregoing manner but rather by Combat 18 because he would not allow them to muscle in on Blood & Honour's lucrative music franchise.

Derby Coroner Peter Ashworth concluded at the inquest: *"We are still no nearer finding out what caused this tragic accident. All we can say is that because of the car's two defects the car became less easy to control.* **But there must have been some other factor which contributed to the crash,** *even if Ian had not grabbed the wheel in a way many others in the same situation would have done."*

Either way, in the far Right all roads lead to MI5 as the instigators behind the operation to murder Ian Stuart but then only he knows the real truth and dead men tell no tales. But across the Western World many thousands of men and women in the far Right adore Ian Stuart as the messiah who came to liberate them from ZOG and I still hear his anthem in their hearts, ***"Hail, the New Dawn!"***

CHAPTER 17

DISRUPTIVE ACTION?

The BNP leadership was searching for political bedfellows in the Tory Party in the early 1990s in an attempt to raise awareness of the BNP's desire *"to go respectable"* as national organiser Eddie Butler put it, but there was also a darker reason for infiltrating the Tories from within. The objective was always clear in our minds from the outset of this surreptitious campaign. The governing Tory Party was the main obstacle to the BNP's growth into a mainstream political force. Even if we failed to take over the levers of power at constituency level, which I believed was impossible, our mere 'radical presence' in the Tory Party would cause significant inner division prompting voters to abandon the Tories and switch their support to the BNP.

A destroyed Tory Party could open an avalanche of support for the only alternative right wing force in the country: a rejuvenated British National Party. It stood to reason really. Right wingers, seeing their votes wasted on a fractured Tory Party could have no choice other than to support the BNP Rightist alternative. We were convinced that this strategy was a vote winner but it was to take years more to materialise under the leadership of Nick Griffin, by which time I was no longer a BNP member.

It is entirely true that we were completely unsuccessful at attracting senior Tories into the BNP (except Alan Clarke's passive support through meetings with John Tyndall) but we enjoyed considerable success with grassroots Tories. Most of our funding came from disgruntled Tories during 1992. Laurence Johnson hatched a plan to infiltrate some of our members into the Tory Party acting on direct orders from BNP head office in London. Our objective was again clear: get some of our more intelligent activists into the Tory Party to sow the seeds of dissension amongst grassroots Tory supporters. These 'Tories', in turn, would voice their grievances with the Tory leadership, causing splits and in-fighting thus weakening the Tories, bringing in a slew of recruits to the BNP.

Most of our middle class members held dual membership of the BNP and the Tory Party, so infiltration was easy. The covert strategy, devised by Eddie Butler at BNP head office, proceeded with progressive success. On a national scale, approximately 300 BNP activists infiltrated the Tory Party during late 1992. We were playing the State at its own game of breaking up 'undesirable' political groups from within – disruptive action. John Tyndall believed that the National Front was destroyed by Special Branch/MI5 agents in 1979. Tyndall would seem to be justified in his belief following the revelations made in the BBC 2 documentary True Spies, broadcast in November 2002. Special Branch admit that its agents helped to bring down the NF causing in-fighting and splits. For Tyndall, counter-infiltration was sweet revenge.

(Eddie Butler, a first class organiser, now back in the BNP at Griffin's invitation)

Our infiltrators, led by Eddie Butler, set about a campaign of murmuring discontent and by late 1993, disaffected Tories were flocking to join the BNP, particularly in the wake of Derek Beacon winning the BNP's first council seat in Tower Hamlets in September the same year. Hundreds of Tories left their respective branches across the country to become BNP members. This minor but significant success gave us political credibility and we understood that the 'destruction' of the pseudo-patriotic Tory Party was a prerequisite to the BNP's eventual *"velvet revolution"*. But there was a great deal more work to do before the BNP formed a government.

For several years John Tyndall was a regular at former Tory Defence Minister Alan Clarke's dinner table and the two men claimed to see things from a similar standpoint. Whether Alan

Clarke helped Tyndall hatch the infiltration plot providing him with 'sensitive' security information remains unclear but help came from somewhere at the very heart of the Tory Party. Naturally, we saw ourselves instinctively if not politically at one with most Tories.

Eddie Butler eventually left the BNP to join the Tory Party in 1994. He was the BNP/Tory link-man until he openly rejoined the BNP in August 2003, after a brief spell in now defunct Freedom Party. Butler was the BNP's long-term agent provocateur, his disruptive 'work' well progressed but incomplete before he rejoined the party at Griffin's invitation. Butler wormed his way into the Monday Club through the far Right Bloomsbury Forum, a front group set up by the BNP to present a respectable face of neo-Fascism and to infiltrate party members into the Tory party for disruptive action. Ultimately, this action culminated in the election of ultra-liberal David Cameron to the leadership of the Conservative Party and the Tories ditched their traditional right-wing policies to become cuddly to the electorate.

The agenda of the BNP infiltrators in the Tory Party was to destroy the Tories from within by maintaining the image of a hard-line Tory Party clearly unacceptable to voters. The BNP sees working-class boy David Davis as the only threat in the Tory Party because of his traditionalist right-wing stance, particularly as the former shadow Home Secretary. And whilst the Tories were becoming ever more unacceptable to the electorate; the BNP accelerated support for its policies by adopting a more media friendly image and toning down its racist policies: voluntary repatriation instead of forced expulsion of immigrant families.

During Iain Duncan Smith's campaign to become Tory leader, Edgar Griffin a Tory activist of 50 years standing and the father of BNP leader Nick Griffin 'was exposed by the media' as a BNP activist. Edgar Griffin claimed that he answered the BNP telephone hotline for his wife Jean, a BNP candidate at the 2001 General Election, quite by accident, claiming his wife was not home to take the call. My direct experience at the time in the BNP throws up a different story with darker tones of cunning, guile and deceit. Nick, Jean and Edgar Griffin decided it was time for Edgar to 'retire' from political work and in so doing damage the interests of IDS and the Tory Party. The Griffins wanted Ken Clarke to win the Tory leadership contest, believing his pro-Euro stance would disenfranchise Tories, leading them into the BNP's camp. As a senior press officer in the BNP I was made privy to these matters some weeks before the revelations made in the press.

A BNP 'activist' was secretly delegated to tip off the national press concerning Edgar Griffin's 'covert' BNP activities. The identity of this activist is more likely than not to have been Dr Stuart Russell/Dr Phil Edwards, a former lecturer at Nottingham University who resigned his post there in the science department on *"political grounds"*. The IDS/Griffin scandal was big news for the best part of three days, damaging the interests of IDS, the Tory Party and put the BNP back in the headlines, just as was planned. During the height of the scandal Edgar Griffin was quoted as saying: *"The two parties are almost the same in terms of long-term plans. In terms of manifestos of the Tories and the BNP, you can hardly tell the difference."* But can the same now be said under the 'leadership' of David Cameron?

I was 'encouraged' by Nick Griffin to resign my Tory Party membership and write a letter of strong complaint to IDS about the sacking of Edgar Griffin. I was a member of the Gedling Constituency Conservative Party during August 2001. Labour MP Vernon Coaker was the sitting MP for Gedling retaining the seat in 2005 with an increased majority against a feeble challenge from the Tory PPC Anna Soubury, a former low-grade journalist, now practising as a criminal barrister and standing at the 2010 General Election as the Tory PPC in Broxtowe.

I duly resigned my membership in 'disgust' at Edgar Griffin's expulsion from the party just as I was 'encouraged' to by Nick Griffin. This ploy simply fools Tory leaders into thinking there is considerably more support for the BNP in the Tory Party than actually exists. As a reward for my 'loyalty' Nick Griffin took me under his wing as his personal press officer. I was able to further infiltrate the BNP and gain direct experience of covert strategy. I also gained a startling insight into the multi-faceted character of Nick Griffin and his Tories in disguise.

Perhaps one of the most stunning episodes in this book came in April 2003, when the Sunday Mercury published a page-lead on meetings between Tyndall and Alan Clarke. [The Sunday Times had previously killed the story as a favour to the newspapers 'friends' in the Tory Party and I was not in the least bit surprised by the rampant nepotism.] Before the story was published, the Sunday Mercury's Tom Wells spoke to Simon Darby on the telephone who denied everything outright and did not address a single point put to him. Instead Darby told Wells that I was currently incarcerated in a mental hospital in Nottingham and nothing I said could be believed. I was actually sat in Nottingham's Central Library at the time and when Tom Wells broke the retort to me, we both had a good laugh.

SUNDAY MERCURY, APRIL 13, 2003   5

British National Party defector blows the whistle on more chilling activities

EXCLUSIVE
BY TOM WELLS

CLAIMS... (right) former Conservative cabinet minister Alan Clark and Welsh campaign chief Edgar Griffin

A HIGH-ranking defector from the British National Party has exposed what he claims are shock new links between the far-right group and the Conservative Party.

Today, in an exclusive interview with the Sunday Mercury, Simon Smith sensationally claims how:

● Former Conservative cabinet minister Alan Clark regularly wined and dined a BNP leader;

● BNP activists have infiltrated the Conservative party to destroy it from within;

● The right-wing party deliberately sought to de-rail Iain Duncan Smith's election as Conservative leader;

● The BNP has actively sought to exploit the Countryside Alliance.

Conservative Central Office has refused to comment on the allegations and BNP leaders have dismissed the claims as the "fantasy of a madman".

But Mr Smith was a senior Midland elections officer for the BNP before he quit last year to blow the whistle on the chilling activities of the group. He has since received death threats.

Elections

The allegations also feature in his new book A Storm Rising which is available on the internet.

NEW SHOCK-CLAIMS

At first said everything I alleged was untrue but then right at the very end of the article he admitted that the centrifugal allegation that Tyndall and Clarke met together was true and that the BNP was proud to be associated with Alan Clark, who said was one of *"finest MPs of modern times."* I expressed astonishment to Tom Wells that Darby had made such a glaring *faux pas* in the space of five minutes and having first denied the two men met, then contradicted himself entirely. It is one of the most memorable acts of stupidity on the part of the BNP leadership during our very public battles.

Darby was also forced into another embarrassing climb-down when I wrote to him at his home address to advise that I was instructing solicitors to sue the BNP if anyone in the party attempted to smear me again by claiming I was *"incarcerated in a mental hospital"*. I explained in graphic detail that a repetition of this vicious character assassination would cause me to initiate litigation for damages against the BNP and because the smear was completely untrue, a High Court judge would award me damages to an extent that would bankrupt the BNP. In the event, Darby took heed of the message and did not repeat the slur in public ever again and my warning to sue over this matter stands to this day.

But things have not always been so acrimonious and on the 28th February 2005, I spoke to Nick Griffin on the telephone for several minutes and swapped notes on State assets masquerading as 'journalists'. The editor of Notes From the Borderland Magazine, Dr

Larry O'Hara has termed these stringers as journo-cops because of the nature of their devious work for HM Government agencies in the press. They are part journalist and part police officer or part spook. In terms of the Daily Mirror's political editor Oonagh Blackman a term applies to that created by O'Hara because Blackman is in fact a journo-spook. This fact was admitted by her colleague Andy Lines in a covert recording of our meeting in London in June 2005. The tape recording is hosted on YouTube and Lines reveals that Blackman has *"supervisory sources at MI5 and the Metropolitan Police"*.

Following a telephone call from Carl Fellstrom, a freelance journalist who claimed to be working for the Sunday Telegraph newspaper, I had cause to speak with Nick Griffin to assure him that I was not part of a media operation to call for the banning of the BNP. In fact, I have never called for any political party to be banned in what is supposed to be a democracy and Fellstrom was deeply angry when I refused to jump on the Establishment bandwagon demanding the BNP be banned. Indeed, all manner of unpleasant occurrences began shortly thereafter and the first among which was my own banning in the media. For refusing to join the criminal gang calling for the BNP to be banned I was subjected immediately to a media-wide 'deny reference' campaign.

In Britain, allegedly a democracy, one should be allowed the right to freedom of speech but because I refused to join the gang calling for the BNP to be denied a right to freedom of speech, my right to work in the media was terminated. I was ostracised without reference and no media organisation would buy my work, not just on the BNP, but on any other subject. Having previously upset the mass media gang by attempting to expose Peter Hill editor of the Daily Express for his unhealthy links to the MI5, I was left with no room to manoeuvre. Knowing full well that I was *persona non grata* and could not earn a living, vested interests reasoned that I would have to back down and come out fighting against the BNP to earn a crust.

The HMG gang and the criminal New Labour regime under Tony Blair thought I would break with ease but in reality I trained my attention away from the BNP and turned my sights on the rotten Establishment. My own reasoning was who was causing me the most serious problems and that question was easy to answer. My public spats with the BNP and Griffin were just that and caused both parties some discomfort. In essence, both gave as good as we got but the Establishment I realised was literally determined to destroy me if I did not join the campaign to ban the BNP. I stuck to my guns and did not yield to any threats and banning and fought back.

From the outset, I had witnessed some particularly unpleasant schemes to destroy the BNP by media organisations and could not consent to work with these animals who cared nothing for the truth. I came across some information in May 2002 about journalists at the News of the World and their scheming against the BNP. I regarded their plan as so low and vicious that I blew the whistle on it directly to Nick Griffin by anonymous email. In fact, this set in motion a train of events that led to me sending Griffin a great deal of material on the media's plans to crush the BNP. My own rationale was that if the material to be published was true then I had no problem with it but in many cases the material was completely fabricated and very nasty.

For almost three years I worked with the national press on BNP and far Right related issues and at the same time blew the whistle on their sordid tactics to Nick Griffin and the BNP stayed one step ahead of the game as a result. I have witnessed dirty tricks in the national media arguably more disgusting than anything I have ever seen in the BNP and could not be party to them. In reality, when Fellstrom approached me to join him in calling for the BNP to be banned, I was being asked if I agreed that the BNP should be destroyed and the answer was NO.

I realised immediately that the public spat with Griffin had gotten out of hand and approached him with a peace offer. I said I would not attempt to embarrass him or anyone else in the BNP again if the party's members and supporters left me in peace. I expected a rather terse rejection but Griffin agreed to the proposal and a ceasefire was arranged and became immediately effective and both sides adhered to the agreement.

Since then I have made no attempts to expose Griffin or anyone else in the BNP and have left them in peace and likewise they have left me in peace. This development encouraged me to belief that Griffin was a man I could do business with and that he was in control of the vast majority of BNP members and supporters. The only aberration came in the form of Calvin Richards and his little private army who continued to issue threats via the intermediary of Dean Hopewell. They had told him to tell me, *"not to think it's over yet because one day we will have him for what's he's done."* I regarded the threats as the usual hot air and ignored them other than to tell Dean that if I caught wind of an attempt to cause me injury, I would immediately launch a pre-emptive strike against the culprits and to hell with the consequences.

The message got home to them and since then there have been no more threats because they cannot or dare not carry out their threats anyway. I have no seen no evidence to link Griffin to these threats and therefore he cannot be blamed. This is quite separate from the purpose of publishing this book and this work is not designed as an attack solely against Griffin and no one should think it is. I have to set the record straight now before time runs out and no man lives forever and that is all I am prepared to say on the matter. I have a clear conscience, I do not suffer from sleepless nights – life is too short for that nonsense – and I take each day as it comes. I do not regret the public spat with Griffin and the BNP because in retrospect it was unavoidable as the closing chapters of this book will prove.

CHAPTER 18

ASSASSINATION

After the Sunday Times and Sunday Mercury exposés, I have experienced a deep and timely sense of release from the BNP - a sense of finality and closure. I cannot go back to the BNP now in any capacity and the show is over. This has been a time of colossal upheaval in every aspect of my personal and professional life. But, release or not, I would be foolish to think that there are no more dramas to come. In reality, this is just the beginning of a new phase with some of the old flavour thrown in. 'The flavour' is far Right intimidation and death threats - not a pleasant taste I can assure you but that's the way it is and it's always best to accept reality for the way it is.

I've got the new house fixed up and secure. I'm going to be in the UK for a few months yet - I've got a book to write and some research to complete as well. Instinct tells me that I should complete the book from abroad but I need to get the sense of things from England. I need to travel to old haunts so I can relive the atmosphere of those places. It's always best to write from the perspective of being there right now.

I've installed smoke alarms at vital points in the house, next to windows and the front door, should a petrol bomb come screaming through one night while I'm in bed. You never know with some of the more extreme factions of the far Right. I know that they're out to get me but I'm not going anywhere until I've finished my work in the UK. Still, I'm fairly confident that they don't know where I live now but who knows. Maybe I'm just being paranoid about the extra security? It's dark now and I've just been to the local Tesco super-market to get some groceries.

The rain is teeming down and I'm walking along the main road which leads to the side road where I live in Nottingham. I scan right and left as I walk to make sure no one suspicious is hanging around. Good, everything's clear but wait... there's a dark green Vauxhall cavalier parked a few yards down from the house on the left hand side of the road and someone is moving inside. It's a man, that much I can see from forty yards away.

The street light just behind the car reflects his face onto the wing mirror and he looks edgy and nervous. I'm starting to think that this is a hit. I'm thinking hard and fast what to do. I decide to hit him instead. I close in on his car walking at rapid speed. His door opens an inch - here we go. I rush forward and kick the door shut with a clang. He looks up at me, confused and scared, his eyes like brown glass - I've seized the advantage but now what. I've got no weapon to use other than my brain. He starts fidgeting in his pocket. A gun maybe or a knife, must be a gun, he can't stab me through a closed window. Now what? I put my face right up to the glass and stare him directly in his frightened brown eyes. I stare and he's transfixed, unmoving, barely breathing.

He puts his hands up to his shoulders to show me he's clean - no weapons. I reach inside my pocket and withdraw my mobile phone and start tapping in 999. He's got the hint now. The engine cracks into life, I step back a couple of feet, and he zooms off along the street in the direction of the cemetery at the top of the road. I chuckle nervously. That was close, too close and I'm lucky that guy was an amateur. I decide not to come home again when it's dark unless I use a taxi. I don't phone the police because there's nothing to report now. I didn't even get the car registration number because I was too fixated on him and his movements. Anyway, I'm alive, so what's the problem.

Better get inside and get the TV on, it's election night and I want to see if the results are coming in yet. This new place is like a fortress and I feel totally secure here. I'm having an Indian meal tonight and strong liquor, not too much though because I've got work to do noting down the election results etc. I'm feeling a little shaky inside after the incident on the street a few minutes ago but life is like this for me now.

The strong beers were too much for me and I fell asleep - I needed it anyway. No real harm done though because I can pick up the results from the internet. I'm online at the BBC website and there we are, the BNP has won three seats in Burnley. There was a dispute over the third seat and after several recounts the BNP nicked the seat by a few votes. I was right: the BNP has won several council seats, just as I predicted. I was told by every journalist I spoke to during the campaign that the BNP would be lucky to pick up one seat. I disagreed with their theories because support and enthusiasm for mainstream politicians is at an all time low. The media is calling the result a 'protest' vote but I think the whole issue is much deeper than that and the BNP will go from strength to strength in the coming years.

The BNP's average share of the vote has risen close to 18%. Is this just a protest vote across the 68 seats they've contested? Or, does it point to the fact that the BNP has won significantly increased support because of three centrifugal issues: Terrorism, crime and immigration. I think the BNP correctly identified the concerns of local white communities and then played up issues from a national perspective but then all politicians do the same. The race riots of last year and the ensuing racial and religious divide in the northern towns, Oldham and Burnley, have been vote winners for the BNP. There are other important factors too. BNP activists have been on doorsteps talking to people about their real concerns and all too often the answer is *"we want the same funding that Asian communities get and an end to crime and immigration"*.

The BNP was always successful at linking crime and immigration as a vote winning strategy and the National Health Service suffering from 'foreign health tourism' from the Third World, this has also become a big vote winning concern. Hitler concentrated on Germany's collapsed economy to win power 1930s but here in the West we have strong economies for the moment, so other socio-economic issues have to be found to campaign on. Mainstream politicians seem to have abandoned the issues of crime and immigration and that's where the BNP comes in and the Lib/Lab/Con Party is to blame for this not the BNP.

Voters are tired of years of sleaze and corruption in the Lib/Lab/Con Party. Throw in the fact that politicians hardly ever honour their election pledges and the BNP's increased vote is assured. I don't think most people who vote BNP actually want to because they know the party has more than its fair share of undesirables but they do so out of desperation and all political parties harbour undesirable elements to some degree. Poverty and crime are narcotic influences on any community, sink estate or not. And let's take that term alone shall we 'Sink estate': A neighbourhood where people live in near Third World conditions of poverty and epidemic high crime rates, where the police have lost the war on crime. That these places of misery should exist in the Western World today is disgraceful and destroys the New Labour fantasy of 'social justice'.

The wealth and power generated in the West is not distributed fairly by any means and the BNP saying that coloured communities get more funding than white communities is a misnomer. Not because it isn't happening, in some areas of Britain it is, but that people should have to live on meagre incomes in the first place is real evidence of a growing void between rich and poor in the UK, irrespective of a person's race, colour or religion. New Labour, contrary to building a society based on 'social justice, have in fact built a sick society where the gulf between rich and poor has widening beyond any injustice inflicted on the nation by Margaret Thatcher.

The mainstream parties have done nothing to redress this unjust socio-economic dichotomy. New Labour talks of 'social justice' but that means nothing to people who live in severe poverty - they don't see any change and that is reality, like it or not! The BNP saw its opportunity to target deprived white areas, threw in the race issue, and won thousands of votes. But the seats they've won in Burnley, are in fairly affluent areas and this factor points to another major problem which in socio-political terms is akin to a storm rising.

Since the beginning of 2001, the BNP has encouraged hundreds of its supporters to join the Countryside Alliance (420,000 CA supporters marched through London in September 2002) to permeate the BNP's policy of Land and People, throughout the rural constituencies, most of them Tory seats. The Land and People programme, with its own BNP website, is no more than a modernised throwback to Hitler's Blood and Soil programme, which brought together German rural and urban communities in the huge *Strength Through Joy* meetings held across the Third Reich.

Griffin sees huge political capital in getting his BNP activists to agitate the Land and People programme in the Countryside Alliance. He hopes to take over the issues affecting rural communities by blaming the ills of rural folk on the European Union and inner cities teeming with illegal asylum seekers. The BNP makes no secret of the fact that its activists are at work in the Countryside Alliance. For years now, the BNP philosophy has been that the big cities are dead in terms of British racial homogeneity and that any British racial revival must be led from rural communities. I am sure Griffin perceives British rural folk as Hitler saw his German peasants: the progenitors of eugenic supremacy, leading a Caucasian renaissance. But the question is whether Griffin can maintain focus on the issue for more than a few months given his past record of switching faces to suit the mood of the day.

The BNP attitude towards the big cities is that they will have to be 'liberated' from ethnic communities by a pure-blooded white country folk. Griffin himself lives in rural Wales on a smallholding, expanded in recent years with BNP money. This reflects the BNP policy of buying up small plots of land across the UK, on which to hold its Red, White and Blue festivals - *Strength Through Joy*. But, in reality the BNP has only one plot of land available for this purpose at this time - Griffin's farm in Welshpool.

But Griffin has big plans to buy more land; another good reason to infiltrate the Countryside Alliance in his eyes. In 2001, Griffin spoke to a BNP meeting on the Land and People issue, saying: *"This then is our task - to build a responsible and powerful nationalist movement which can unite town and country, and bring together the rank-and-file of the old right with the voters of the old left. We are going to create a fusion of racial nationalism and social justice. And when that is done, we are going to win!"*

And the BNP has started winning by using this strategy to its full effect. As a politician, Griffin is all things to everyone at any time, simply to advance his career and the BNP's electoral success which he sees as synonymous. But, as a man, I really don't want to comment on what I actually think of Griffin; that would present him with an easy opportunity to sue men and attempt to injunct this book, so I'll refrain. But I will not refrain on speaking the truth about the BNP and as usual Griffin and his BNP supporting lawyer Phil Sloan, can threaten what they want.

Following the Sunday Times exposé, Calvin Richards promised to sue the newspaper for libelling him - no such legal action was instigated by Richards and he made no complaint to the Press Complaints Commission either - a fact that speaks for itself. But the BNP did make an official complaint to the Press Complaints Commission, over another exposé I did with the Sunday Mercury in Birmingham. After careful consideration the PCC threw out the BNP's complaint as being groundless.

When I first joined the BNP's Media Monitoring Unit in the summer of 2000, I was advised by Dr Stuart Russell of the finer points of the MMU's strategy. Namely, should any national or regional newspaper or other media organisation, publish defamatory comments about the BNP, we were to write to the organisation concerned and threaten an official complaint to the PCC or Broadcasting Standards, backed up with the threat of legal action. Threats, threats, threats - is all you get from the BNP when you're a journalist working to expose this, that or the other aspect of the party's real polices. I have not given in to BNP threats and have no intention of doing so and this does not make me a hero or a martyr in the making.

It's late May 2002, and Bob Haywood, the Sunday Mercury's news editor has just phoned me to ask how I'm coping with the pressure of far Right threats since I 'outed' myself, as it were. The paper is going to do a follow up story on the death threats I've received. I've told him that I'm not giving in to far Right threats and that I have done the right thing by coming forward to speak the truth about the real BNP.   Bob told me to take up clairvoyance instead of journalism because my prediction that the BNP would win several seats has come true. Bob was not convinced that the BNP would win seats and told me so. I told him that I knew the BNP would win seats because I've been out campaigning with the BNP and sensed the public's mood and clairvoyance has nothing to do with anything in this respect.

In the real BNP, when supporters think no journalist is around, they reveal their true feelings on mainstream politicians, journalists and immigration. The common policy on which all BNP supporters agree is the desire for revenge on the leaders of the corrupt Lib/Lab/Con Party. The mainstream political leaders are seen as traitors in the BNP and without question they would face charges of treason under a BNP government. If the BNP took power today, emergency 'social justice councils' would be set up to administer the BNP's desire for justice and/or revenge. These would be little different than the Bolshevist revolutionary councils which sprang up after the 1917 Bolshevik Revolution to administer their desire for justice/revenge.

On the issue of the European Union and the Single Currency, mainstream party leaders are regarded as anti-British traitors, plotting and scheming to ensconce Britain into a federalist empire or the Soviet [European] Union. Their punishment for treason in the BNP's eyes is life imprisonment. On immigration, all three leaders favour more immigration into the UK, so they're already convicted in the eyes of BNP supporters. The BNP is no ordinary democratic   political   party   committed   to   preserving   liberal democracy. Its members are violent, frequently talk about buying guns and crossbows for the 'race war' and sometimes they do buy weapons for this purpose. The Nazi Nail Bomber David Copeland was a BNP member in 1996 but left after saying the BNP was 'too soft' for him. He joined Combat 18 and the British National Socialist Movement and these organisations 'refined' his racial hatred in acts of murderous terrorism.

Copeland, like so many far Right fanatics, believed he was given a mission from God to destroy coloured people and homosexuals, who he believed were destroying Britain. In reality, he was given a mission by Combat 18 to 'bomb, maim, kill and destroy the enemies of the white race'. Since late 1997, when

Combat 18 recovered from its leadership 'contests', the Single Cell Strategy was adopted by neo-Nazi radicals across the world. It works like this: four man active service cells are easy to infiltrate and compromise. Intelligence Services have found it easy to smash these cells in the past. But a 'lone wolf' is virtually undetectable and can wreak massive chaos and carnage before he is caught or stopped. C18 provides training - The Terrorists Handbook, freely available on the Internet - and gives 'advice' on how to carry out terrorist attacks.

Combat 18 has hundreds of fanatics across Europe and the US, training and arming to the teeth for this purpose. The implosion point for each fanatic is reached when he sees something deeply wrong in society and decides to destroy it acting alone but under the guidance of his inculcated ideology. He is given no orders to kill anyone by C18.The forces of law and order cannot prosecute C18 leaders on terrorist conspiracy charges, because there is no evidence that they had any role in such attacks. C18 call this strategy 'leaderless resistance'.

David Copeland was a 'lone wolf' and he imploded in 1999, planting bombs across London which wreaked terror and murder among the capital's ethnic and gay communities. His third and final bomb, at the Admiral Duncan pub in Soho, killed three people, one of them a pregnant woman. Each bomb caused misery and suffering for 'The Cause' and was 'justified' as a legitimate military action against the enemies of neo-Nationalism but the BNP quickly denounced the attacks. It is an important point to make at this juncture that the BNP had nothing to do with the attacks.

In July 2002, another C18 'lone wolf' set out to assassinate President Chirac at the Bastille Day parade in Paris. Maxime Brunerie, 25, a member of Bruno Megret's extreme right MRN party, was 'upset' that Jean Marie Le Pen lost the presidential contest to Chirac a few weeks earlier. He took it upon himself to assassinate President Chirac and left a message on the Combat 18 website the night before, which read, ***"Watch the TV tomorrow, this Sunday. I will be the star. Death to ZOG, 88!"***

Brunerie was wrestled to the ground by onlookers and arrested but not before he loosed off a single shot from his hunting rifle at President Chirac - he missed. Just imagine the destabilising effect on European societies if a major EU leader is assassinated by a Combat 18 'lone wolf'. The BBC dubbed Brunerie the 'amateur jackal' but if he had succeeded Brunerie and Combat 18 would have made front page news on every newspaper in the world. The stated aim of C18 is to assassinate senior EU leaders, an act of terrorism which the fanatics believe will cause a civil war across the hated European Union.

Writing in The Preachers of Hate, published in October 2002, the BBC's Europe Correspondent, Angus Roxburgh, suggests that 'far Right political parties across Europe have no Paramilitary wing'. His naivety and arrogance is a warning to all journalists 'investigating' the far Right. Angus Roxburgh has made a 'valuable' contribution to the far Right 'debate' with his work but he sees the far Right from the perspective of a journalist 'invited' to press conferences to interview far Right politicians in public. At no time does Angus Roxburgh get to see the real far Right in action. Enough said.

Far Right political groups across the world and their approximate numbers:

BRITAIN: British National Party, approximately 12,000 members and over 1 million supporters and growing rapidly. Nick Griffin's recent surrender to the Racial 'Equality' Commission to allow non-whites to join the party has caused the BNP to haemorrhage approximately 10% of its members to the National Front in protest. Blood & Honour (UK based) 2500 members and over 800,000 hardcore supporters across the world.

FRANCE: Front National, 50,000 members and 3 million supporters. Jean Marie Le Pen retains his position as the central leader of the French far Right and continues to shock the French Establishment with soaring elections results.

GERMANY: Deutsche Volksunion (DVU) & Nationaldemokratische Partei Deutschlands (NPD), 40,000 members and over 1.5 million supporters combined but NPD is strongest of the two groups in terms of members and supporters with radical elements well connected to Blood & Honour.

AUSTRIA: Freedom Party (Freiheitliche Partei Österreichs, FPÖ), 30,000 members and 600,000 supporters. Vote fell from 21% in January 2000, to 10% in November 2002, after an unsuccessful period in coalition government with the conservatives. In April 2005, former party leader Jörg Haider and other leading party members defected from the FPÖ to form a new party, the Alliance for the Future of Austria (BZÖ). In 2008 the Austrian far Right picked up 857,028 votes, 17.5% of the national share of the vote and this gave them 34 seats in the National Council of Austria *(Österreichisches Nationalrat).*

(Jörg Haider's car wreck in which he was killed on 11th October 2008. The vast majority of his supporters assert that he was murdered by Israeli MOSSAD and his death was no accident)

BELGIUM: Vlaams Blok, 30,000 members, 761, 407 votes in 2003. On November 14, 2004 the party changed its name to Vlaams Belang *(Flemish Interest).* From its creation in 1978, it was the most notably militant right wing of the Flemish movement. All significant Flemish political parties were reluctant to enter coalitions with the Vlaams Blok. Following the agreement, known as the cordon sanitaire, Vlaams Blok never entered any level of government. As of 2006, this agreement still applies to the successor party, Vlaams Belang, although a coalition exists between the Vlaams Belang and the lesser known right wing party VLOTT.

Together, they stood at the 2006 municipal elections. An appeal court in Ghent, Belgium, in April 2004 ruled that some of the party's organisations had breached the 1981 law on so-called racism and xenophobia. As a result of the loaded process against them, Vlaams Blok changed its name to Vlaams Belang. Vlaams Blok's track record in the Flemish and Belgian parliament elections was strong. The election campaigns consisted mainly of the immigration and law-and-order theme, combined with the desire for Flemish autonomy (e.g. it abstained from a crucial vote on splitting the unified electoral district of Brussels-Halle-Vilvoorde).

SWEDEN: The SD (Sverigedemokraterna) was founded in 1988 and describes itself as a nationalist movement. Polling data throughout the summer months of 2008 showed the party approaching the 4 percent threshold necessary for entry into the Swedish Parliament, notably reaching 4.4% in both August and September. In a March 2010 poll the party reached 7.6%, their best poll result to date. As of 2010 the party claims 4,571 members, a 26% increase from the year before. There are thirteen district party associations in Sweden for the SD, as well as around one hundred local or municipal associations. Young members are organised in the Sweden Democrat Youth. The current Youth Organisation was founded in 1998. The party also distributes a newspaper to its members, *SD-Kuriren*. Since 2005 the paper has been printed in tabloid format, and approximately 28,000 copies have been published. Polls indicate that there is a strong possibility that the Sweden Democrats could break the 4% threshold and enter the Swedish parliament for the first time at the 2010 Swedish general election.

In June 2003, two members of the Aryan Brotherhood were arrested at a flat in Karlstad, northwest Sweden. The police discovered a 'cleverly constructed' video bomb destined for a senior police commander in the town. Since the assassination of two policemen and a trade unionist in 1999, Sweden has become calmer in terms of terrorist incidents but racially-motivated violence is on the rise. Swedish Nationalists have identified radical Muslims as the greatest threat to their race and culture. In 2006 whilst *en route* to meet leaders of the SD, Nick Griffin survived an assassination attempt by Marxist terrorists who tried to bomb the train he was travelling on.

DENMARK: The Danish People's Party (Danish: *Dansk Folkeparti*) has risen to prominence on a anti-immigration ticket buoyed up the Islamic terror threat. In the parliamentary elections in 2007, it took 25 seats in the 179-member Folketinget (an increase of 1 seat), with 13.8% of the vote, remaining the third largest party in Denmark. Its chairwoman and founder is Pia Kjærsgaard. Since 2001, the party has supported a government consisting of the Liberal and Conservative parties. While not being a part of the cabinet, the Danish People's Party maintains a close cooperation with the government parties on most issues. In return for their parliamentary support, the party has required a legislative effort for a strict policy towards immigrants and potential refugees. The DPP has been described as a right-wing populist party. It is generally more populist than traditionally right wing, being a strong proponent for some social programmes, such as pensions and other benefits for seniors. In the 2009 elections for the European Parliament the prime candidate Morten Messerschmidt won his seat in a landslide with 284,500 personal votes; thus giving the party a second seat (which went to Anna Rosbach Andersen).

SPAIN: Democracia Nacional (Spanish for *National Democracy*) was founded in 1995. It is modelled after the French Front National (FN) and grew indirectly out of several defunct parties like the CEDADE group and Juntas Españolas. Their leader is Manuel Canduela Serrano, a former member of Accion Radical (a neo-Nazi group active in the Valencian Community that was involved in the murder of Guillem Agulló i Salvador, for which Canduela was in the prison for half a year). Some of their members have been identified as being related to the white power Blood & Honour skinhead groups of the early and mid 1990s. In the 2004, Spanish general election, the party got 15,180 votes throughout Spain, amounting to a 0.06% of the total vote. In the 2008 Spanish general election, they got 12,588 votes, amounting to 0.05% of the vote.

Democracia Nacional has been criticised for being xenophobic and racist, partly due to their poster showing white sheep in an aggressive attitude towards a black sheep. This image had previously been used both by the suiss SVP and the German DVU. In November 2007, the magazine *Interviú* published a report including a recording from a concert organised by the youth section of the party, in which shouts from the crowd could be discerned as "Heil Hitler", "Sieg Heil" and "Duce". On 11th November 2007, Carlos Palomino, a young member of an anti-fascist organisation, was murdered in Madrid, near a demonstration organised by Democracia Nacional against illegal immigration. Palomino was stabbed by Josué Estébanez, a member of the armed forces who was going to the demonstration. Estebanez was not a member of Democracia Nacional because members of the armed forces are prohibited from having any political or syndicalist allegiances. Growing steadily but progress slowed by the painful memory of Fascist dictator General Franco.

ITALY: Alleanza-Nazionale & Lega Nord, both successful but Lega Nord proposes independence for Northern Italy - separatist. LN has 20,000 members and more than 100,000 supporters. AN is a one nation party, with 50,000 members and 300,000 supporters.

PORTUGAL: Partido Nacional Renovador (Portuguese: *Partido Nacional Renovador.*) In the 2005 national elections the PNR obtained just under 0.2% of the vote, failing to elect any deputies to Parliament by a wide margin. In the 2009 European Election the party had about 13 thousand votes having 0,37% of the vote, the party had its higher results in the districts of Lisbon and Setúbal.

SWITZERLAND: Swiss Peoples Party, Christoph Blocher's. The CVP holds roughly 15% of the popular vote. In 2003, it held 28 mandates (out of 200) in the Swiss National Council (first chamber of the Swiss parliament); 15 (out of 46) in the second chamber (largest party in this chamber) and 1 out of 7 mandates in the Swiss Federal Council (executive body). In 2005, it held 20.7% of the seats in the Swiss Cantonal governments and 16.7% in the Swiss Cantonal parliaments (index "BADAC", weighted with the population and number of seats). At the last legislative elections, 22 October 2007, the party won 14.6 % of the popular vote and 31 out of 200 seats. This was a gain of 3 seats, ending the long-term decline of the party and it was the only one of the four largest parties besides the Swiss People's Party to gain votes and seats.

HOLLAND: The Fortuyn List led by Pim Fortuyn, was Holland's premier Nationalist group with 20,000 members and 70,000 supporters until its leader was assassinated in 2002 by a Marxist terrorist. Analysts thought the far Right in Holland was finished after Fortuyn's murder, which was the objective of his killing, but the remaining Nationalists found inspirational leadership in the direction of Geert Wilders. Under the direction of Wilders Holland has experienced a huge upsurge in support for the far Right. He now leads the official opposition Freedom Party (PVV) , riding high on the crest of a wave of anti-Islamic feeling in the once liberal haven, now a hotbed of religious unrest with homosexual men and scantily-clad women targeted by Islamists.

(Pim Fortuyn assassinated by neo-Marxist gunman on 6th May 2002)

SOUTH AFRICA: AWB was led by former policeman Eugene Terre Blanche until his murder in 2010. The AWB want a separate homeland for Afrikaan whites (Voorstat) but the ANC regime will never yield to the demand of the Boers to live in their own homeland. At its high watermark in 1994, the RWB had around 50,000 supporters but was never able to attract the power-bloc of Dutch speaking whites away from the National Party that it needed to become a national force. The RWB at first insisted that the only people who could join had to be of Dutch descent and thus alienated many thousands of white South Africans of British-

English origin. The membership restriction was nonsensical given the fact that the parents of the RWB leader were French. The group had a strong anti-English vent from the outset and as such was doomed to the fringes. In 2002, twenty-two members of the radical Afrikaner group Boeremag, were arrested on charges of conspiring to bring down the South African government by plotting to destroy a network of dams nationwide which would have opened the gates for racial/civil war. The Boeremag (Boer Force] men were put on trial, charged with treason in Pretoria in September 2003. European neo-Nazi groups Combat 18 and Blood & Honour have sent volunteers to patrol white owned farms in South Africa since 2002.

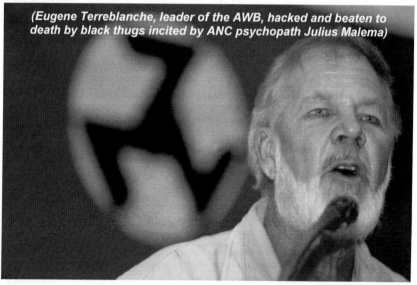

(Eugene Terreblanche, leader of the AWB, hacked and beaten to death by black thugs incited by ANC psychopath Julius Malema)

AUSTRALIA: The former British colony has witnessed a large upsurge in racial violence since 2008 and Melbourne has witnessed large-scale race riots. The policy of successive Australian parliaments over the last 10 years has been to introduce the strictest immigration controls in the Western World. One Nation and Australia First, carry around 40,000 members between them and over 250,000 supporters.

UNITED STATES: Too many groups, mainly survivalist, to list individually here. A total of around 500,000 supporters and activists is probably the true mark of their total strength but it is impossible to determine their actual strength given the disparate state of their groups and sub-groups. Because the First

Amendment in the United States guarantees freedom of speech and little or no fear of prosecution, far Right groups have failed to break through because they are viewed by the mainstream whites as being too extreme and vulgar. The US groups are highly belligerent, a phenomenon that reflects US society at large and its well documented gun culture. Blood & Honour has spread rapidly over the last 10 years and neo-Nazi skinhead gangs are on the rise, particularly in the old states of the Confederacy. The most significant far Right leader in the USA was David Duke but he has gone into the wilderness in the same manner as Pat Buchanan.

(Russian National Unity parade in Moscow)

RUSSIAN FEDERATION: In 2009, Russia's neo-Nazis killed 71 people, mostly non-white immigrants. Blood & Honour has exploded in the country and Alistair Bulman is often telephoned by far Right MPs in the Russian Parliament to thank him for his support. Across Russia there are an estimated 50,000 neo-Nazi skinheads and they represent the most violent form of neo-Nazism in the world. It is a paradox given the fact that Russia was the centrifugal force behind the Soviet Union and its fight against the Third Reich that its sons and daughters are now the most dangerous ultra-neo-Nazis in the world.

Russian skinheads are studying and copying the tactics of Al

Qaeda in preparation for the clash of civilisations or 'race war'. In 2008, Ross Kemp on Gangs visited the Moscow suburbs to report on the training being undertaken by the skinhead gangs and later commented that the most dangerous people he had visited in the entire TV series were the Russian neo-Nazi gangs. The BNP under Nick Griffin as eschewed official ties with the Russian far Right so as not to damage their image any further with UK electorate but British Blood & Honour are highly active and influential in Russia today.

CHAPTER 19

A PROFUSION OF PLOTS

Chris Jackson challenged Nick Griffin for the leadership of the BNP, lost the vote and was subsequently expelled from the party on trumped-up disciplinary charges.
But Griffin still has the audacity to claim the BNP is 'democratic'.

In June 2007 and with Griffin's popularity riding high, he was challenged for the leadership of the BNP by North-West organiser Chris Jackson but no one expected the *"scheming upstart"* to win the ballot. But the scene was set for Jackson to push forward the reform agenda and highlight the considerable weak points in Griffin's leadership. Seemingly, everyone expected a fair contest and that transparency and equanimity between the candidates would prevail. They were soon disappointed and Jackson sealed his fate as the Griffin faction plotted to destroy him, not just to win the ballot, but to remove Jackson from the party for daring to challenge their beloved leader.

Griffin, who claims to be a democrat, has practised a policy since 1999 of expulsion against anyone in the BNP who dares to criticise his 'leadership' of the party. In each case, he has claimed one or the other expelled member has been involved in a dastardly plot to destroy him by spreading lies from within and scheming to overthrow his faction at the head of the party. Griffin created the laughable 'Advisory Council' Simon Darby to give the party a veneer of democracy in the eyes of its members but he has never taken any notice of the Advisory Council and remains *in situ* for show. Anyone on the council who has dared to challenge him has been expelled from the party and character assassinated beforehand for good measure. Naturally, Griffin, a dictator who won the majority of votes from the BNP membership hates any form of criticism.

(Sadie Graham and Matt Single conspired and failed to defeat the Griffin faction in 2007 but the split was a big setback for the BNP)

In expelling the faction around Sadie Graham in December 2007, it quickly became clear that the Griffin faction had bugged the laptop computers and mobile phones supplied to leading activists by the BNP leadership. Griffin proudly announced that his security department had detected the threat to the 'elected leader' of the BNP and his forces moved quickly to remove the Sadie Graham faction, including herself and lover Matt Single and cohort Kenny Smith. It was claimed by the Griffin faction that Graham had been plotting with Searchlight to destroy the BNP but in reality her small faction was not prepared to tolerate the embarrassing antics of Mark Collett.

Since Griffin and Collett were acquitted twice of inciting racial and religious hatred, Collett began to believe in his own invincibility and further enraged the more stable Graham faction with heavy drinking and dating sexy teenage girls. In response to the arrogance and contempt Collett showed to leading party members Griffin did precisely nothing. As usual, and the same happened in my case with the Calvin Richards faction, Griffin made sensible noises that Collett would be brought under control and calmed down. Nothing happened and decent BNP activists could see only too well that their hard work was going down the drain every time Collett played up to the press as the petulant and immature clown lined-up to replace Griffin as the leader of the party.

(Mark Collett, far right, was expelled from the BNP in April 2010 for plotting to overthrow Nick Griffin in the latest palace plot)

The Sadie Graham faction, far from being the employ of Special Branch as subversive agents in the BNP as claimed by NFB Magazine and its editor Larry O'Hara, were simply trying to remove the faction gathering around the wild and calamitous Mark Collett. Anyone with half a brain cell at the top of the BNP could see that Collett was a dangerous nuisance and a disaster waiting to happen for the BNP. Anyone that is apart from his patron Nick Griffin who was grooming Collett as his replacement as 'elected' chairman of the party. Having made repeated attempts to persuade Griffin to honour his promise to deal with Collett and having received no constructive response with words backed up by actions, they moved on the Griffin faction but did so in the most amateurish manner that there defeat was guaranteed from the outset. Their plot, if it can be called a plot, was stillborn because the plotters relied on information technology supplied by the BNP and 'trusted' that the equipment had not been tampered with.

(Arthur Kemp, former South African Intelligence Officer, who Griffin trusts more than anyone in the BNP to detect palace plots)

Had the Graham faction displayed anything remotely resembling professionalism, Griffin would have been toppled and the BNP would have split into two different political parties. Even if the plotters had succeeded, it is highly likely that Griffin would have mounted a challenge in the High Court and been reinstated as chairman as a result. Nonetheless, the BNP would still have been split and the Graham faction would have commanded a large groundswell of support in the new faction. It was not to be and Griffin successfully had the dissidents arrested by the police but at no time did the police ask anyone in the BNP about the illegal bugging of telephones and laptop computers. Nottinghamshire Police, revealed repeatedly at the bottom of police performance tables, either not ask the question or ignored the illegal bugging on political grounds because of the opportunity to inflict harm on the party in the public domain.

In the event, Matt Single took the blame for illegally distributing the entire BNP membership list on the internet and the mother of his child Sadie Graham walked away without any blemish to her character. Whilst Graham avoided criminal charges and prosecution, her reputation was destroyed in the BNP and the couple moved from Nottinghamshire to southern England, apparently out of harm's way. It has to be wondered what extent of 'cooperation' Sadie Graham gave to the police to escape without a scratch and Matt Single go off leniently. But the real issue of the leak of the BNP membership list was Griffin's failure to secure the party's highly sensitive data. His 'intelligent' response was to have a T-shirt made carrying the slogan 'proud to be on the [BNP] list'.

No one other than his sycophantic supporters could have there was currency in lame response that showed-up Griffin and the BNP as being clueless in the security department. The release of the membership list, apparently by Single, was an act of revenge and one that had been coming for at least two years. Had Griffin not thought to have membership list secured so that no one could access it without the access codes of other trusted key holders? A perfect example is the IronKey system that prevents data loss and disclosure by ensuring all key holders have to agree to the access to the data. This elementary line of defence in information technology and data preservation was completely beyond Griffin's intelligence. The failure exposed him as a man whose only understanding of security is in the form of surrounding himself with muscular heavies.

I was contacted by a Griffin sycophant claiming to be the Italian Fascist Giuseppe De Santis. I contacted Larry O'Hara at NFB Magazine and he was convinced that De Santis was in the employ of MI5 but offered no real evidence to prove his suspicion. I was also unable to find any evidence linking De Santis to MI5 and agreed to cooperate with him. At the time, another split in the BNP was emerging in the struggle for power in the party's Solidarity Trade Union for British Workers.

I explained to De Santis the finer points of protecting the BNP's data, particularly the membership list but after several weeks he replied to the effect that no one in the BNP was intelligent enough to understand how to build up an effective counter intelligence unit and would I consider doing the job. I replied to say that I could not serve in the BNP under Griffin and that it was time he evolved into the modern world and took his party with him. But it was clear that Griffin and Arthur Kemp, a former South African intelligence officer, did not know how to lay the foundations of a counter intelligence unit to protect the party from infiltrators from the far Left, HMG agencies and the national media.

I saw then that the BNP would be beset with further data losses and infiltration by its enemies would go undetected because the party leadership could not be bothered to learn how to protect the party's inner security sanctum. With the leak of the membership list, the poisonous New Labour regime and assorted media hacks launched a massive campaign to smash the BNP and several party members were attacked or had their property damaged by far Left terrorists egged on by the State and the mass media. It was embarrassing to see the BNP humiliated in this manner and media groups were calling for the BNP to be banned. It at once became clear that the Establishment was waiting for the membership list to be leaked before launching an offensive against the BNP.

(2008 saw HM Government wage a failed all out war against the BNP)

This development showed a degree of orchestration, or what Jung called synchronicity, between Matt Single's leak of the list and the State's campaign to destroy the BNP. Was Single working with agencies of the State to smash the party or did the State simply latch on to the membership leak and launch a all out war against the BNP? No one has yet uncovered evidence to prove that Single was working for the State before the plot to oust Griffin and likewise there is no evidence to prove that he was working for the State after the leak of the membership list in November 2008.

But what can be resolved without a great deal of effort was that Griffin was the cause of the BNP's embarrassment because he failed to resolve the problems caused by Mark Collett. As a result of refusing to tame Collett, the Sadie Graham faction launched a palace plot and it set in motion a sequence of events that culminated in the 2008 witch hunt against the party by HMG agencies and their mainstream media puppets. This could have been avoided had Griffin had acted against Collett earlier but the leader proved to be impotent and the BNP almost broke apart as a result. The Griffin faction have proved themselves to be adept at bugging the technology supplied to its employees and activists to spy on their activities should they dare to criticise the leadership – a throwback to the Soviet Union one could argue – but where it comes to real security and counter intelligence, Griffin and the BNP are lost.

And Griffin seems to have learned little from the profusion of plots against him because when he appeared on the BBC's Question Time current affairs show in October 2009, another leak was made on the internet of the updated BNP membership list. This caused nothing like the embarrassment of the first leak but Griffin again responded with a 'proud to be on the list' T-shirt. What does this show about Griffin's mentality regarding the privacy of BNP Members?

If anything it shows childishness and outright abject stupidity from a man who knows that he is out of his depth. It also sends a message to anyone considering joining the BNP: Your name will appear on the internet at intermittent intervals on a leaked BNP membership because the leadership is not interested in protecting your privacy and we don't know how to even if we wanted to. Who would want to join a political party that operates like a gang of childish rebels who confront such serious threats with 'proud to be on the list' T-shirts.

The law of averages dictates that eventually one of the many plots being formed in the BNP at the moment will succeed and Griffin will be toppled but this is the wrong way forward for the plotters. Griffin has to be beaten in a straightforward and legitimate leadership contest that is based on the vote of the entire BNP membership. Anything else will not be acceptable and will in turn destroy the BNP and split the party into several factions. Not to mention the fact that Griffin will employ litigation in the civil courts and bring in the police to assist him in defeating any illegal coup. After all, at the moment he is the elected leader of the BNP and even though he behaves like a dictator he has to be beaten at the ballot box before he will ever accept defeat.

And beating Griffin in an internal leadership contest under the rules of the BNP constitution is not as difficult as the plotters think.

His appalling performance on BBC Question Time in which he showed himself up as an awful embarrassing waxwork of a man, nervous, snarling, slimy and evasive has set in process his downfall. The halo surrounding him was blown apart on Question Time and for the first time the BNP membership saw Griffin ridiculed – by his own actions and words – and event broadcast to millions of viewers across the UK showed that Griffin was deeply vulnerable. His immediate response to the Question Time humiliation was to claim that he had been lured into a bear pit and attacked by a nasty pack of wolves.

(A nervous and slimy Nick Griffin makes a fool of himself on BBC Question Time and in turn harms the BNP again)

To those of us who know Griffin it was clear that his shoddy explanation for his erratic performance was entirely typical of a man who lost the ability to be self-effacing. Appealing to a misplaced and misguided 'sympathy' vote he claimed support for the BNP had gone up overnight by about 10% but provided no incontrovertible evidence to support his fanciful claim. In Essex the day after the show Griffin was blubbing like a schoolboy and had no credible explanation to give for his crushing defeat before the entire nation. He appealed to the British love for the underdog and managed to con most BNP members that they had to sympathy for their glorious leader who had fought to bravely against overwhelming odds and been slaughtered in the process of defending 'liberty' and 'justice'.

It was a sickening sight and behind the scenes plots were forming to destroy Griffin and replace him as the BNP leader but the problem with the plot was that it was to be lead by his little protégé Mark Collett. Murmurs of deep discontent rose up in the part ranks but Collett did not capitalise on the brewing desire to topple Griffin and instead reverted to character. The 'plot' culminated in March and April 2010 as the BNP entered the final phases of its plans to field over 300 candidates at the Parliamentary elections on 6th May. Clearly, Collett and company could not have picked a worse moment to try and bring down Griffin and his faction were on to the plot from the outset. It was a foregone conclusion that Collett would fail and he did.

In April, after it was revealed that the Griffin faction had a tape recording of Collett plotting to overthrow the leader, Collett was expelled from the party and the police were called in to investigate. Collett was arrested on suspicion of making death threats against Griffin in a palace plot designed to put Collett in charge of the BNP; a far worse disaster than Griffin as the leader and the party rose against Collett to back Griffin but the mortal wound has now been inflicted. Collett should have paid attention to the eternal maxim that **'he who wields the knife seldom wears the crown'.**

A clever leader in waiting would have manipulated a situation whereby stalking horses were trained and instigated to challenge Griffin for the leadership and then sat back watched the contest unfold. Stalking horses also never win leadership contests are there merely to unmask a desire to replace the leader and make the leader look weak. The real leader in waiting sits back and waits for his moment to strike and only then when the sitting leader is weakened and the party is in a state of revolt and desiring unity. Collett was not intelligent enough to become leader because he did not have the intelligence to comprehend the unwritten laws of plotting for political power. Likewise he did not prepare the groundwork and instead acted as a reactionary to Griffin's outright surrender to the Racial Equality Commission's litigation for the BNP constitution to be changed to allow coloureds to join the party and destroy it from within.

Griffin's decision not to fight the case and to cave-in without a fight caused serious splits within the BNP and was part of the Commission's objective. Throughout the litigation Griffin portrayed himself and his team as mounting a brave fight to save the BNP and the core principles of its creation. In reality, from the outset Griffin believed he could not win the battle and began negotiating with his hated enemies to strike a deal to save his own leadership and to hell with the BNP constitution. He betrayed his members and supporters by telling them he was resisting the legal action but in reality he had already sold out to the Commission and the bent British Establishment. He lied through his back teeth, not an uncommon trait for Griffin, and began the process of agreeing the sum the BNP had to pay for the Commission's legal fees.

There was no squabbling and no brave resistance as he claimed and the litigation, such as it was, merely determined the amount the BNP should pay the Commission in legal fees for bringing the dictatorial litigation in the first place. This latest betrayal and abject surrender was worse than Griffin's appalling act of political suicide on BBC Question Time and Collett was not going to tolerate the stab in the back. He could have succeeded had he laid the groundwork for revolt and began recruiting supporters to assist him for an *Ides of May* revolt to usurp Griffin and save the BNP from the outright humiliation in having to allow the worlds' humanity into the party.

Griffin secured his leadership at a time when he was selling the constitutional change to the membership of the party and did so with apparent ease. He made himself look good because the candidate against was an amateur but against a professional Griffin will be humiliated and he knows it. At a Sky News press conference on 14th February 2010 he sold the change in the party's constitution to the viewing nation and lied by saying the entire party was behind his change. In reality, over 10% of the BNP membership had quit the party and joined the National Front because the NF refused to change its own party membership rules whereas Griffin caved-in without a fight.

Griffin explained to the membership that the party did not have the money fight the Commission's litigation and that he was acting in their best interest by selling out to the Establishment to secure his leadership of the party. In reality, the BNP has never been in better shape financially and easily raised the requisite funds to contest the 2010 General Election with ample reserves for emergencies. With both Griffin and Andrew Brons now drawing large incomes from the European Parliament; the party's finances are in good shape and can be seen at the Election Commission. The deeply unpalatable truth for BNP members is that following Griffin's criminal trials and his self-inflicted political suicide on Question Time, he no longer has the backbone or willingness for a big battle with the Establishment. He has also set a benchmark for the BNP's future conduct of legal challenges by the Establishment: The BNP under Griffin's leadership will surrender to any outrageous demand and the Establishment gang are only too well aware of his fatal weakness. Griffin has lost the ability to fight and instead portrays himself as the 'saviour' of the BNP against the 'evil' Marxist Racial Equality Commission. But the reality is that Griffin capitulated to the Marxist gang and so doing threw up the fundamental question of why the BNP exists?

The BNP was formed to fight for race and nation and allowed only people of indigenous British descent to join the party in the fight to save race and nation from destruction at the hands of the One World capitalists and neo-Marxists. Why does the BNP still exist now that it has sold out to the Globalists? The answer is that party is nothing more than a vehicle for Griffin's political ambitions and founding principles have been raped by its own 'leader' because he had not the stomach or the knowledge to fight and beat the Racist Equality Commission. The BNP is not heading for power and will never form an elected government in Britain under Griffin so what is the point of his leadership? The answer is self-interest, money and his declared intention to retire at 55-years-old on the back of the money he has made from the BNP.

In the photograph above Griffin launches the BNP's manifesto for the 2010 General Election campaign. This event quickly descended into farce on St George's Day when Griffin walked into the venue flanked by a man wearing an old tin helmet that looked like an old tin pisspot and wearing a gown that looked like an old pair of curtains hastily misshaped into a design resembling the flag of England. It was another cringe making session for the BNP and one could not help but be astonished and deeply amused by the stunt. How can the majority of electors take the BNP seriously when it is led by a chinless clown who prefers self-humiliation?

According to Ann Marie E. McSwain, Assistant Professor at Lincoln University, *"leadership is about capacity: the capacity of leaders to listen and observe, to use their expertise as a starting point to encourage dialogue between all levels of decision-making, to establish processes and transparency in decision-making, to articulate their own value and visions clearly but not impose them. Leadership is about setting and not just reacting to agendas, identifying problems, and initiating change that makes for substantial improvement rather than managing change."*

The foregoing passage shows that Griffin does have the leadership skills needed to transport the BNP to national government. He is incapable of listening to the wise counsel of others and his complete lack of a professional stratagem to win power at the ballot box shows up his glaring weaknesses. The stunt at the launch of the 2010 General Election manifesto was just another immature act of crass stupidity that smacked of an amateur organisation wanting to play in the big league of national and international politics. Can anyone with half a brain envisaged a time when the tired old waxwork of Nick Griffin will become the Prime Minister of the United Kingdom? If the answer is no and you are a BNP member then the time is right for you to demand his resignation.

Griffin may think he is smart and highly intelligent but in this book I have exposed his many faults and fundamental inability to build a leadership cadre when he eventually retires from the BNP. The reason why Griffin has not built-up a network of leaders to replace him is because he cannot tolerate anyone in his party who has strength of character and real leadership qualities. He moves against such people and expels them from the party, first subjecting them to character assassination to keep the deluded membership on side. This crazy conduct is not the statesmanship-like quality required of a leader who knows that one day his time will come to stand down and allow young blood to lead the party.

Griffin's conduct is that of a nasty, vicious and slimy creep who adores himself and expects everyone else to do the same or face the consequences. He turned the same tactics on me after the exposing his rotten clique in 2002 but in the event he was dismayed that I fought him and his entire organisation to a standstill and forced them to the negotiating table. At his disposal Griffin had thousands of BNP members and supporters and a large reserve of money but still I was able to beat him and became his nemesis but my intention was never to challenge him for leadership of the party. On my side I had a handful of like-minded others and a small purse of funds but even so Griffin was beaten. His fanatical members, after accepting Griffin's advice to end the war against me, declared that they would take care of me at some time in future.

(Griffin appeared like a cardboard cut out on Question Time)

They were disgruntled and defeated and deeply angry at their inability to terrorise me into silence. I proved myself to have more backbone and intelligence than the Griffin faction and to this day they seethe with hatred. The reality is that most his clique want me dead – so much for their peace loving reincarnation as democrats – but I shall not yield to the BNP under Griffin and will put up a fight for the truth whereas he collapses under considerable strain. I have no ill feelings towards the general BNP membership because they are only now waking to the real Nick Griffin and it's a disturbing sight.

When the BNP eventually elects a leader with high intelligence and charisma, then the Establishment will shudder with fear and realise they have a serious enemy that can beat them and their misrule and greed. The Rotten Parliament between 2005 and 2010 should have propelled the BNP to the corridors of power and seen them knocking on the doors of Whitehall has a government in waiting. But Griffin's appalling Question Time performance has seriously hindered the BNP and harmed its chances of winning real political power. People will not forget the awful self-humiliation by Griffin but in essence this merely exposed him for what he is.

EPILOGUE

The first edition of this book was met with a storm of death threats against me by the more fanatical members of the BNP. Calvin Richards left a voicemail on the answering machine of Alistair Bulman's telephone stating that I had written a book exposing the far Right and that I needed to be "dealt with". But Alistair Bulman is anything but the fool that the BNP took him for and saw that Blood & Honour was being manipulated to kill me and do the BNP's dirty work in the process. Naturally, Blood & Honour leaders would have been arrested in the event of my murder and faced criminal trial and imprisonment but Bulman would not do the BNP's dirty work. Instead he came to me and told me the truth and that his movement would not act against me but that he could not help me against the BNP.

In many ways, I am alive today because Alistair Bulman advised Blood & Honour not to take violent revenge against me. Likewise Bulman finally told me the truth about Gordon Jackson and today we have no axe to grind against one another and I remain in his debt for telling me the truth. Former colleagues in the BNP, including Calvin Richards, knew what had happened in the Jackson appeal and his death and not one of them so much as whispered a word of the truth to me. They were deceitful and as such in real terms I have not betrayed anyone in the BNP by writing this book. By definition, there can be no loyalty to the disloyal and I feel not an ounce of regret for exposing the truth about the real BNP under both John Tyndall and Nick Griffin.

There is only one man in the British far Right that I respect and that is Alistair Bulman who has not once compromised over principle and policy and continues the fight for his true beliefs and does not seek to hide the truth from the public. Can the same be said of the vile and treacherous Griffin faction in the BNP who have sold out the founding principles of the party. And at no time have I have sold out to the agencies of the State in their campaign to destroy the BNP. In October 2003, I was approached to work for MI5 as a desk officer investigating the far Right and rejected the overture out of hand. The same was also true when approached by MI5 and Special Branch satellite Searchlight Magazine.

I told Nick Lowles of Searchlight Magazine that I did not share his agenda against the BNP and the wider far Right and rejected his offer to promote the book. I have no doubt that had I accepted the offer, a great deal of money would have come my way and I would have been given protection from the BNP thugs threatening me and my family. Calvin Richards confronted my brother, a former boxer, in a Nottingham supermarket and was forced to back down or get knocked down. Since then the BNP bullies have not dared to threaten anyone in my family and have been made aware of the consequences for crossing the Rubicon again.

In May 2002, I also rejected a publishing deal offered by John Blake of Blake Publishing because his editor Nick Davies wanted to fabricate events in the book for public consumption. I lost out financially but retained my respect and honoured my principles which are not for sale and the Daily Mail learned this painful lesson in July 2004 after publishing a nasty smear article against me across two whole pages. I complained to the PCC and the complaint was upheld. I then promised to sue the Daily Mail on the grounds of libel and the newspaper settled my claim before court proceedings became necessary and issued a public apology in the newspaper.

I have never compromised over principle and have not sold out to the Establishment and its ruthless mass media machine to destroy the BNP. Griffin and his little gang tried to convince the

BNP membership that was an MI5 agent and ultimately failed. When this tactic backfired, Griffin and Simon Darby then began telling journalists that I was detained in a mental hospital in Nottingham and when I threatened to sue them, they were forced to back down in defeat. I have no respect for anyone in the Griffin faction and hold Griffin beneath contempt on the foregoing grounds. His failure to stop me from publishing this boon on two occasions is another sign of his impotence and the truth will out.

The BNP's first attempt to litigate against this book was withdrawn by Nick Griffin and he claimed Tony Lecomber had no authority on the BNP's part to threaten litigation against the book. The possibility of a BNP litigation against me on the grounds if libel was stillborn from the outset. How could a man like Lecomber, convicted of racial violence and attempting to bomb the office of a left-wing newspaper, hope to win a libel action for damages after the damage he has heaped on the BNP? The very suggestion was laughable but portrayed Griffin's real BNP in its true light and I am grateful to them for handing me such an easy victory.